PAPAW

A novel about God's power of forgiveness

David R. Kosak

ISBN 979-8-89243-521-5 (paperback)
ISBN 979-8-89243-522-2 (hardcover)
ISBN 979-8-89243-523-9 (digital)

Copyright © 2024 by David R. Kosak

All rights reserved. No part of this publication may be reproduced, distributed, or transmitted in any form or by any means, including photocopying, recording, or other electronic or mechanical methods without the prior written permission of the publisher. For permission requests, solicit the publisher via the address below.

Christian Faith Publishing
832 Park Avenue
Meadville, PA 16335
www.christianfaithpublishing.com

This is a work of fiction. Names, character, incidents, and places are either the product of the author's imagination or used fictitiously. Any resemblances to persons living or dead, business establishments, events, or places is coincidental. Jesus, however, is real.

Printed in the United States of America

For my wife Donna who is the greatest Christian I know and showed me the light. I love you.

CHAPTER 1

D-Day, Northern France, June 1944

On May 10, 1940, as Germany's battle for France commenced, Winston Churchill became prime minister of Britain. Churchill would soon endure a humiliating but miraculous evacuation of Dunkirk. The Battle of Britain started a month later. Fought entirely in the air, the outnumbered British fighter pilots bravely battled and defeated Hermann Goring's Luftwaffe, thus thwarting Hitler's attempt to force Britain to sue for peace.

Both battles proved to be triumphs for Britain. Neither, however, turned the tide of the war. To that point, Germany's ill-fated invasion of the Soviet Union had not begun, and America was still a year and a half away from entering the war. Britain's fate appeared bleak.

Not until November 1942, during the Second Battle of El Alamein, would Britain see her first real victory. By November 1942 the tide of war shifted in favor of the Allies. Under pressure from Joseph Stalin, the leader of the Soviet Union, the Allies decided to open a second front. An invasion of France and Normandy would be the location.

While planning the invasion of Normandy, the Allies faced two and a half years of bloody fighting. On June 6, 1944, within a narrow window of favorable weather, Operation Overlord, the largest amphibious assault in history, got underway. By the end of the day, it was hoped a second front would be established.

Once Overlord got in the hands of men who would do the fighting, Eisenhower grew concerned over its outcome, and he prepared a statement accepting full responsibility for its failure. Thankfully, the world would never hear the statement. Operation Overlord was, notwithstanding heavy casualties, successful. The Allies established a second front, and the five beachheads (Gold, Juno, Omaha, Sword, and Utah) were consolidated into one front on June 12.

Miserable weather after the landing tempered the success of Overlord. The hedgerows of northern France also plagued the Allied armies pursuing retreating Germans. These mini jungles of thick trees and undergrowth, lining many of the roads, provided excellent cover for the German army. Countless Allied soldiers, including many Americans, lost their lives fighting Germans who were entrenched in these hedgerows. Therefore, a breakout became the highest priority.

War-weary men, mostly teenagers or in their early twenties, knew the war ended in Berlin. Many of the battle-hardened Americans were fighting since America's entry into the war. Their European counterparts, however, had been fighting since the start of the war. Therefore, the hedgerows were little more than a frayed rope that soon would break under the strain of the advancing Allies hungry for victory.

The Germans, fighting a defensive war on two fronts, were on their heels. The Russians were moving in from the east and the Allies from the west. The once-mighty Luftwaffe no longer had an offensive capability in the skies, and the U-boat war on the Atlantic was rendered ineffective. The thousand-year reign of the Third Reich, of which Hitler boasted, was about to collapse. Only German soldiers, who fought to the death, remained.

Even after the successful landings on the beaches of Normandy and as the Allied army fought their way through hedgerows, Hitler clung to the fantasy of an invasion at the Pas-de-Calais, the narrowest point between England and France. Eisenhower and his staff understood that Hitler would eventually realize his error and move to reinforce his armies near Normandy.

The Allied leaders were anxious for a breakout.

CHAPTER 2

Opportunity

GENERAL CLARENCE HUEBNER rarely second-guessed himself. This morning, a battle plan he put together on short notice was the root of his concern. Huebner, who came from humble origins, entered the Army as a private. He earned a regular commission in 1916 and distinguished himself during the First World War, earning several medals, including two Distinguished Service Crosses, a Distinguished Service Medal, and a Silver Star. In 1943, General Omar Bradley, commander of the American forces in Europe, placed Huebner in command of the First Infantry Division, also known as the Big Red One. A move that would instill discipline. Huebner, on June 6, 1944, led the Big Red One onto Omaha Beach during the D-Day landings.

Shortly after the landings, Allied reconnaissance spotted a weakness. A small salient, or bulge, appeared, exposing two flanks in the German line. Bradley tasked Huebner with putting together a battle plan to exploit this weakness. A bridge at the center of the salient was the focal point of the plan. Huebner made good use of his organizational skills and devised a plan to accomplish a near-impossible feat. He would move a battalion into striking distance of the German line undetected. If successful, this surprise assault would capture the bridge intact and punch a hole in the German line. Hopes were high for a successful outcome.

Huebner, fresh off the costly struggle on Omaha Beach, paced anxiously in his tent. Surrounded by maps and frontline dispatches, he waited on word from the battalion commander, Lieutenant Colonel Joshua Hendrix, for a progress report. Tech Sergeant Neal Hill entered Huebner's tent with a radio over his shoulder. He reached out with the receiver in hand and said, "Sorry, sir. It's Colonel Hendrix. I knew you'd want this."

"Okay, sergeant, let me have it," replied Huebner. He barked into the receiver, "Josh, what the hell's goin' on down there?" Lieutenant Colonel Joshua Hendrix, called Josh by his fellow officers, served under the general in various capacities since America entered the war.

Sergeant Hill listened to General Huebner, attempting to glean information. The general nodded and, in mechanical monotones, repeated, "Uh-uh, uh-uh." A smile washed over the general's face. "Good God, how in hell did ya pull that off?" The general listened and again said, "Uh-huh, uh-huh." He shouted into the receiver, "Damn it, make sure this operation starts on time! No later than 7:00. Got it!" After a brief pause, he said, "Okay, good luck." He turned to Sergeant Hill and said, "That bastard moved four companies within a thousand yards of the German line undetected. Now it's up to Baker Company."

"That's good news, sir. I served with Captain Jones. He's a good man," replied Sergeant Hill.

"Sergeant, I hope you're right."

CHAPTER 3

A Beautiful Day for a Battle

Danny thought, *"I should have married Anne."* He slowly rotated his head from left to right scanning the valley, then he reconsidered, *"Hell, I did the right thing. I'll be dead in thirty minutes."*

Squad leader Sergeant Jerome Daniel Shykes, Danny to his friends, crouched low at the edge of an aspen forest. Spindly white shafts towered into the sky. The crowns of the trees, high in the air, tangled into a thick mat, blocking the morning light, and within the confines of the forest, there was an eerie darkness Danny found comforting. Crows cawed to one another, communicating the presence of the men of Baker Company. The men were spread out in a thin line at the edge of the forest. Danny nervously scanned the gently sloping hillside and river before him. Except for a few cows grazing lazily, it was barren. A smattering of trees dotted the riverbank, and a small hamlet lay on the opposite side of the river. On Danny's side of the river, next to a bridge, a Tiger tank sat menacingly, and a few German soldiers milled about. These were the only indications of war.

Danny's squad acquired five replacements after the heavy losses suffered while taking Omaha Beach. Their uniforms were fresh, like their young faces, and added to the surreal scene in front of him, which troubled Danny more than the horror of the beach landing ten days earlier.

"No noise. No explosions," Danny thought. *"The Germans are clueless. If only those damn crows would shut up."*

He muttered, "Just plain creepy. Goodness, those bastards'll see us for sure. I don't like it."

Danny, who looked more like his Italian mother than his Irish father, removed his helmet with his right hand, exposing a thick crop of wavy black hair. He wiped his brow with his left arm, scratched his square jaw blanketed with stubble, and shot a cynical look at his wartime friend, Sergeant Reginald Smith, known as Smitty.

The two met during the North Africa campaign and marveled at their good fortune. They were alive and unhurt. The scene below indicated to Danny that things would soon change—and change for the worse. It was too quiet and too nice; even the smell was too sweet. No booming artillery or rattling of machine guns, not even in the distance; just silence. It seemed as if the war had paused for some inexplicable reason, and Danny found it unnerving.

Smitty, of average height and build with shaggy blond hair and large brown eyes, was, like Danny, ruggedly handsome. Always the optimist, Smitty reassured Danny that it was their destiny to make it home. To him, the war was a noble cause as well as an adventure. Smitty's optimism did little to allay Danny's concerns.

Danny, the pessimist, felt their time was up. The fact they made it this far meant that in the rifles slung over those Germans' shoulders were bullets with their names. In fact, after they miraculously survived Omaha Beach, he confided to Smitty that a Stuka dive bomber would drop a bomb right on his head.

They were certainly opposites, but if opposites attract, that would explain why these two were such good friends. Both pined to be with the girlfriends they left behind and thus shied away from the youthful exploits of other soldiers in their platoon. Smitty, two years older than Danny, was like an older brother, but they had a bond like identical twins.

Danny furrowed his brow. "I can't believe I volunteered for this. How'd the hell did I let ya talk me into this numbskull idea?"

Smitty pointed at the bridge in the valley and laughed. "Danny ole boy, in just forty-five minutes, we'll be standin' on that bridge, an' you'll be thankin' me. Scuttlebutt has it the volunteers for this mission are goin' to the rear. Hell, Danny, all we gotta do is get to that bridge an' clear the charges. You get one side. I get the other, just like the ole cap'n said. Then we set out the rest 'a the war an' be some generals' driver. Hell, you may even be Ike's driver, maybe even Churchill himself."

Danny glared incredulously at his friend, not saying a word.

Smitty grabbed and shook his filthy tunic. Bits of dry mud fell to the ground, and he said, "It'll be worth it if all we get's a hot shower."

Danny shook his head in the negative. "Yes, if we don't get kilt. Do ya realize we're the only two stupid enough to volunteer? This's the dumbest thing I've ever done."

Smitty lifted his head, rolled his eyes, and snickered. "Ya got it all wrong. Look at it this way. The war's goin' on for another year, hell, maybe two. Do ya have any idea how many bullets or Stuka dive bombers you'll face?"

Danny stared at Smitty with a furrowed brow.

Smitty continued, "Today we'll do it all at once an' get it over with. The odds are in our favor this way. I did the math in my head." Smitty, grinning like the Cheshire Cat, said nothing more and stared at his friend.

Danny paused and thought, *This stupid idea has a sliver of sense. Hell, all his stupid ideas do.*

Danny glared at Smitty. "Goodness, Smitty, you're serious. You're REALLY serious. It's scary enough that you believe the horseshit you're spreadin'. What's scarier is that ya think I'll believe it. My friend, you'll have a good future as a politician. I bet you'll be president someday."

Smitty busied himself sighting his Thompson. "Trust me, just trust me. A half an hour from now, forty minutes tops, we'll be outta this ole war."

Danny shook his head skeptically in the negative. "We'll just run down there, charge the damn bridge, and say excuse us. Fritz, my friend, I have a job to do. Then clear it of explosives. Sure, a lead-pipe cinch."

Thinking cultivated fear, but Smitty trusted his friend in tight situations. There was no logical explanation that would comfort his friend. Danny needed to hear and see confidence.

Smitty rested the Thompson on his right thigh, glanced at Danny, and with a cocky smirk said, "Yeah, somethin' like that." Smitty furrowed his brow and looked into his friend's eyes. "Danny, you're goin' home. I promise. You'll see your Anne. That beautiful gal you keep goin' on about, get married, an' have lots of kids, an' tell 'em 'bout your ole pal Smitty. How you an' I won this here war."

Danny replied, "Hope you're right. We had plans, ya know. Then came this war. Anne wanted us to get married, but I told her we needed to wait till I returned. I wish I listened to her but didn't want to make 'er a widow. I miss 'er."

Smitty said, "Yeah, I know what ya mean, ole boy. I think of Jean all the time. What'd we do without 'em?"

"All I know is Anne kept me alive, an' it ain't goin' to be over anytime soon."

"I think this'll be our last one."

A gentle rustling of low-hanging branches preceded a firm whisper. The deep Southern drawl could only be their platoon leader, twenty-three-year-old First Lieutenant Leon Kaminski.

"Okay, you jokers, the cap'n is ready. This way, stay low, an' be quiet!" exclaimed the young lieutenant. Smitty and Danny followed, making their way toward the captain's position.

CHAPTER 4

The Baptism of Private Johnathan Knox

SAVORING THE SILENCE and enjoying a pleasant break from the lousy weather, Baker Company Commander Captain Eric Jones trained his field glasses on the valley below. To the left, a small road, upon which his company made its way, emerged from the trees and parted the open, gently sloping pasture evenly. It led to a small truss bridge, the target of Baker Company's mission.

Interconnecting iron beams that formed triangles over the truss bridge were in harsh contrast to the quaint French countryside dotted with small farmhouses, many dating back to the eighteenth century. It spanned the narrowest and straightest point of the river, which, except for two patches of wooded areas near the bridge, was without trees. One of Germany's latest tanks, the Tiger II, guarded the bridge.

The open ground before the men of Baker Company sloped a thousand yards to the river's edge. Among the farmhouses and barns on the other side of the river, cows and horses were grazing, and like the German soldiers, were unconcerned. Captain Jones trained his field glasses on three civilians riding a small cart pulled by a donkey. They just crossed the bridge, moving deeper into the German position. He thought, *"A man, a woman, and a young adult female. Could they be a family? There's nothing I can do."* A moral debate ignited within the young captain, but the machinery of war and the greater good of the mission kept him focused. To the young captain's relief, they continued moving. He looked at his watch; it showed 6:40.

He thought, *"They'll be okay. They've gotta be."*

Unlike Danny, Captain Jones felt energized by the nice weather. He scanned the valley and watched the German soldiers calmly walking about. *"Everything's as it should be. Just like reconnaissance said it would,"* he thought.

Captain Jones led his company, four platoons in all, on a forced march that began at 1:00 a.m. His weary men, cloaked in darkness, formed a semicircle at the edge of the forest, waiting to fight in an unforgiving battle. The morning sun shone through startlingly clear blue skies, drenching the valley in warmth. The lack of exploding artillery and gunfire created a peaceful silence. In spite of the mission and his role in its outcome, Jones, riding an escalating wave of optimism, found pleasure in the beautiful morning.

Standing six feet, two inches tall and weighing two hundred and thirty pounds, Captain Eric Jones was easily found on the battlefield. An imposing man referred to as Preacher because of his strong Christian faith. An accomplished athlete, having played fullback on his college football team, he displayed no vices. In spite of his athleticism and size, the soft features of his bookish face made him appear more at home in a library than on a football field.

When America entered the war, the soft-spoken captain from east Tennessee was a CPA and worked at his father's accounting firm, which he would someday take over. After the attack on Pearl Harbor, he told his father he intended to enlist in the Army. Reluctantly, his father gave his blessing and hired an accountant to fill in for his son. After basic training, he applied to officer training school. After officer training, he was sent to North Africa as a second lieutenant.

Jones soon discovered, after surviving his first battle, that the brutality of war exceeded the glamour depicted in recruiting posters. He watched countless men, mostly young boys, die under his command and honed one idea to a razor edge: *kill or be killed.* After countless firefights, a crust of cynicism shielded the young captain's humanity. His job was to vanquish evil while keeping as many of his men alive as possible. This required the taking of human lives. The noble aim of America's involvement in the war reconciled this concept with his Christianity. Yet he could not banish from his mind the thought that those he killed could, under different circumstances, be friends. He often pondered how they felt and understood that, like him, they had mothers and other loved ones. While he could kill them, he could not hate them.

The war matured Jones beyond his twenty-eight years, and hints of gray streaked through his black hair. With maturity came increased confidence and decisiveness under fire. His confidence was forged during the ill-fated Battle of Kasserine Pass in North Africa and the successful Italian campaign. These attributes served him well when he stormed onto Omaha Beach on June 6, 1944 as a captain and company commander. The enlisted men under his command held him in high regard. He was tough, fair, and regarded their lives as highly as his own.

Now in France, he found himself positioned on the high ground, planning to attack and capture a bridge. It was the most important moment of his short military career—the moment he longed for. When he enlisted, he never imagined he would lead men in a desperate battle—a battle that, at least in his mind, had a purpose. His confidence in the planned attack grew as he watched the enemy below.

Poised and ready to strike were Captain Jones and 150 men of Baker Company, the tip of an allied juggernaut. The Germans, unaware of the looming battle, were milling about. Like Jones, they were enjoying a rare and beautiful spring morning. Baker Company's position could not have been better.

Jones paused, scanning the valley to take in its beauty. The sounds and smells of spring conjured pleasant thoughts that took over his mind. The men were in position, and he wanted to savor the silence, and in his mind, he saw his wife sipping coffee and his two daughters playing under his favorite oak tree. This was his time, even if only for five minutes. The war could wait.

A hushed voice broke the silence. "Cap'n, suh, we caught Jerry with his pants down." Captain Jones returned from his brief break to find his XO, Lieutenant Kaminski, staring with wide eyes. With him were Danny and Smitty. Kaminski turned to the two sergeants and continued, "We're ready, suh, the men're in place. Danny an' Smitty are chompin' at the bit. Jist like my ole coonhound, Beauregard."

Danny glanced at Smitty, who, in turn, sarcastically rolled his eyes. "Still can't believe we got this close. Hell, Cap'n, ya must have an angel on yer shoulder. But we can't hold this position much longer."

Captain Jones turned his attention to Danny and Smitty. "Ah, you two. The only ones to volunteer." He furrowed his brow cynically. "Now, just why DID you volunteer for this job?"

Danny regretted his decision to volunteer, glaring and clenching his jaw so tight the muscles in front of his ears bulged, eager to hear what his friend was about to tell the captain.

Smitty glanced at Danny, smiled, winked, and turned to Captain Jones. "Well, sir, Danny an' I feel like it's a worthy an' important mission. Besides, we're best for the task."

Smitty and Danny had been with the young captain since North Africa, who was relieved after they volunteered. Captain Jones said, laughing, "Great, 'cause ya know there's this crazy rumor that the volunteers for this mission are goin' to the rear. I know you two are too smart to fall for something like that."

Captain Jones caught Danny mothing, "Fubar."

Captain Jones shot a skeptical look at Kaminski. The captain said, "Sergeant Shykes, would ya care to share your thoughts with me an' the lieutenant?"

Danny, in low tones, said, "Well, I was just tellin' my good friend Smitty here that him talkin' me into such a noble mission was a good idea. I can't wait to get to that bridge. Reckon this's a once-in-a-lifetime opportunity." Jones laughed and returned his gaze to the bridge and the Germans below.

"Shush, quiet!" Captain Jones exclaimed in a whisper.

Who-wee-who-who-who.

"Hear that?" Captain Jones asked, seeking acknowledgment of the strange sound.

Straining to hear enemy activity and to no avail, Lieutenant Kaminski replied with a puzzled look, "Well, suh, no." The puzzled men stood in silence, looking at each other. The sound came again.

Who-wee-who-who-who.

PAPAW

Astonished that he was the only one to hear the sound, Captain Jones repeated his question. "There! Hear it?" he proclaimed with a smile. "It's a mourning dove. Haven't heard one since I left home." A relieved chuckle erupted from Danny, Smitty, and Kaminski.

"Kinda peaceful, suh. Reckon he don't know all hell's 'bout to break loose. Kinda like those Krauts down thar," said Kaminski.

Danny turned to Smitty and said, "Ya gotta love the cap'n. We're 'bout to go into a meat grinder, an' he finds a bird."

"Yeah, the cap'n is a good man. I'd follow 'im into the jaws a hell," said Smitty.

Captain Jones returned the field glasses to his eyes and resumed scanning the valley. "Today's goin' to be a good day." He glanced at Kaminski and said, "When we're standing on the bridge, Kaminski, you can tell me how a Polack ended up in Georgia."

Kaminski said, "Suh, guess I was lucky. Don't ya think it's too nice a day to fight? Seems to me everyone's kinda enjoy'n the mornin'. Let's go fishin'."

Captain Jones paused the scan. "That'd be nice, Lieutenant, but I don't think the old man would like that. The high command's watchin', even Bradley. I'd rather get shot than screw this up."

Captain Jones, with his elbows on a fallen tree, trained his field glasses on the bridge and carefully worked the focusing knob back and forth with his fingers. Three German officers walked onto the bridge, halted halfway, and one spoke to the others. Captain Jones continued to work the focusing knob, straining to identify the officer giving instructions.

"Oberstleutnant! Battalion strength. For once, recon got it right," whispered Jones. The German officer speaking pointed to a clump of trees on the west side of the bridge. The captain whispered, "Yes, Herr Oberstleutnant, I see that machine gun. Right where recon said it'd be." The German officer turned to the east side of the bridge and pointed to another clump of trees. Jones swung his field glasses and focused on the clump of trees.

"What're ya lookin' at, Herr Oberstleutnant?" whispered the captain as he nervously worked the focus knob. "I don't see anything. Gotta be somethin' there." A glint of sunlight reflected off a bespectacled gunner sitting in a machine gun nest. "Aha, Herr Oberstleutnant, a second machine gun. Thank you," whispered Jones.

"Kaminski, look!" exclaimed Jones, handing to the young lieutenant the field glasses.

"Can't see nothin', suh," replied Lieutenant Kaminski, looking through the field glasses.

Captain Jones gesticulated frantically. "Over there, in that clump of trees on the small mound. Look close. See it?"

Lieutenant Kaminski looked at the clump of trees and focused on the machine gun. "Oh shit, that's a nasty surprise. Ya don't reckon it's a forty-two, do ya? We'd get chewed up good. Damn, jist when ya think ya have it all figgered out. What's the plan, suh?" Lieutenant Kaminski said, handing the field glasses to Captain Jones.

"Don't have to tell ya, both machine guns gotta go. Just hope there're no more surprises."

Kaminski said, "Not one to bellyache, but with the tank, Romero'll have his hands full."

"'Fraid so."

Danny looked at Smitty and said, "We damn near run into that thing. I knew it couldn't be that easy. Always somethin' goin' wrong."

Smitty said, "Relax, ole boy, the cap'n knows what to do. Hell, we've seen worse."

Platoon leaders Lieutenant Romero of the first platoon, Lieutenant Jackson of the second platoon, and Lieutenant Powell of the third platoon joined the four men. Lieutenant Kaminski led the fourth platoon. Kaminski said, "Hate to say it, Romero, but your job just got harder."

Captain Jones confirmed Kaminski's sentiment, handing Lieutenant Romero the field glasses. "I'm afraid Kaminski's right, Romero. We spotted a second machine gun. Look at that clump of trees over there."

Lieutenant Romero took the field glasses, looked where his captain directed, and said, "Sir, two machine guns, a tank, an' one bazooka. The math ain't good."

Jones replied, "Now ya have two bazookas." He turned to Kaminski and said, "Kaminski, have Corporal Johnson report to Romero."

"Yes, suh, Cap'n."

Jones's eyes widened. "Let's go over this one more time. Romero, your job's to knock out the tank an' both machine guns. Ya have two bazookas. The first two rounds gotta hit the machine guns, then go for the tank. Aim for the tracks, am I clear? Get the guns, then the tank. After that, you're to support the main assault behind Powell and Kaminski."

"Yes, sir, Cap'n, the first two rounds go to the machine guns, then the tank. Don't worry, we'll get 'em," replied Romero.

Captain Jones turned to Lieutenant Jackson. "You keep your platoon in reserve until we see how it goes. Lieutenant Romero'll holler at ya if he's in trouble. If ya hear nothin' after five minutes, go to the bridge, got it?"

Lieutenant Jackson replied, "Yes, sir, five minutes, charge the bridge."

Captain Jones issued his final instructions to Powell and Kaminski. "Powell, you an' Kaminski'll lead the main assault. I'm goin' in with you guys. Our job's the bridge. Danny an' Smitty are on me till we clear the bridge."

Yes, sir, Cap'n," replied Lieutenant Powell.

Jones looked at Smitty and Danny and asked, "We gotta clear the bridge. Do ya have any questions?"

Danny and Smitty stepped forward, and in unison, snapped to attention and delivered a textbook salute. Smitty said, "No, Cap'n, we're ready to go."

Captain Jones said, "Knock it off, boys. No time for that nonsense. I want to thank you an' remind you the bridge is the mission. We must capture it intact." Captain Jones looked at Danny and asked, "Aren't you from my neck 'a the woods?"

Danny replied, "Yes, sir, I'm from Townsend, Tennessee."

"I'm from Alcoa. I grew up there. That makes us neighbors," replied the captain.

"Yes, sir, Cap'n, maybe we can go fishing when we get home."

Jones replied, "I'll take ya up on that. There's some good trout fishin'. Now, we have a war to win. Any questions?" Danny and Smitty stood silent. Jones added, "The three of us been together a long time."

"Since Kasserine. That was a tough one, sir," said Smitty.

"This'll be nothin' like that. Those Krauts are gettin' tired of war. I feel good 'bout this one." Captain Jones softened his tone. "I want ya to know it's been a pleasure to serve with ya."

Danny said, "It has been OUR honor to serve under your command."

Jones said, "It's time to get the bridge. Care to join me?"

In one voice, Danny and Smitty said, "It'll be a pleasure, sir."

Quick steps and snapping branches startled the gathering. A young private rushed forward, catching Lieutenant Jackson by surprise. Jackson grabbed the soldier by the scruff of the neck and said, "Whoa, Private, what're you doin'? You're goin' to get us killed. Get back to your position."

Captain Jones, startled by the young boy, thought, *"Goodness, they're getting younger. Did they even check his birth certificate?"* The replacement, yet to see combat, came after the Omaha Beach landing. His unflawed skin, small nose, and bright blue eyes, which peeked through a helmet that appeared two sizes too big, betrayed innocence. He was a small lad, and Captain Jones said, "It's okay, Jackson. Step forward. What's your name? How old are you?"

The nervous private snapped to attention and gave a sloppy salute. "Johnathan Knox an' I turned eighteen las' January, sir."

Jones, who could not believe he was old enough to be drafted, thought, *"Goodness, I've been out here too long. He doesn't look a day older than sixteen."* He asked the private, "What's on your mind, son?"

"Sir, the men say you're a preacher. Is that true?"

Captain Jones replied, "That's what the men call me, Private, but I'm not a preacher. I'm a deacon. But more important, I'm a believer. What can I do for you?"

The private pushed his helmet back, exposing pleading eyes. "Did ya bring Jesus with ya, sir?"

PAPAW

The innocence of the boy's question caused the captain to set aside the mission. He said, "No, soldier, I didn't. Jesus was here before we arrived." Jones pointed to the bridge they were about to attack. "Jesus is everywhere. Why he's even down there with Jerry."

Lieutenant Jackson snapped at the young private. "Be quick, boy. We don't have much time. Those Krauts'll spot us any moment. Get to the point."

The teenager fumbled with a sheet of paper he pulled from his pocket. With a trembling hand, he handed it to Lieutenant Jackson and pleaded with the officer. "If I get it, could someone make sure my mother gets this letter?"

"Is this what all the fuss is about?" laughed Lieutenant Jackson. "Hell, I'll make sure, Private. Unless I get it."

The private continued his plea. "But, sir, the letter says Cap'n Jones baptized me. Please, Cap'n Jones, I give my mother a lot of worry, an' I never got baptized, sir. I promised I would, but I got drafted, then it was too late. Isn't there something you can do, sir?"

Captain Jones checked his watch; it read 6:50. He then reached for his canteen and reassuringly told the boy, "Okay, kid, settle down. I'll baptize ya. Your mother's important, Knox, but ya need to do this to save YOUR soul. Are ya comin' to the Lord, son?"

Relieved, Private Knox replied, "Yes, sir. Does this mean you'll do it?"

Lieutenant Jackson, who never questioned his captain, asked rhetorically, "Sir, you're not goin' to go through with this, are ya? I mean, I love Jesus. We all love Jesus—even Shykes loves Jesus—but we can't hold this position much longer. We have to move now. I'm Baptist too. If he's saved an' gets it, he's bound for glory an' don't need to be baptized. Sir, you know it."

Kaminski supported Jackson's plea. "I have to agree with Jackson on this. We're lucky we got this far. Now the sun's shinnin', an' if we lose the element of surprise, we'll all meet Jesus, an' the mission'll fail."

Danny looked at Smitty and said, "First, a machine gun. Now this. I don't like it, Smitty. I don't like it one bit. We're doomed. We just need to get on with it."

Smitty spoke reassuringly, "Ya worry too much. It's goin' to be fine. Just wait an' see. Trust the cap'n. He's done good by us."

Captain Jones loved any opportunity to minister to the men. There was no doubt in his mind that a divine force was at play. It was just too perfect. He thought, *"Maybe this's what the men need before entering battle. Maybe it's something I need. Who am I to question fate?"*

Captain Jones looked at his watch and proclaimed, "Gentlemen, if we end up meeting Jesus, then nothing of this mission'll matter, will it? The way I see it, we still have ten minutes with nothing to do. I can't imagine spending these few minutes in a better way, or for that matter, on anything more important." Lieutenant Kaminski and Jackson stopped the protest, realizing nothing could be said to change the captain's mind.

While the captain's decision to perform the ritual lifted an enormous burden from the boy's shoulders, it served to only intensify fear among his lieutenants of discovery by the enemy. Captain Jones returned his attention to Private Knox. "Will this mean a lot to your mother? Are you truly saved? Is Jesus Christ your personal Lord and Savior?"

"Yes, sir, I'm saved."

"Under the circumstances, a sprinkle'll have to do."

"Yes, sir."

Captain Jones got started. He counseled the young private while Lieutenant Jackson and Kaminski sought counsel with their eyes. The captain said, "Don't worry, it's goin' to be a good day. I feel it in my bones. One day you guys'll be talkin' to your grandkids 'bout this moment."

Lieutenant Jackson, reassured by the captain's words, relaxed and said, "Yes, sir, I reckon we need God on our side. It'll be fine." Smitty and Danny, along with the other lieutenants, buoyed by the confidence of their captain, found peace.

Captain Jones began. "Johnathan, do you believe Jesus Christ is the Son of God, and do you acknowledge Jesus died on the cross and was resurrected so that all sin would be forgiven for those who accept Jesus Christ as their Savior?"

"Yes, sir, I do."

PAPAW

"Do you acknowledge that his blood cleansed your soul of sin, and you ask forgiveness and repent of your sins?"

"Yes, I do."

Jones opened his canteen, and with a sudden snap, broke the cap from its chain. He poured water into the cap and addressed the men. "Today, Private Johnathan Knox testified before God and man that he is a follower of Jesus Christ.

"For God so loved the world that he gave his only begotten Son, that whosoever believes in him will not perish but have eternal life. Johnathan Knox, do you put your faith in Jesus Christ as your Lord and Savior?"

"Yes, I do."

"Johnathan Knox, upon your profession of faith, I baptize you in the name of the Father, Son, and Holy Spirit." Captain Jones poured the water on the private's forehead. The men, circled around Captain Jones and Private Knox, were overcome with emotion. In a matter of minutes, many would be dead.

Captain Jones said, "Let us pray." Without regard for the surroundings all the men removed their helmets, bowed their heads, and went to their knees. Captain Jones prayed.

"Our Father, who art in heaven, hallowed be thy name. Thy kingdom come, thy will be done, on earth as it is in heaven. Give us this day our daily bread, and forgive us of our debts, as we have also forgiven our debtors. And lead us not into temptation but deliver us from evil. For thine is the kingdom, and the power, and the glory, forever. Dear heavenly Father, you are the master of the universe, and we are your creation, and we know your will shall be done. We pray for the knowledge to understand your will and the courage to see it through. We are about to engage in battle. Lord, we ask for your guidance during this battle, so we may triumph over tyranny. Protect us, Lord, and give us the strength to forgive our enemies. It is in the name of Jesus Christ, our risen Savior, that we ask these things. Amen." The men responded with a quiet amen.

Smitty looked to Danny and said, "This may be the greatest moment of the war for us."

"Yeah, Smitty, I gotta agree. Just wish I could see Jesus down there like you an' the cap'n. I'll be glad when this whole mess is over."

"Jesus is with us. You'll see," Smitty replied.

Private Knox said, "Thank you, Jesus. Thank you, Captain."

Captain Jones replied, "You're welcome, soldier, an' may God be with us today."

Jones returned his attention to the platoon leaders. "See, all's well. Now we have a job to do. Any questions? Don't worry, Able Company and Charlie Company will move in from the west an' keep that battalion pinned down."

Lieutenant Powell voiced concern. "Sure hope so, Cap'n. If they don't, we're dead."

Jones said, "Gentlemen, don't worry. Everything'll be fine. Move out. Remember, your best defense is speed. Attack when you hear the artillery. Good luck." The lieutenants returned to their platoons. Powell, Kaminski, Danny, and Smitty stayed with Captain Jones.

CHAPTER 5

Taking a Bridge

CAPTAIN JONES RUMMAGED through his pockets for a strip of beef jerky; after biting off a piece, he reexamined the map. With everything in place, the captain could do no more. In spite of the difficult battle ahead, Captain Jones felt certain the men of Baker Company would succeed. Still, he could not help but think the success of this first mission and the lives of his men were in his hands. The young captain, riding a wave of hope, checked his watch; it read 7:00. The brief tranquility he cherished would morph into a frenzy of violence and death in a matter of seconds. He grasped the walkie-talkie and dropped it. After regaining composure, he picked up the radio and called for the planned fire mission. He inhaled deeply and spoke loudly into the radio.

"White-Eagle-Five, this's Baker-One. Fire for range, over," said Captain Jones.

The radio crackled, "Roger, Baker-One, White-Eagle-Five. Fire for range, over."

"Grid 63253, direction 5200, distance 4800, over," said Captain Jones.

"Roger, Baker-One. Grid 63253, direction 5200, distance 4800, over," replied White-Eagle-Five.

Captain Jones said, "One panzer, danger close, 650 yards. Fire at my command, over."

"One panzer, danger close, 650 yards. Fire at your command, over," replied White-Eagle-Five.

Captain Jones said, "Fire one round, wait for adjustment, over."

"Fire one round, wait for adjustment, over," replied White-Eagle-Five.

He turned to Lieutenants Powell and Kaminski and said, "Hold steady until I give the command."

"Yes, sir."

Captain Jones picked up the field glasses and fixed his attention on the German position just beyond the river. The first round shrieked overhead.

Swooosh.

The round fell short of the river, giving a loud report and sending a plume of dirt and smoke into the air. The young captain thought, *"I can't believe my luck."* Jones had no time to contemplate his good fortune. He turned to his lieutenants and said, "Gentlemen, today's our lucky day."

The captain grabbed the walkie-talkie. "White-Eagle-Five, this is Baker-One. Add two hundred yards, and fire for effect. Say again, add two hundred yards, and fire for effect, over."

"Roger, Baker-One, add two hundred yards, and fire for effect, over."

"Roger, over and out."

Lieutenant Romero gave the command to open fire. Two rockets from the bazookas, launched in rapid succession, roared into the targets. The machine gun nests and the German soldiers manning them exploded into a shower of debris. White-Eagle-Five opened fire. Shells from their howitzers rained onto the German side of the river. In less than ten seconds, the chaos of battle enveloped German troops, who, only moments ago, were enjoying the beauty of a sunny spring morning. They scrambled to their positions as a cloud of smoke produced by exploding artillery shells drifted lazily over the valley toward the men of Baker Company.

Captain Jones shouted, "It's our turn. Kaminski, lead your platoon with Powell's to the right of the bridge! We'll follow. Move fast!"

PAPAW

"Got it!" Kaminski and Powell raced to their platoons.

The captain turned to Smitty and Danny. "You two're on me. Let's go."

Danny said, "This's it, Smitty."

Smitty replied, "We gotta bridge to get, let's go. It'll be okay, just follow me, an' run like hell." He added, "We have to die of somethin'."

"Let's not die here. I wanna die an old man sittin' on a porch with a beer in my hand," said Danny. The fear and apprehension Danny felt contemplating this moment left him; he was about to die. Danny and Smitty fell in behind their captain and the men of Baker Company.

Captain Jones's exposed force could do nothing but run to the objective. High-pitched whistles and shrieks filled the air. Rifle fire from German soldiers and pre-targeted mortars wreaked havoc on the advancing Americans. The tank rotated slowly on its tracks toward their position, preparing to open fire with its machine gun. Shrapnel from exploding mortar rounds rained down upon the men of Baker Company; the blasts sent soldiers to the ground, and many died.

The captain felt the fear of his men course through his body like an untamed horse that required breaking. He broke the fear and used it like any other weapon. His faith became a weapon as well. Before every battle, he turned to his faith, where he found great comfort, and in his faith, courage and strength. The ability to harness his fear and faith earned him a Silver Star for valor at the Battle of Kasserine Pass and would serve as an example for his men. Like the others, however, he wanted to be standing when the guns fell silent. To a man, nothing was more important.

Captain Jones possessed the speed of a star fullback. Danny and Smitty struggled to keep up. They ignored the cries of the wounded; only a decisive victory could save them. Two bazooka rounds screeched overhead, and as planned, hit the tracks of the tank, rendering it immobile. Unforgiving artillery fire from White-Eagle-Five fell from the sky. The exploding rounds landed behind the German line beyond the river, reducing buildings to splinters. Dirt, rocks, and shattered boards flew through the air, thwarting attempts by advancing German infantrymen to support their comrades.

Fighting intensified as Kaminski and Powell led their platoons to the bridge. They closed in and tightened a noose around a squad of defending German infantrymen. Advancing on the objective, Captain Jones, Danny, and Smitty ignored bullets and exploding shells. Lead elements of the assault hurled the surprised enemy back across the bridge in confusion.

Bullets buzzed through the air like angry hornets. A round pinged Danny's helmet as he fought to keep up with Smitty and their athletic captain. Enemy artillery shrieked overhead, followed by deafening explosions, choking dirt, and smoke. Danny's eyes and lungs burned. The ground shuddered with each explosion, and Baker Company's losses mounted.

One round exploded close to Captain Jones, sending him to the ground with a bounce. The concussive force threw Danny and Smitty to the ground on their backs. Momentarily dazed, they scrambled to their feet and retrieved their helmets. Amazed to be unhurt, they ran to their captain, whose body lay prostrate.

Smitty squatted on his haunches, flipped the body over, and became lost in contemplation, descending into shock. Danny stood over his friend, who was oblivious to the battle. Shrapnel tore a jagged gash in Captain Jones's neck. His tunic was soaked in blood, and his eyes were locked open. Smitty ran his trembling fingers through his captain's hair and stammered, "He, he, ja, ja, just baptized a young boy."

Danny thought, *"I've never seen Smitty like this. He got us through one tight spot after another."* Danny stepped up for his friend.

"Come on, Smitty, the war's over for the cap'n. He's gone to a better place. We've gotta job to do. Let's go. We'll die if we stay here. Think of Jean an' your daughters. It's what the cap'n would want." Smitty turned from the captain, and with blank eyes, stared. Danny grabbed Smitty by the shoulders, pulled him to his feet, looked into his eyes, and shook him. "DAMN IT, SMITTY, SNAP OUT OF IT!"

Smitty's eyes widened, and a smile came to lips. "I'm okay, ole boy."

PAPAW

Danny thought, *"Thank God. He's back."*

Danny gesticulated toward the bridge. "Let's finish the mission."

"WAIT!" shouted Smitty. He reached and retrieved the captain's canteen.

Danny shouted, "HURRY!" Smitty fumbled with the canteen while Danny anxiously rocked from one foot to the other, watching.

Smitty twisted the cap from the canteen, put it his pocket, and said, "Let's go."

When they reached the bridge, Danny and Smitty encountered three German infantrymen emerging from behind the tank, leveling their rifles at them. Smitty shouted, "I GOT THIS! MEET ME AT THE BRIDGE!" Danny gave an affirmative nod and continued.

Smitty shouldered his Thompson, squeezed the trigger, and swung the weapon from left to right like a door on a hinge, raking the infantrymen with a spray of bullets; they fell to the ground. He replaced the magazine and ran toward the tank. The tank crew flung the hatch open, attempting to escape the burning hulk. Smitty fired a short burst at one crewman climbing through the opening, and the German soldier slumped over the turret, dead. He thought, *"I better clear the tank."*

Smitty jumped through smoke and flames, scrambled to the turret, and drew a grenade. Frantic voices shouting in German came from within. He pulled the pin, dropped the grenade through the hatch, and jumped from the burning tank. A panicked hand reached out of the turret, grasping at his dead comrade, and a head followed. A muffled explosion knocked the turret from its mount, and the eighty-eight-millimeter cannon, which struck fear in the hearts of Allied tankers, slumped to the ground. Smitty watched the soldier sink into the turret as gray smoke billowed as if coming from a chimney.

Smitty muttered with a chuckle, "Poor bastards."

He found the bridge under the control of Powell and Kaminski; their men were busy pursuing retreating German soldiers. He ran to Danny and shouted, "YOU GOIN' TO STAND AROUN' ALL DAY? TAKE THE RIGHT. I'LL TAKE THE LEFT."

They dropped their Thompsons and extra weight and swung over the side of the bridge, dangling freely from the girders. Driven by fear and fueled by adrenaline, they raced like crazed gymnasts toward the center of the bridge in a frenzied hand-over-hand motion.

The two, locked in a deadly competition, dangled from the bridge, not looking at the slow-moving current thirty feet beneath. Danny glanced at Smitty, who was busy cutting wires. Danny turned his attention to his task and spotted the second charge. Upon reaching it, he clipped the wires, and, like Smitty, threw the bundle of explosives into the river.

Lieutenant Jackson, along with Lieutenant Romero, led his platoon across the bridge. With the added pressure of Able Company and Charlie Company and the enemy in full retreat, the American attack on the German position became a rout. Smitty and Danny, their mission complete, frantically made their way to the other side of the bridge while bullets pinged off supporting girders.

Smitty flashed Danny a thumbs-up, and the latter returned the gesture. Their relief at the completion of the mission was thwarted by a bullet that struck Smitty in the chest. Danny dangled from the bridge, watching helplessly as his friend splashed into the river. A round hit Danny, shattering his left wrist, and he followed, crashing into the frigid water. His senses intensified with the surge of cold water. His boots and uniform became an anchor, and he continued to sink until he bounced off the bottom.

Danny thought, "*I'm goin' to drown!*"

He tumbled along the bottom, disoriented. Water pressure felt like nails being driven into his ears. Trying to get to the surface, he flailed against the powerful current, but the river refused to relent. Terror, claustrophobia, and death gripped Danny.

Anne came to him in a vision, standing at the bus stop, saying goodbye. She beckoned, *"Come home. It's not your time. I'm waiting."* The image of Anne strengthened his resolve. Just as quick, Danny found his feet on the riverbed. He pushed with all the strength he could muster and fought his way to the surface, recovering his composure. Gasping for breath, he found Smitty floating downstream, struggling. He swam to his friend and wrestled him to the riverbank on the German side of the river.

Smitty's heart pushed blood through a gaping chest wound with each beat, and his confident face turned ashen. Life faded from eyes that, only fifteen minutes earlier, sparkled with confidence. Death would take his friend in moments. Danny, in spite of seeing death on a vast scale, could not bear to watch his friend die. But the bond between the two chained Danny to his dying friend. He called out, "MEDIC, MEDIC." Danny turned to Smitty and said, "Hang on, Smitty. I'm goin' to find a medic."

Smitty's eyes widened. Through coughs he said, "No! There's no use, ole boy. Don't leave. Don't let me die alone."

Danny wore a shell of indifference and shied away from the men in his squad. Such indifference would normally protect him from what he was about to endure. However, while in North Africa, the outgoing Smitty sought Danny's friendship and broke through his indifference. Smitty's infectious confidence drew Danny in, and they became close wartime friends. Now Danny had to confront what he dreaded most: saying goodbye.

"Okay, Smitty, don't worry. I'm not goin' anywhere."

"I've gotta confession to make," said Smitty with a weak smile.

Danny lowered his ear to Smitty's mouth and prepared for the confession. "Go ahead, I'm listenin'."

Smitty coughed and laughed weakly. "I'm afraid of water. I can't swim. Looks like I owe ya one, ole boy."

Danny laughed and said, "Figures. I told ya this was a numbskull idea. Let's just call it even. You saved my ass a few times."

Smitty, struggling to speak, said, "I know, but the thought of drowning's scary. Hell, when we hit the beach, I wasn't scared of the Krauts. I was afraid the water would be over my head. I was always afraid of drowning. That water's so damn cold. Did ya get hit?" Danny held up his left wrist for his friend to see.

Smitty looked at Danny's hand. "The million-dollar wound, ole boy. See, told ya it'd work out. An' ya thought this was a numbskull idea." Danny let his friend talk.

Smitty reached into his pocket and retrieved the cap he took from Captain Jones's canteen. "Look, the sun. It feels good. Goin' to be a nice day." He pressed the cap into Danny's hand. "I'm feelin' a little woozy. Keep this. I have a feelin' you'll need it someday. It'll help ya remember that you can find God anywhere—even in war. Find Jesus, Danny. All this is not his fault."

With his remaining strength, Smitty squeezed Danny's hand. "Keep it."

"I'll keep it, Smitty." Danny felt Smitty's grip weaken.

"Tell Jean I didn't suffer, an' I love her."

"I will."

"If I hurry, I can catch up with the cap'n. I'd love to go through them ole gates with 'im. I'm goin' to the Lord. Tell 'em…" Smitty became limp, and his eyes remained open and still. Smitty died.

Danny slumped over his dead friend, and through heavy sobs, said, "Don't worry, Smitty. I won't let 'em forget."

In less than twenty minutes, Danny lost two close friends. He looked at the sky. "Some God you are. With the snap of your finger, you could stop all this. Why Smitty an' the cap'n? Why not me?"

The fighting ceased. After the brief and deadly encounter, dead bodies and wounded soldiers from both sides littered the once pristine hamlet. Charcoal smoke hung over the river in the still air like a shroud. Scores of artillery and mortar rounds gouged craters into the once smooth pasture, and shattered buildings burned. American commanders milled about, questioning local civilians, while enlisted men gathered abandoned weapons left by the retreating German soldiers. Support and medical personnel rushed in to secure the objective, treat the wounded, and sort out the dead. The horrific scene reminded survivors, with a visible testament, of the horrible cost of war.

Except for the occasional pop of rifle fire and the roaring engines of jeeps and trucks, silence reclaimed the land. Danny held his dead friend in his arms. Among the garbled voices, "Hey, Shykes, ya call for a medic?"

Danny gently rubbed the cap that, only a short time ago, Captain Jones used to baptize a scared private. He thought of his captain and Smitty. He looked at the medic and said, "He's gone."

Danny held Smitty as the medic looked down, and the medic replied, "Is that Smitty? Smitty's dead? You two been together since Africa."

Danny's emotions erupted, and he shouted, "DAMN IT! HE'S GONE, NOT DEAD!"

Danny turned back to Smitty, softened his tone, and said, "He told me he went to find the cap'n."

CHAPTER 6

July 1979

Nine-year-old Ricky, captivated by Danny's story, sought confirmation and asked, "Mr. Shykes, did it really happen like that?"

Tim, Danny's grandson, looked at Ricky incredulously. "Yes, it's true. All of it. Papaw's got a Silver Star to prove it."

The children's innocent voices returned Danny to July 1979; in solemn tones, he replied, "Yes, Ricky. I'm afraid that's how it happened. A lot of brave men died. I lost two of my best friends, and it was the last time I saw action."

Ricky asked, "Were ya scared? I bet ya weren't. Don't think I could run that fast."

"Yes, I was scared. Once we got started, I was so busy I forgot I was scared. But me an' ole Smitty had a job to do. I never saw men run so fast in my life. It was the fastest I ever ran, an' I never run that fast since." After a brief reflective pause, Danny added, "Of course, I was younger."

Danny's left hand, along with his youth, were long gone. His hair went from black to gray to white over the years. He exercised regularly, and except for a small beer gut, maintained good muscle tone. Good investing and modest living allowed him to retire early from his job as a park ranger. He intended to spend his retirement traveling with his wife, Anne. The plans fell through after Anne died tragically, along with their son-in-law, in an automobile accident.

PAPAW

Danny made a small apartment for himself in the basement of his spacious farmhouse and asked his daughter, Carol, and his grandchildren to move in. Having the children around eased the loneliness and depression. The arrangement worked out for Carol; the children loved their papaw, and her career as an emergency room nurse required shift changes that made finding day care difficult.

Tim, his nine-year-old grandson, and Mary, his eight-year-old granddaughter, idolized Danny, now sixty. The children, cute and well-mannered, had sparse patches of freckles that ran across the bridge of their noses. Mary, with blond hair and blue eyes, favored Carol, her mother. Tim, with a crop of thick black hair and brown eyes, favored his late father, Tom.

Danny's small farm provided ample space and horses to ride. Anne started to teach Tim and Mary about horses as soon as they were able to walk. God and horses were Anne's passions. She often used horses as a gateway to Jesus and derived considerable joy from teaching children horsemanship. Her plans were to make Tim and Mary excellent riders and the latter a barrel racer. Danny felt Anne's presence through the children's love of horses.

The children became the brunt of Danny's many pranks and an eager audience for his wartime stories. The children loved the stories, and most of all, the bridge story, which he told many times. Today, two of Tim's friends, Ricky and Hunter, joined his grandchildren.

Ricky, gregarious, confident, and large for his nine years, walked with a confident swagger, which amused Danny. His father, a Marine, kept Ricky's brown hair cut in a scalp-hugging burr that felt gritty to the touch. The leader among the children, he enjoyed fishing and hunting small game.

Hunter, tall, skinny, and also nine, sported a pageboy haircut, resembling Buster Brown. However, Hunter stood in sharp contrast with the mischievous comic strip character. Large buck teeth dominated his face, causing him to pronounce the letter R and, sometimes the letter L, as a W. Hunter's overprotective parents, who taught at the local university, tried to shelter Hunter from influences they deemed beneath the intellect of the child, who loved to read about history, play chess, and stargaze. Plagued with numerous allergies, he required a great deal of oversight, especially when eating. He felt out of place around those he did not know and became the target of bullying. Ricky looked after him with the same care he would give to a younger brother. Hunter loved spending time with Tim and Ricky, but most of all, he loved the rough-and-tumble play forbidden by his parents. His pleasant and unassuming personality endeared him to the other children as well as Danny.

Danny's five-year-old Jack Russell terrier, a gift from his late wife Anne, sat patiently among the small gathering, ready to play. Danny named the dog Ike after Dwight David Eisenhower, Supreme Allied Commander during World War II. Anne chose the terrier for its feisty personality and excellent ability as a ratter. Rats were the only animal for which Danny had no empathy, and he enjoyed watching the small dog hunt the rodents while he drank beer. The spirited little dog was never far from his side, except when Mary and Tim were nearby.

During this rendition of the bridge story, the children, apart from Mary and Hunter, were equipped with broomsticks used as makeshift rifles. Metal cooking pots, which Tim procured from the kitchen, adorned their heads. The handles, jutting out to the sides, tilted their helmets to varying degrees. Danny, amused at the strange sight of his small squad, looked at his granddaughter and asked, "Mary, where's your helmet?"

Before she could reply, Tim said, "She's a girl, Papaw. There weren't no girls in the Army."

Indignant, Mary shot back, "Was to!"

Ricky, in support of Tim, said, "Was not."

Danny jumped in. "Now, now, boys, calm down. Yes, Ricky, you're right. During World War II, women didn't fight in the American army." The boys turned to Mary and grinned. Their long-running argument finally came to an end. Danny noticed Mary's crestfallen look and added, "However, girls did all kinds of things to help us in battle, like take care of the wounded, drive supply trucks, and some were even flight instructors. Do not forget about the French Resistance." The smiles on the boys' faces left and found Mary's face.

PAPAW

Hunter entered the debate. "The Fwench Wesistance was an undergwound army that fought against Germany when Fwance fell."

Rick snapped, "Quit bein' a brownnose," then shot an incredulous look at Danny, seeking confirmation.

Danny turned to Hunter and said, "Ya know what? Hunter's right. Before we invaded France in June 1944, the French had a secret army that fought the Krauts. They fought bravely by knocking out telephone lines, blowing up trains, an' hid our pilots who were shot down behind enemy lines. They did anything they could to harass the enemy, an' guess WHAT?"

In one voice, all four children asked, "What?"

Danny leaned over and patted Mary on the head and said, "Girls fought in the French Resistance. The girls were some of the toughest fighters on either side."

Mary beamed with pride and looked at her brother and proclaimed, "See, I told ya so." The boys now had to openly accept Mary into the group.

Danny noticed a small cross drawn in red crayon on Hunter's makeshift helmet. "Hunter, looks like you're the medic, right?"

Sheepishly, Hunter said, "Yeah, Mom won't awow me pway with guns."

Tim echoed, "Yeah, Papaw, his mom won't even let him play with a broomstick."

Danny laughed. "Not even a broomstick."

"No, not even a broomstick. He's our medic," said Ricky.

"Boys, let me tell ya. Medics were the bravest of the brave," said Danny. He tapped at the red cross drawn on the pot. "Why, a Kraut sniper would use that cross as a target. The bullet would enter from the front, pass through the helmet, an' explode out the back, spewing blood an' brains. A mess, for sure. Medics were very important. I thank God they were there."

Danny's daughter Carol interrupted his graphic tale. "Tim, tell your friends it's suppertime. They've got to go an' come back tomorrow."

"Awe, Mom, can't they stay a little longer? Please?" Tim pleaded.

Carol gave in. "Okay, fifteen minutes, an' that's all."

Mary cast her gaze on Danny's hook. "Papaw, can you make your hook shoot lightning?"

Tim said, "Yes, show Hunter an' Ricky. They never seen nothin' like it."

Danny fancied himself an engineer who loved to tinker, and constructing rat traps occupied much of his free time. He conjured up every conceivable design. One such trap, called "walk the plank," consisted of a large bucket half full of water, a ramp, and a hinged plank baited with peanut butter. Like the name suggests, rats would make their way up the ramp and onto the plank. When the rat reached the peanut butter, the plank would fall away, dumping the rat into the water and causing its death by drowning. Danny even built a guillotine rat trap, a detailed replica of the one used to execute Louis XVI, king of France, in 1793, complete with little steps. The rat would climb the steps and stick its head through a slot while reaching for a baited wire, which triggered the blade, dispatching the rat. Danny loved the model. However, due to its messy nature, he rarely used it.

Most of all, Danny loved watching Ike. On many nights, Danny would take a chair and a cooler filled with beer to the barn, then turn Ike loose. The dog had a sixth sense for finding rat burrows. Danny derived great pleasure from listening as Ike scampered through the barn, letting out an occasional bark. When the barking stopped, Ike was feverishly clawing at the ground. Then, for Danny to see, the dog would pop out with the unfortunate rat tightly clenched in his jaws. As if on cue, Ike would dispatch it by violently shaking the helpless rodent. The little dog's head became a blur as he shook the rat. After a few seconds, he would check it for life by prodding the dazed creature with his nose. If the rat showed any sign of life, Ike repeated the process. After determining a rat was dead, Ike would prance with the rat in his mouth and drop it next to Danny. One night, Ike piled up five rats.

His latest trap, the centerpiece of the impromptu demonstration, was an electronic trap. Danny had been working on it for several weeks. It would dispatch a rat with a high-voltage jolt of electric-

PAPAW

ity. He loved to show it off to the children by placing his hook near it, triggering an arc and a loud pop.

"I think we have time," Danny said with a fiendish grin, lifting his hook and twisting it to and fro to show the children.

The children erupted with excitement. Danny rose, walked to his workbench, picked up a wooden box one foot square, six inches high, and within the box was a complex array of circuits, capacitors, and wires. A metal probe protruded from one side of the box, and from the other side, an electrical cord dangled.

Tim cried out, "I get to push the button first, Papaw."

Danny laughed and said, "Let Hunter go first. Everyone'll get a turn." Hunter burst with joy.

Danny plugged the cord into a wall socket and told Mary, "Push the red button." Mary pushed it as instructed. The basement was quiet except for the high-pitched whine of capacitors charging. "Okay, Hunter, when the green light comes on, it'll be ready. When I say, 'fire in the hole,' push the blue button. Got it?"

"Yes, sir, Mr. Shykes, got it."

"Fifty thousand volts! Ricky! Hit the lights!" Danny said as the capacitors charged. Ricky ran to the wall and flipped the switch. Darkness overtook the basement. Suddenly, the whining stopped—not a sound. With the capacitors fully charged, the children were awash in an eerie green glow.

Tim whispered, "It's ready, Papaw. It's ready."

Danny said, "Okay, be careful, an' wait till I give the word." With careful deliberation, he positioned his hook for maximum effect. He remained silent, milking the moment. The children sat quietly, fixated on Danny's hook. Their eyes were wide and still, and their faces glowed green.

"FIRE IN THE HOLE!"

On cue, Hunter pushed the blue button, and electricity arced from the probe tip to Danny's hook. The flash looked like a tiny lightning bolt, and for an instant, engulfed the basement in bright light.

Crack.

The children's screams were followed by raucous laughter, and Danny asked, "Who's next?"

The screaming caused Carol to stop dinner preparations. She walked to the door leading to the basement. "What're youins doin' down there? Anyone hurt?"

Fearing his mother was about to put an end to the fun, Tim said, "No one's hurt, Mom. We're fine." He turned to Danny and whispered, "Quick, Papaw, tell Mom it's okay. Quick."

Like a child beseeching their mother, Danny said, "It's okay, jist usin' my rat zapper to make lightnin' with my hook for the kids."

Carol admonished her father. "Dad, be careful. Remember when you accidentally set it off an' got electrocuted? You were out cold. Had to have EMS come out. Took 'em fifteen minutes to bring ya around. I thought you were dead."

Danny reassured his daughter. "Yes, I remember. Goodness, I just tripped. It won't kill anyone, jist rats." Danny repeated the exhibition; with each rendition, the children erupted with laughter.

Hunter asked, "Mr. Shykes, how come ya don't get hurt?"

Danny slapped his knee with his good hand. "I'll jist tell ya." He removed the hook. The stump dressed in a rubber boot stretched over a sock fascinated Hunter and Ricky. "Ya see this?" Danny asked rhetorically, lifting his stump in the air for all to see. "Look at this rubber boot here," he said, stretching the rubber and letting it snap back against his forearm. "It's called an insulator. That means electricity won't pass through to my arm. Without it, I'd get knocked flat on my ass." He looked at Tim and Mary. "Don't ever come down here an' play with this, got it?"

"Okay, Papaw, we won't," replied Tim and Mary.

Tim looked at Hunter and Ricky. "We gotta eat."

Ricky asked, "Can we come up tomorrow?"

"What about it, can they?" Tim asked.

"It's okay with me, but ya need to ask your mother," insisted Danny, and he led the children upstairs to the kitchen.

Tim asked his mother, "Mom, can Hunter an' Ricky come up tomorrow morning?"

PAPAW

Carol, scheduled to be off, answered, "Sure, if it's okay with your papaw."

Ricky said, "We'll be up in the morning."

Tim turned to his mom and asked, "Can we have breakfast?"

"Sure, why not."

Hunter and Ricky could not believe their good fortune. "See ya in the morning," and they ran out of the house.

CHAPTER 7

Anne and Danny's New House

CUMULUS CLOUDS DRIFTED lazily across the sky as two hawks searching for prey, riding thermals, drew large circles overhead. April 1946 had been unusually dry and warm for east Tennessee and the foothills of the recently created Great Smoky Mountains National Park. The mountains stood as a silent reminder to Danny of the beauty he longed for while fighting in North Africa, Italy, and France. The sounds and smells of death forever tainted the beauty of those nations. Danny would never entertain any desire to return to Europe.

A year earlier, as the war wound down, Danny anticipated resuming his life with Anne while recovering from wounds sustained battling for the bridge. As he waited to go home, minutes became hours, and days became weeks. Now home and Anne his wife, weeks became days, and hours became seconds. Time flew by, and he wanted to squeeze as much life as he could into every second.

The 1939 Ford coupe, a wedding gift from Anne's father, kicked up a cloud of dust as they made their way to an old, run-down farmhouse. Danny pined for the little farm ever since he started to drive. The property, in Wears Valley and unoccupied since before the war, lay between Pigeon Forge and Townsend, Tennessee. With the war behind him, he had Anne and his dream job as a park ranger. Soon he would have the old farmhouse and a perfect life.

PAPAW

He pushed the accelerator to the floor. They sank into their seats under the force of the car's acceleration. Danny turned to his beautiful wife and said, "Feel that! Just listen to that V8."

Anne, with a confident smile, asked, "Goodness, Danny, what's the hurry?"

After a moment, Danny slowed the car and pointed to the farm. "We're here."

Anne's excitement intensified when Danny turned onto the plain dirt driveway that passed between two stately oaks standing like sentries. It led to a dilapidated three-story white Victorian house built in 1890 and situated between two five-acre tracks enclosed by a split-rail fence in need of repair. Massive pecan trees surrounded the old house, which had a large wraparound porch forming an L running from the front and along the left side. Weeds overtook the lattice and grew through the broken planks. The house had no electricity or plumbing, and much of the split oak clapboard siding had rotted, and the old roof needed repair. Danny saw beyond the washed-out white paint, broken planks, and overgrown weeds to the splendor of the magnificent structure.

A barn, almost as large as the house, seemed larger than necessary for the small farm and was in good shape other than needing some paint. A forty-acre pasture, framed with barbed wire and forming a nearly perfect square free of trees, opened behind the barn. Perfect for cattle, it sloped gently up toward the foothills. The property line to the south bordered the Smoky Mountains, ensuring complete privacy.

Danny slammed the brakes, skidding to a stop. He leapt out, ran to the other side, and opened the door for his wife. Anne reached out and gently clasped her husband's hand, more as a ritual of courtship than a need for assistance.

Anne looked into Danny's eyes. The war matured him. Not yet thirty years old, he had streaks of gray running through his jet-black hair. The cocky boy she met was gone. Years of marching and fighting, along with a sparse diet, kept Danny fit and muscular. In his rugged face, with a square jaw and large deep-set brown eyes, the confidence of his waning youth sparkled—something war could not take from him. He dressed in a simple attire consisting of a loose-fitting, unbuttoned, untucked gray denim shirt with sleeves rolled to the elbows that draped loosely over faded blue jeans. Nevertheless, Danny appeared to Anne as a chivalrous knight returning from battle to reclaim his life and take his prize.

Anne emerged from the car with the elegance of a queen or grand head of state. She rested her arms on the open door, leisurely surveying the vast rolling landscape dotted with barns, and to the south, foothills covered with a carpet of fir trees. Anne, because of her beauty, found herself at the center of attention. She never sought the attention she drew. Only from Danny did she seek attention, yearning to be at the center of his earthly world. Anne, however, was ready to build a new world with Danny—a world with Jesus at the center.

The sight of Anne standing by the car took Danny's breath. Her subtle intelligence and wit, however, drew him to her. Anne, an extrovert who knew something about everything, never shied away from expressing her opinion when asked. She enjoyed everything he enjoyed, including the outdoors—horses, fishing, and camping—but when the occasion required, she welcomed the opportunity to adorn herself with the latest fashions. On such occasions, she acquired a mature elegance that exceeded her youth—elegance only found on the cover of a fashion magazine. Her faith in Jesus, however, moored her to humility. Like Danny, Anne cherished this moment. In her mind, their life together was a gift from God, and both would require a lifetime to understand.

Anne, dressed to the nines, wore a knee-length, form-fitting white cotton dress with a cross-V neckline trimmed in navy blue. A navy blue belt cinched snugly above her hips intensified her figure. Navy blue slingback pumps on one-inch block heels adorned her feet. She removed a large floppy, navy blue toyo straw sun hat trimmed with a simple white bow, exposing pinned-up blond tresses, and tossed the hat into the car. Deep blue eyes sparkled against a dark complexion and delicate features.

Danny asked rhetorically, "How'd I get so lucky?"

PAPAW

Anne threw her arms around Danny's neck. "Don't think about it. Just kiss me. God brought you back to me an' wants us together."

Danny kissed Anne and said, "You really believe that. You sound like ole Smitty. Him and Cap'n Jones were holly rollers, just like you. Lotta good that did 'em. Here I am, an' they're dead. Just can't see God. Not after all I saw. But if all that makes ya happy, I'm happy."

"That makes me happy, an' one day you'll see. There's a plan."

Danny leaned over Anne. "Shhh. Listen."

"I don't hear anything."

"The wind," Danny said. "Feel the breeze. It's blowing through the trees." He tilted his head back and took a long, deep breath through his nose. "Smell that! Trees, dirt, an' fresh air—no stench of death, no explosions, just the sound an' smell of nature. I love it."

Danny's happy banter reassured Anne. If the war changed him, maybe it was for the better. Any task or challenge they faced, in Anne's mind, could be overcome. "You're incredible. Looks like that ole house'll keep us busy," said Anne.

Danny grabbed Anne's hand, and they ran to the old farmhouse. "On account of me bein' in the war, I gotta good deal. This's our house now. That's if ya want it. I'm goin' to build ya a home fit for a queen. Do ya wanna help me fix'er up?"

Anne replied, "Yes, I'll help ya. You're stuck with me." Anne looked at the large old farmhouse. "You wouldn't be thinking of little ones, would you?" Danny smiled mischievously.

Anne wanted to get married before Danny left. He would not have it for fear of leaving a widow behind. While he fought in North Africa, Italy, and finally northern France, he had second thoughts and longed for his fiery blond-haired, blue-eyed beauty. While Anne waited for his return, she prayed daily, hanging on to any news from the Army. Time, separation, and distance would not squelch the love they had. Now Anne stood in front of the old farmhouse, feeling Danny's excitement, convinced Danny was worth the wait.

The war, a gaping wound in Danny's mind, would take years to heal. He studied Anne and the house, contemplating Smitty and Captain Jones, and thought, *I don't understand. Why did I get to come home? Why not Smitty or Captain Jones?*

Danny said, "Come on, I have a lot to show ya." They ran to the house and flew up five steps onto the front porch. Danny threw the door open and, forgetting his wife, charged in.

Anne stood, arms akimbo, and said, "Hey, Mac! Aren't ya forgetting somethin'?"

He looked back at his wife's silhouette through the door and stepped toward her.

"Oh, forgot."

Danny swept Anne into his arms and carried her through the door. He put her down and held her in his arms, running his fingers through her hair, releasing it from its restraints. Anne's hair fell to her shoulders. He looked deeply into her eyes and kissed her as if it were for the last time.

"I'll never let you go."

"I think I'm going to like this," said Anne as Danny pulled back. "You better not let me go, Daniel Shykes. All this's your fault, ya know. You made me fall in love. I just can't help myself. I'm at your mercy."

Danny brushed her cheek with a finger and said, "You were with me the whole time. When I was shot an' fell into the river, I was gonna die. But you came to me, an' I went to you." His eyes moistened with emotion. "You told me to come home. Without you, I would've died. You kept me alive through the hell an' uncertainty of war. You kept me goin' when death came near. Now it's my turn. I'll always be here for you. I'll protect you as you did me."

Anne said, "I didn't keep you alive. God did. Every day, I reminded God how much I loved you. Guess God saw things my way. I don't know what God has planned, but God's not through with you. One thing I know, part of your purpose is to love me. So, Mr. Shykes, tell me, what's the plan?"

"Well, Mrs. Shykes, as you noticed, this house needs lots of work—a new roof, new windows, and the whole inside needs to be redone," said Danny as he tapped the floor with his hook. "The foundation, floors, and walls are in good shape. The supporting structures are solid as a rock. I checked it out. Let's look at the barn." Danny grabbed Anne's hand and guided her through the front door, and they ran to the barn.

When they entered the barn, pigeons scattered, drawing attention to the rafters and crossbeams. Anne examined an old, rusty bow saw hanging on the wall and gently ran her hand over a supporting beam. "It may be in better shape than the house. We could move in here. What about it?"

"In Europe, this would've been a luxury. I just wanna be with you, even if it's in a barn." Danny's eyes stayed on his beautiful wife. "I'll fix a place in the house while we work on it." He pointed toward the front of the barn. "We can put our tack over there."

Anne replied, "That's a good spot. This barn'll make a good stable for the horses."

Haw, haw, haw, hee haw, haw, haw, haw.

Anne, attracted to the braying, asked, "Is that what I think it is?"

She dashed for the sound, and upon exiting, much to her delight, stood a gray-dun donkey. Its muzzle and belly were white, and a thin black line of fur ran across its shoulders. Another thin line of black ran down the center of its back, forming a cross. At the end of a gray tail was a tuft of black fur. A short black mane contrasted with its dusty gray coat. At the sight of Anne, its long gray ears with black along the edges stood erect. The docile animal, seeking attention, stared with unflinching eyes, its tail swaying from side to side and its head stretched over the barbed wire fence. Anne could not hide the love she instantly felt for the donkey.

She ran to the donkey as if she found a million dollars and gently rubbed his muzzle. "Look, Danny, he's beautiful. He's a jack. What's his name?"

The sight of Anne with the animal charmed Danny. "That's Donkey."

"Don't be silly. I know it's a donkey, but what's his name?"

"His name's DONKEY."

Anne continued to rub his muzzle. "Well, his name's Jack now."

Danny intended to let Anne decide if they should keep the animal. He could not, however, resist the opportunity to string her along. "Don't get too attached to 'im. He won't be here long. I'm goin' to get rid of 'im. We don't need a donkey. All he'll do is take space. Space I can use for a cow."

Anne protested, "Oh no, Danniel Shykes! We're keepin' Jack."

"The Jenkins widow, you know Margaret, said she would take 'im back if I didn't want 'im. Her husband, Lee, died a few years before the war. This used to be their farm, but it was too much for her to handle by herself." Danny ran his hand through his hair and looked Anne in the eye. "She told me Lee, he was in the first war, suffered from shell shock an' since he returned, was never the same. She said he saw a lot of bad stuff. Then shortly before he died, she got this little donkey foal, and somehow, he came out of his shell. She said that the last two years of his life were as if he were normal an' happy. I guess she figured that I suffered from the same problem, an' the donkey would help me like he helped Lee. But I'll not need 'im. I think I'll fence an acre for Margaret, an' we can return the donkey to her."

"His name's Jack, an' we're keep'n 'im, an' that's final."

Danny had no intention of giving the animal away. He loved watching Anne make the case for the donkey and continued to milk the moment. He said, "Goodness, Anne, are ya serious? We have no use for a donkey. There's nothin' wrong with me. I'm fine. Look at those stupid ears. Can ya tell me what he's good for?"

Anne rubbed Jack behind the ears. "There's NOTHING stupid about Jack. His ears're fine, an' he's good for plenty."

"Just name one thing."

"For one thing, he'll protect your cattle from coyotes. Besides, he's a noble animal. Don't you know it was a donkey that carried Jesus into Jerusalem?"

Danny scratched the back of his head with his hook. "I figured you'd work Jesus in."

Anne pointed to the donkey's back. "Look, see that? It's the mark of the cross. All donkeys have that mark. I don't suppose you've heard of the legend of the cross?"

Wishing to prolong the moment, Danny made his way to Anne and Jack. He scrutinized the animal's back. "I'll be. There's a cross on his back. Tell me about this legend."

Anne pulled from her pocket a small Bible, flipped through the pages until she found Matthew 21:1–11, and read from it. "As they approached Jerusalem and came to Bethphage on the Mount of Olives, Jesus sent two disciples, saying to them, 'Go to the village ahead of you, and at once you will find a donkey tied there, with her colt by her. Untie them and bring them to me. If anyone says anything to you, say that the Lord needs them, and he will send them right away.'

"This took place to fulfill what was spoken through the prophet: 'Say to Daughter Zion, 'See, your king comes to you, gentle and riding on a donkey, and on a colt, the foal of a donkey.'

"The disciples went and did as Jesus had instructed them. They brought the donkey and the colt and placed their cloaks on them for Jesus to sit on. A very large crowd spread their cloaks on the road, while others cut branches from the trees and spread them on the road. The crowds that went ahead of him and those that followed shouted, 'Hosanna to the Son of David! Blessed is he who comes in the name of the Lord! Hosanna in the highest heaven!'

"When Jesus entered Jerusalem, the whole city was stirred and asked, 'Who is this?'

"The crowds answered, 'This is Jesus, the prophet from Nazareth in Galilee.'"

Anne returned the Bible to her pocket. "Legend has it, the donkey Jesus rode followed him to Calvary, an' he was so sad at the sight of his master on the cross that he turned and looked away, but the little donkey would not leave his master. As a reward for the loyalty and love the donkey showed, the Lord caused the shadow of the cross to fall upon the animal, an' to this day all donkeys wear the cross."

Danny replied, "Goodness, can't argue with that. I guess if Jack makes ya happy, we can keep 'im. Besides, I don't want God upset."

Anne pressed for more. "I think Jack's lonely. Let's get 'im a companion."

Danny, bested by Anne, got serious. "You're not suggesting we get another donkey, are ya?"

"Jack needs a girl donkey."

"One's enough! The cows'll keep 'im company."

"Danny, it's not the same." Anne smiled and said, "Besides, there is nothing as cute as a little donkey."

Danny's pleasant little game with Anne turned against him, and he decided to cut his losses. "If this keeps up, I'll end up with a donkey farm. Okay, one more, but that's it! He's your responsibility." Anne confidently smiled over a victory that, from the start, she won.

With the donkey issue settled, he laid out his plans. "We've got enough space for horses an' a few head a cattle." He pointed to a sunlit place one hundred feet behind the house. "That's where we're goin' to put the garden." He turned to Anne. "What're thinkin'? Do ya like it?"

"I love it. Ya got it all figured out."

Danny took Anne into his arms and said, "All ya gotta do is tell me what ya want, an' it'll get done. You're the boss." He kissed Anne and pulled back. "I forgot about children. Are ya ready?"

Anne smiled.

CHAPTER 8

The Sinking of U-1206

DANNY SAT STARING into his plate.

"Papaw! What's wrong? Why aren't ya eating?" Mary asked.

Carol walked by her father and touched his shoulder. "Dad, are ya all right?"

Danny broke free of his pleasant daydream. "I'm fine. Just thinkin' 'bout your mother an' the first time she saw this house. It sure was a mess." After a moment of silence, he added, "I promised to be there for her. She was there for me. Should've been with her that night. She'd be alive."

Carol took a seat and grasped her father's hand. "It's tough. We all miss Mom. I know it's harder on you. But you're not responsible. There's nothin' you could've done. Mom knows that. I miss Tom. We gotta have faith that we'll see 'em again."

Carol's husband, Tom, was like a son to Danny. He worked as a police officer, and they spent a lot of time together hunting and fishing. On the evening of the accident, Anne had been babysitting Tim and Mary, and in spite of the storm, Anne wanted to go home. Even though Anne and Danny lived down the road, Tom insisted on driving. A drunk driver, traveling at a high rate of speed, lost control of his car and crossed into their lane, hitting them head-on. Tom and Anne died after their car rolled into a rain-swollen stream at the bottom of a small ravine.

Although Carol's words were comforting, Danny thought, "*I should've picked her up.*"

Since her death, that thought greeted Danny every morning. Anne suggested, "*No need to get out. Tom'll bring me home,*" remembered Danny. But he succumbed to his weariness and let Tom bring her home.

Swift and unexpected, the accident wrenched from his heart his greatest love, and for the first time, Danny found himself alone. The thoughtless incursion of a stranger robbed Danny and Anne of their remaining life together. The nightmare of that evening greeted him every morning. *"If only I had gone, maybe Tom and Anne would be alive, or at least Tom would be alive, and I would be with Anne."*

During the war, Danny had Anne. He did not understand, but she was with him even as death tugged at his heels. Her promise that he would return saved him. In June 1944, while fighting for a small bridge, he found himself sinking in a river, wounded and fighting for his life. As he sank into the cold water, Anne beckoned to him, "*Come home to me, Danny.*"

When he returned from the war, he promised her, "I'll always be there for you." After the accident, he could not move beyond his promise—a promise forever unkept and plans left unfulfilled. Danny would never see Anne, and it was his fault. After the accident, Danny suggested Carol and his grandchildren move in. He needed to hear their sounds; their games and bickering kept Anne close and Danny sane.

Danny changed the subject. "After supper, we're goin' to the store."

Tim and Mary lit up. Mary asked, "Are we gettin' a toy?"

"Maybe," said Danny. "We ain't doin' nothin' till you two eat."

Danny ate his hamburger, turned to Carol, and said, "Aren't ya goin' to eat?"

"Remember, I have a date."

Danny reassured his daughter. "I forgot. It's been long enough. Ya need to get out. You're still young, an' your life's in front of ya."

"I know, Dad, but it's still hard. We're just goin' to dinner."

"No hurry. Who's this guy? What's he do for a living?"

PAPAW

"His name's Michael Paulson. His sister's a friend of mine. He's an engineer over R and D."

Danny perked up. "Engineer! R and D! Where?"

"At a place called Hydro-Dyne," replied Carol.

Danny cast his gaze at Tim and Mary and admonished them. "If you two wanna go to the store, ya need to eat." Danny turned back to Carol. "Never heard 'a Hydro-Dyne."

"Me neither. All I know is they have several contracts with the Department of Defense. It's near Oak Ridge. Not sure what they make. All I know is it has to do with water. It's a big company. They even have a plant in Germany. You can ask 'im yourself. He'll be here anytime."

Danny's mind raced. *Did he design ships, maybe some kind of turbine or sonar?*

Tim interrupted Danny's contemplation. "We're done eatin'."

Mary chimed in. "Yeah, we're ready to go get a toy. You promised."

Carol said, "You can wait a few minutes an' keep Michael company while I finish gettin' ready." A knock at the door interrupted the conversation. Then she turned to her father. "Dad, can ya get that? Tell Michael I'll be ready in a few minutes."

Danny let Michael in and led him to the living room. "Carol'll be ready in a few minutes." Danny reached out to shake Michael's hand and said, "You must be Michael. I'm Carol's father."

Michael took Danny's hand and said, "Hello, Mr. Shykes, I'm Michael Paulson. Just call me Mike. Nice to meet ya."

Danny showed Mike to the sofa. "Okay, call me Danny."

Michael Paulson, called Mike by his friends, was thirty-three, small, and athletic. A handsome man and former army ranger, he kept his thinning blond hair cropped short, betraying his military bearing. His glasses, with a square dark frame, gave him a cerebral look. Tim and Mary joined them.

Mike greeted the children with a warm smile. "You must be Mary an' Tim."

"Yes, sir," replied Tim while Mary remained silent.

Danny started his fatherly interrogation. He last performed the ritual twelve years earlier when he met Tom. "Mike, I understand you're an engineer."

Mike replied, "Yes, I am—"

Danny jumped in before Mike finished. "Carol said ya work for Hydro-Dyne. Had somethin' to do with water. What do they make? Don't reckon I've heard 'a that outfit. You're over R and D, right?"

"Yes, Hydro-Dyne deals with anything that has to do with water. Most of our business involves defense contracts. I'm over R and D, and I supervise ten engineers. In fact, we're working on a contract for the latest nuclear submarine," replied Mike.

Danny asked, "Submarine?"

"Yes, sir, we're a subcontractor for General Dynamics. There's not a lot I can say. It's all classified." The children were fixated on their grandfather.

Danny scratched his head with his hook. "Can ya tell me what it is you design? Torpedoes, turbines, some kinda sonar?"

"Not exactly. I don't see the harm in telling ya what we make. I'll just show ya." He stood up and asked, "Where's your bathroom?"

Caught by surprise with Mike's query, Danny got up and said, "This way."

Mike followed Danny to the bathroom with the children close behind. Upon entering the bathroom, Mike scrutinized the toilet, looking into the tank and lifting the seat. Danny and the children were mesmerized at the sight of their guest. He retrieved a penlight from his shirt pocket, got down on his haunches, and looked at the bottom of the tank. Mike stood up and looked at Danny.

"Oh, my! You've gotta Hydro-Dyne 500. That's a very good toilet." The children giggled at their grandfather's crestfallen face.

Unable to contain his disappointment, Danny said, "Toilets. I thought ya did work for the Department of Defense."

With pride, Mike explained, "We do, but we also work in the private sector. The Hydro-Dyne 500 was the first toilet I designed. Worked on that sucker for over a year. We wouldn't stop until it was able to flush a bucket of golf balls with less than two gallons of water.

PAPAW

It took several redesigns, but we finally got it, an' it worked like a charm. Even today, it's our best toilet."

Danny interrupted, "Who shits golf balls? Jack Nicklaus or Lee Trevino?" Tim and Mary giggled.

"I'm not sure 'bout that, but I can assure ya this little beauty can take whatever YOU can throw at it an' then some." Mike laughed and said, "I designed it seven years ago, an' it was the top of toilet technology at the time." Mike patted Danny on the shoulder. "That launched my career. Now I'm over research an' development. Hydro-Dyne has one-third of the total toilet production in the country. We do other things, like bathroom an' kitchen sinks. We even design wastewater disposal for labs an' for the military."

Danny asked, "You're telling me you design toilets, correct?"

Mike said, "Yes, you're correct, but we're working on specially designed toilets for submarines. Of course, the toilet is only the visible part of a complex system of waste disposal in a submarine. It's not very glamorous, but even the most powerful nuclear submarine'll be rendered useless if ya can't get rid of waste." An air of confidence came over Mike. "Take the tragic tale of U-1206."

Upon hearing *tragic* and *tale* fall from Mike's lips, Mary and Tim fell under a spell. Danny's curiosity arose as well, and all three, anticipating a grand tale, became awestruck.

"Well," began Mike, "engineering is all about trade-offs. For a German U-boat design, one such trade-off was the holding tank for waste. Their subs had no holding tanks. This meant the crew of a German U-boat could not use the toilet while submerged."

"What'd they do?" asked Mary.

Mike laughed. "They used buckets."

"They shit in buckets," Danny replied.

"I guess if they had to." Mike continued, "They used the saved space for more fuel and supplies."

Tim asked, "What'd they do with the buckets?"

Mike said, "When they surfaced, they dumped 'em. After much complaining, the engineers came up with a solution. Not holding tanks. Instead, a new flushing system that allowed them to flush at depth." Mike, with his eyes squinted to narrow slits, turned to Tim and Mary and said, "Now, the tale of the sinking of U-1206, the only ship in maritime history to sink due to faulty toilet design."

Mike rendered the infamous tale of the sinking of U-1206.

"Toward the end of the Second World War, German engineers designed a submarine that solved the problem of disposing of waste at depth while not requiring a holding tank. The problem was that at depth, the exterior pressure became too great to discharge wastewater. Submarines of the United States Navy, for example, utilized holding tanks to capture excrement and other waste. The holding tanks were emptied after the submarine surfaced. Crews on German U-boats, on the other hand, had to suffer the misery of relieving themselves in buckets when at depth. After surfacing, the buckets were emptied, and they could use the toilet.

"Fitted with a newly designed flushing system, the U-1206 could flush wastewater at depth, eliminating the need for a holding tank. However, it required a complicated procedure of opening and closing valves in sequence. Two specially trained members of the crew had to flush the toilets.

"On April 14, 1945, less than a month before Germany's surrender, submarine U-1206, was on patrol off the coast of Scotland at a depth of two hundred feet. Captain Karl Schlitt, in command, decided to use the toilet. When he learned that both technicians were busy with other problems, he decided to flush it himself.

"Schlitt failed to follow the proper flushing sequence, and water surged into the submarine at a high volume. He summoned one of the trained technicians, but it was too late. Schlitt ordered the submarine to surface. Things went from bad to worse. Upon surfacing, the U-boat came under attack by the Royal Air Force (RAF). Bombs dropped by the RAF left U-1206 mortally wounded, and Schlitt ordered his men to abandon ship and scuttle the submarine. Three men drowned, and the remainder of the crew were captured. U-1206 lies at the bottom of the North Sea to this day."

Mike with a chuckle said, "That's the tale of the sinking of U-1206."

Danny said, "Poor bastard sank his sub takin' a shit." Tim and Mary giggled hysterically at their grandfather's paraphrasing.

PAPAW

Mike said, "That's one mistake I don't intend to make. Woe to anyone who loses a billion-dollar submarine because of a faulty toilet design. I'm working on such a system now. We'll use holding tanks. I'm testing ten prototype toilets in the lab."

Danny asked, "How the hell ya test a toilet? Ya have ten guys sitting on it smoking an' reading the paper?"

Mike laughed and replied, "We use a special gel that simulates fecal material. I'm heading the development team. The Hydro-Dyne 600 is being developed for military applications, specifically submarines. According to our engineering trials, it can move five pounds of fecal matter with just a half gallon of water. Can't tell you more than that. It's all TOP SECRET. The next phase will be field trials."

Playing to his grandchildren's adoration, Danny replied, "Top secret. Field trials. How will ya do that? Find someone who can shit five pounds at a time? Not sure even I could do that."

Mike replied, "These designs are overengineered. Under normal use, it'll never be required to move that much material. We'll put 'em in ten homes an' see how they function under normal operating conditions, an' we'll collect data."

Carol stepped out of her bedroom and found everyone huddled around the toilet. "I'm ready to go. What're youins doin'?"

Excited, Tim turned to his mother. "Mike makes toilets. Papaw showed 'im our toilet. He said it's a good one. You can put golf balls in it, an' it can handle anything Papaw can throw at it, an' a German sank his sub taking a shit! He's designing a toilet for a sub now."

Aware of the source of Tim's bad language, she furrowed her brow, glared at her father, and said, "GOODNESS, TIM! Where did ya hear such awful language?"

Tim shouted, "PAPAW!" Mike laughed hysterically.

"Well, if Papaw jumped off a cliff, would ya follow 'im?" Carol kept her eyes on Danny while addressing her son. "Don't let me catch ya using that kind of language again."

Feigning shame, Tim replied, "Okay, Mom, I won't."

Danny grimaced like a boy caught stealing a cookie. He looked at the children and said, "Okay, you two. It's time for us to go."

Carol grabbed Mike's hand and said, "Yes, it's time to go." Carol turned to her children and said, "Be good for Papaw. Dad, watch your language."

Mike reached to shake Danny's hand and said, "It was nice to meet ya, Danny."

Danny replied, "You two have fun." He turned to the children and said, "Okay, time for us to go to the store an' after we're done get ice cream."

CHAPTER 9

The Implements of Death

Danny turned his 1957 Chevy Bel Air into the Walmart parking lot. He owned the car, his pride and joy, since 1960. After guiding the car into a spot near the entrance, he turned to Mary and Tim and said, "We lucked out. Not far to walk." Before the car came to a complete stop, Tim threw the door open and, along with Mary, bolted for the store. Danny shouted, "Stop! Slow down, that store ain't goin' nowhere." Mary and Tim ignored their grandfather and moved as if shot from a cannon.

Danny made his way to the toy department, where he found the children with shrink-wrapped packages in their hands. They hit pay dirt and were delirious with joy; within Danny's soul, satisfaction reigned. His mind conjured the joy Anne felt when she first saw her beloved donkey, Jack. He thought, *"Like Anne, years ago, they found the Seven Cities of Gold."*

Tim raised the package for Danny to see. Believing it too good to be true and preparing for a negative response, with pleading eyes he asked, "Can we get this?"

Danny took the package from Tim, looked at Mary, and asked, "This's what ya want?"

Mary, wishing for the toy, answered, "Yes! I'm in the uh. Uh, what's that you said I was in?"

Danny snickered. "The French Resistance."

"Yeah, that's it!"

Danny examined the package. Emblazoned on the cardboard within the shrink-wrap was a picture of a soldier dressed in World War II garb, his arm cocked about to hurl a hand grenade, and the words in bold black print, "Combat Action Play Set," caught his eye. It contained two plastic grenades, a helmet, one bayonet, and best of all, a plastic Thompson submachine gun. The words "Try me" in white block lettering were near the trigger of the Thompson and meant to lure unsuspecting children to compel reluctant parents into a purchase. Danny pushed his finger through a small opening and squeezed the trigger.

Rat-tat-tat-tat.

Danny said, "If you're goin' to kill Krauts, you're goin' to need the right tools."

Tim shouted, "Yes! A Thompson just like yours!"

Danny turned to Mary and asked, "Are you SURE this's what ya want?"

"Yes, Papaw."

Danny found a cart and grabbed four play sets. Then he picked up a pair of toy walkie-talkies and said, "If you are goin' to call in a fire mission, you'll need these." He threw the walkie-talkies into the cart with the play sets. The addition of the radios sent the children over the moon.

Danny looked at Mary and said, "We need one more thing. Follow me." With the children close behind, Danny left the toy section and made a beeline for the section of girl's clothing. He zeroed in on a rack of hats and frantically rifled through them.

Tim asked, "What're ya lookin' for?"

Danny ignored Tim and continued his frantic search. A saleswoman approached and asked, "Sir, may I help you?"

Danny turned to her and said, "I was looking for a beret. I can't find any." The saleslady led Danny to the end of the rack.

She found two berets, one red and one black, and said, "All I got are these."

PAPAW

Danny replied, "That'll have to do," and took the black beret, kneeled close to Mary, and placed the beret on her head. The child stood still as Danny adjusted the hat. "Perfect. Just perfect."

The saleslady said, "My, aren't YOU a pretty young lady."

Mary said, "I'm in the French Resistance. Tomorrow we're goin' to kill Krauts."

The saleslady chuckled and said, "You can check out over there, sir."

Danny said, "Mary, you're in the French Resistance."

Tim said, "Ya look cool! Papaw, can we get ice cream?"

"Sure! We're done here. Let's get ice cream."

CHAPTER 10

The Joy of Bacon

Saturday morning at seven, Tim and Mary, normally awake, were asleep. Carol found Danny in the living room, asleep on his recliner. She gently shook her father's shoulder, rousing him, and said, "Dad, they called me in to cover a shift today, so I won't be here this morning. Can ya handle things?"

Danny rubbed his eyes and asked, "What?"

"I won't be here this morning. Can ya handle things?"

Indignant, Danny snapped at his daughter, "Damn it, Carol, I've got a Purple Heart an' a Silver Star. I chased Krauts across Europe, an' then came home, rescued lost people, an' tracked criminals in these mountains. I think I can handle a few little kids. For goodness sake!"

"Okay, okay, I didn't mean it that way. I know you're capable," Carol reassured her father. "I was just making sure you're good with it."

Not over his indignation, Danny shot back, "You can go to work. Everything'll be fine here. Oh, by the way, how'd the date go?" Before Carol could respond, Danny smirked, getting in a small dig. "Did he promise ya the moon, or even better, that ya would sit on his throne someday?"

A quiet chuckle came from Carol. "Funny, Dad, but you should know he's working on a navy contract for toilets. A special toilet for the latest nuclear submarine. It's all top secret. He even had to get a security clearance. That's why he couldn't say anything last night. That's all he could tell me."

Danny rolled his eyes. "Top secret, goodness."

"Mike asked me if you'd mind trying out his newest prototype. I told 'im you'd be happy to. Don't worry, they'll put it in."

"You two must've hit it off. Nothing says love like a new toilet."

"Now's your chance to do your part. Just think of it as your contribution to fighting the Cold War, an', yes, we DID hit it off. We're goin' out next Saturday."

"I'm not goin' to shit my way to Moscow. If I'm goin' to fight Ruskies, I'd rather have my trusty ole Thompson an' a few grenades."

Carol turned to leave. "By the way, I bought an extra pound of bacon for breakfast tomorrow an' some fruit for Hunter. I almost forgot. Hunter's lactose intolerant. He can eat your pancakes, but he can't drink milk. He's not allowed any sugar either, so I got 'im sugar-free orange juice. Let 'im put fruit on the pancakes instead of syrup. Also, he's allergic to anything with peanuts an' bee stings. He carries a special syringe if he gets stung. Don't worry, he can tell ya how to use it, but he'll still need to get to the ER. The Carlsons are vegetarians, an' Hunter's not allowed to eat meat of any kind. No eggs either."

The indignation that left Danny returned in full. "Goodness, Carol, what am I goin' to do with the little bastard? He can't eat, can't play…"

Carol interrupted Danny. "He can't help it. You told me a long time ago, ya can't pick your parents. His parents are good people. They're just a little different than us. Mr. Carlson's a dean at the university. He's over the sociology department." Carol went on, "Besides, Hunter, like the rest of these kids, thinks the sun rises an' sets on you. One other thing—and I hate to bring this up—but can you watch your language? Last Sunday, Mary referred to Alice Huntington's little boy, Pastor Gamble's two-year-old grandson, as a cute little bastard. OH! I almost forgot. No GUNS for Hunter! The Carlsons' are pacifists. Remember, he's the medic, okay?"

Exasperation gripped Danny like a vice as he reassured his daughter. "Don't worry, no meat, no guns, no sugar, an' watch my mouth. Why don't I put a bag over his head an' stick 'im in a closet till he's ready to go home?"

Carol said as she walked out the door, "I wrote it all down with a phone number an' stuck it to the fridge in case you forget. Oh, maybe you can go to church with us tomorrow."

Pretending not to hear, Danny said, "Don't work too hard," and turned his attention to breakfast.

Danny always cooked breakfast, a Saturday morning ritual. He could cook anything related to breakfast. But he took great pride in his pancakes and constantly tinkered with his recipe, adding this or that to achieve a unique flavor. Today, he would keep it simple. He retrieved a container of chocolate chips to add to the batter. Expectations were high, and in just a short time, he would have a house full of little ones clamoring for his special pancakes. Danny got busy.

The aroma of bacon filled the air, and little feet hit the floor. Suddenly, Mary and Tim were standing next to the stove, waiting to sample the freshly cooked bacon. Tim asked, "Where's Mom?"

Danny said, "She was called in to work. I'll be watchin' ya today."

Mary said, "Papaw's making pancakes."

Danny replied, "You two need to get your clothes on an' comb your hair. Your friends'll be here soon."

Mary and Tim headed to their rooms. Danny heard a knock on the front door, and found, as expected, Ricky and Hunter. Ricky charged in with Hunter at his heels, greeting Mr. Shykes on the fly. "Hello, Mr. Shykes. Can we come in?"

Hunter strutted by Danny, saying, "Hi, Mr. Shykes."

"Hello, Hunter. Hello, Ricky. Tim and Mary'll be down in a minute."

Hunter looked about, turned to Danny, and with a puzzled look asked, "Mr. Shykes, what's that smell? It smells good."

Ricky, perplexed and amused at what he heard, asked Hunter, "Haven't ya ever smelt bacon before?" Ricky turned to Mary and

PAPAW

Tim, who just joined them, and said, "Hey, Hunter doesn't know what bacon is."

Upon seeing Hunter's embarrassed expression, Danny interjected, "I'm sure Hunter knows what bacon is." A sheepish grin came over the child's face, indicating quiet gratitude for Danny's timely intervention.

Tim asked Danny, "Did ya make chocolate chip pancakes?"

Mary answered, "Yes! With whip cream." The children made a mad dash to the table and found pancakes, whipped cream, real maple syrup, eggs, sausage, and a plate full of bacon. The children tore into Danny's breakfast offering.

Mary shouted, "Wait! Wait!" She asked her grandfather, "Papaw, we have to ask the blessing. Can I? Can I ask the blessing?"

Danny shouted, "Stop! Mary's right!"

The children stopped and became quiet.

"Mary, ask for the blessing."

Mary asked for the blessing. "Dear, Jesus, let us give thanks for this food an' that you bless it. We ask in the name of Jesus." Mary turned to Danny, "See, just like Mom taught me."

Recalling Anne, Danny said, "Yes, Mary, an' just like your mamaw taught your mom." Danny tapped a butter knife on the table. "Everyone, dig in."

A joyful racket overtook the silence. Friendly banter filled the air while the children loaded plates. Danny cast his gaze toward Hunter, then the plate of fruit Carol prepared. He retrieved the plate, handed it to Hunter, and said, "Hunter, this's for you." Hunter, enchanted by the bacon, could not hide his crestfallen face from Danny, who, in turn, became enchanted by the boy, astounded someone could exist who never ate bacon.

Like a swarm of locusts, the children ripped through everything. In the wild dash, however, a single strip of bacon was left unclaimed. Hunter eyed the strip of meat, trying to conceal his lust for the treat. After working up the courage, Hunter asked, "Mr. Shykes, can I have the wast piece of bacon?" Danny continued to stare in silent amazement as the child explained, "I never ate bacon before."

Danny looked at the plate of fruit, then at the rest of the children, and found himself at the center of a moral dilemma. On one hand, Hunter was not allowed to eat meat, and his daughter provided an alternative. On the other hand, he saw a small, well-behaved child wanting a treat. He thought, *"Surely one piece of bacon couldn't hurt. What harm could there be?"*

Danny, racked with indecision, returned his gaze to the fruit. Pity gripped him, and he relented. "Go ahead, Hunter, take it. I don't see any harm in just one piece of bacon. This'll be between me an' you." Danny watched Hunter eat the bacon. Not since the war, when he gave a child a Hershey bar, had he witnessed a child experiencing such heavenly joy. Danny was happy.

Hunter savored the bacon, overcome with intoxicating delight. "Can I have more? This's the best thing I ever ate."

Danny remembered the extra bacon. *"When the children go home, I'll run to the store and replace it, an' no one'd be the wiser,"* he thought. *"Besides, all these kids'll have no problem eating a pound of bacon."* He broke out the bacon and fried it.

Hunter asked demurely, "May I have some pancakes?"

Danny remembered what his daughter said about the pancakes. This decision would be easy, and with gusto, he said, "Sure, kid, knock yourself out. Eat all the pancakes ya want."

"Thanks, Mr. Shykes." The child loaded his plate with pancakes and reached for the maple syrup.

Tim shouted, "PAPAW! HUNTER AIN'T ALLOWED TO HAVE SYRUP!"

Danny again found himself at the crossroads of a moral impasse. "It's okay. A little syrup won't hurt. Let's not make a big deal over it."

Mary chimed in. "Hunter isn't allowed to eat any of that, Papaw."

Danny parried his granddaughter's admonishment. "It'll be okay this time."

Mary continued to press the issue. "What if he gets sick?"

Ricky said, "He might die, Mr. Shykes."

Danny scrutinized the boy, who, unaware of the discussion underway, was lost in a private indulgence of pancakes and maple syrup. Danny snapped, "For goodness's sake! He won't get sick, an' he won't die! Now you guys need to eat, an' let me worry 'bout all this! For cryin' out loud, knock it off, an' eat!"

Danny placed a fresh plate of bacon on the table. Hunter, with no regard for the others, raked half of it onto his plate. "This's the best thing I've ever ate, Mr. Shykes," said Hunter. To Danny's horror, the bacon became a gateway drug to self-indulgence.

Danny, spooked by the escalating crisis, ran to the refrigerator and looked at the note Carol left. He thought, "*There's no mention of a bacon allergy. Goodness! He's diabetic.*"

After reviewing the note, he mumbled, "Is there such a thing as a bacon allergy? Did I miss something? If there is, I've never heard of it. There is no mention of 'im being diabetic." His tacit approval created a nightmare.

Fighting panic, Danny rushed back to the children and thought, "*I've got to get a handle on this.*"

"Hey, I fried more bacon." His hopes that the children would eat it were dashed.

Ricky said, "You an' Hunter can eat it, Mr. Shykes."

Tim added, "I've had enough."

Mary said, "I'm done, Papaw."

Hunter asked, "Can I have more bacon, Mr. Shykes?"

Danny, in over his head, lost control. "Haven't ya had enough?" Danny asked Hunter rhetorically.

"No, Mr. Shykes. Bacon's the best thing I've ever ate."

"I guess it's okay," Danny said, surrendering to the will of the child. "Go ahead."

Hunter laid claim to the remaining bacon. All Danny could do was hope for the best.

Hunter, working on the bacon and pancakes, said, "Mom never cooks wike this."

Ricky cried out, "Wow! Hunter ate all that bacon."

Danny saw trouble on the horizon, but it was too late. He cast his gaze on the plate with one strip of bacon and retrieved it for himself.

Danny replied, "He didn't eat all of it."

"Papaw, you're in big trouble," said Mary.

Tim and Mary finished breakfast and ran upstairs to retrieve the new play sets. Mary returned wearing her beret and shouted, "Look at what Papaw got us!"

Holding a play set in the air, Tim said, "There's one for each of us."

Ricky said, "Look, helmets, grenades, an' a Thompson. Cool."

Christmas in July for the children. They frantically tore the toy implements of death from the packaging, and cellophane flew through the air.

Rat-tat-tat, rat-tat-tat, rat-tat-tat.

While Hunter finished breakfast, the children were brandishing Thompsons, aiming, and shooting each other. Danny found their antics a welcome distraction from his dilemma involving Hunter.

Tim pulled out the walkie talkies. "Look, walkie-talkies."

Mary snatched one, turned it on, and shouted into it. "Hello, hello."

Danny said to Tim, "Turn on your walkie-talkie."

Tim turned on the walkie-talkie. Mary repeated, "Hello, hello."

Tim said, "You're not comin' in."

Ricky said, "Ya gotta key the mic."

Mary asked, "What?"

Exasperated, Ricky said, "Girls don't know nothin'. Push the red button while ya talk."

Mary pushed the button, "Hello, hello."

"I hear ya! You're comin' in loud an' clear," said Tim. He pointed to the front door. "Go outside an' try it."

Danny said, "That's a good idea. Ya'll can go out. I'll be out directly. Leave me a radio. I'm White-Eagle-Five." The children gathered the weapons and left one play set behind for Hunter.

Hunter finished breakfast and made his way to the remaining play set. He looked over the Thompson, bayonet, and grenades. Adrenaline coursed through the child's body. He thought, *Today, I'm not the medic.*

Danny approached Hunter and asked, "What're ya looking for?"

"I don't want to be the medic today, Mr. Shykes."

PAPAW

"Then don't. Ya got everything ya need to kill Krauts."

Hunter grabbed the bayonet, tucked it in his belt, placed the helmet on his head, and took the Thompson. The child, over the moon with joy, looked at Danny and said, "Thanks, Mr. Shykes." He noticed a paper bag in Danny's hand and asked, "What's in the bag?"

Danny opened the bag, so Hunter could see. Inside were twenty M-80 firecrackers—a large, powerful firecracker, an inch-and-a-half long with a half-inch diameter. Prized for its deep and loud boom upon detonation. They, along with others like them, including cherry bombs and silver salutes, were banned in the early 1970s. Danny obtained the contraband fireworks from a nefarious source in Gatlinburg.

Danny replied, "Artillery."

"Cool," said Hunter, and he bolted for the front door.

Danny shouted, "WAIT A MINUTE!" Hunter stopped dead in his tracks. "Aren't ya forgettin' somethin'?"

Hunter looked at his Thompson, felt his head for the helmet, checked his belt for the bayonet, and replied, "Don't think so."

With a menacing look, Danny said, "Grenades."

"Oh yeah, I forgot."

Hunter, amazed at the toy grenades, picked one up and held it in his hand as if it were gold, rubbing it between his fingers. His eyes widened, and his mind raced with excitement. He, like Danny, was in the Army. His mother would not approve, and the child found himself at the crossroads of his own moral dilemma. But the temptation of playing like the others took hold, and he succumbed. Hunter looked at Danny.

"GWENADES!"

Danny handed the other grenade to Hunter. "Ya gotta be careful with those."

Hunter hooked the grenades on his belt and ran for the door. Danny shouted, "One more thing!" Hunter stopped and faced Danny. With one quick movement, Danny snapped his right hand to his forehead and offered his salute, "Good luck, Lieutenant Carlson."

"Don't worry, Sergeant Shykes, we'll get the bwidge," Hunter said, snapping his small right hand to his forehead to return Danny's salute. Hunter departed to join his friends in battle.

Danny turned on his walkie-talkie and watched Hunter catch up with the others and thought, *"I forgot somethin'."* He returned to the kitchen, retrieved a cooler, and filled it with beer and ice.

"Now, I'm ready." He walked to his favorite tree and took a seat in the shade.

The radio crackled to life. Tim had the radio and said, "White-Eagle-Five, we need ya to shoot your cannons."

Danny picked up the radio and answered, "Roger, Baker-One, waiting for the coordinates."

Mary snatched the walkie talkie from Tim. "It's my turn." The radio crackled. "Papaw, Papaw over here." Mary pointed at the footbridge that arched over the small stream.

Ricky admonished Mary, "He's NOT Papaw. He's WHITE-EAGLE-FIVE. Give 'im the coordinates."

"What're coordinates?" asked Mary.

Ricky shouted at Mary, "GOODNESS! JUST TELL 'IM TO START SHOOTIN' THE CANNON!"

Mary calmly keyed the mic and said, "White-Eagle-Five, shoot the cannon." She turned to Ricky. "Is that good enough for ya?"

Ricky mumbled under his breath, "Girls."

Danny pulled a Zippo from his pocket. He carried the reliable lighter during the war when he smoked. With his right hand, he flipped the lighter's lid, spun the wheel to create a flame, and inserted the lighter into his hook. He reached into the bag and pulled out an M-80. After igniting the fuse, he tossed it as far as he could. One after another, he would light and toss them. Small explosions echoed in the valley.

Hunter charged the bridge with his Thompson blazing, yelling, "WE GOT JERRY ON THE WUN, MEN! LET'S GET 'EM!"

Ricky shouted at Hunter, "I GOT THIS SIDE OF THE BRIDGE! YOU TAKE THE OTHER SIDE!"

With a wide, arching motion over his head, Tim hurled a grenade. The plastic grenade bounced off a small boulder near the bridge. He yelled, "I GOT THE TANK! MARY, YOU GET THE MACHINE GUNS!"

Mary raised the Thompson to her shoulder and laid down withering imaginary fire; German soldiers fell before her. Hunter observed Tim and Mary advancing toward the bridge. Wishing to support their advance, he drew a grenade from his belt. He pulled the pin with his teeth and cocked his arm back to throw.

"I'M HIT!" Tim cried out, and he fell to the ground clutching his right thigh.

Mary ran to Tim, kneeled beside her brother, and asked, "Where'd ya get it?"

Tim said, "A Kraut sniper got me! My leg! Get Hunter! I need a medic!"

Mary shouted at Hunter before he could hurl the grenade, "MEDIC, HUNTER, I NEED A MEDIC!"

Hunter stopped and looked at the grenade and thought, *"Great."*

Weary of being their medic and not wishing to relinquish his new role, he raised his Thompson, waving it around in the air as an act of defiance, shouting, "I'M NOT THE MEDIC ANYMORE!"

Mary shouted, "YOU'RE THE ONLY ONE THAT KNOWS WHAT TO DO!"

Exasperated, Hunter said, "Aw-wight, I'll wook at it," and ran toward Tim, who was flat on the ground, holding his leg, and thrashing about in pain. Hunter kneeled to examine the leg, with Mary looking on. "I don't have any sulfa or bandages. Don't worry, you're wucky. It's just a fwesh wound. Another half inch, you'd be a goner." Tim got to his feet, hooking his right arm around Mary's shoulder.

Rickey took the radio. "White-Eagle-Five, we got the bridge."

Danny replied, "Roger, Baker-One, well done. I'm sending in the reserve platoon. Hold until you're relieved."

Ricky said, "Roger, White-Eagle-Five, will hold until relieved. Request permission to reconnoiter the woods when the reserve platoon arrives."

Danny answered, "Roger, Baker-One, this's White-Eagle-Five. Permission's granted to reconnoiter the woods. Don't go beyond the big rock. Repeat, don't go beyond the big rock. There're bears out there."

Mary cupped her mouth with her hands and shouted, "Okay, Papaw."

Danny reached into the cooler and retrieved a beer. He heard the chatter of toy machine guns dispensing death, children's voices, and Ike darting by in a sudden flash. The small dog, barking frantically, wanted in on the action and rushed to join the children. The innocence of the children's mock battle had a calming effect. Through Danny's story, they knew Smitty and Captain Jones and, in their own way, paid tribute to Danny's friends and those who never came home. Danny wanted them to remember the sacrifice. He thought of his promise to Smitty:

"I'll never let 'em forget."

A blue Ford LTD turned onto Danny's driveway and made its way up the gravel road, stopping short of his perch. Unaware of who owned such a vehicle, he immediately recognized James Gamble, the pastor of Owl Creek Baptist Church, exiting the car from the passenger side. He had been the pastor of the church for as long as Danny could remember. Anne and her family belonged for years while Danny never joined, even after they got married. He did, however, attend Sunday services with Anne on a regular basis until her passing. A man climbed out of the driver's side. Danny did not recognize the forty-year-old of average size and athletic build.

Pastor Gamble, approaching Danny, felt as though he were entering a lion's den. But the God-fearing man was on a mission. "Hello, Danny, is Carol here?"

Danny thought, *"Why's he here?"* He replied, "No, she was called in to work."

The pastor, visibly disappointed, said, "Oh, sorry. She said we could drop by."

Danny, sensing an agenda, gathered his thoughts. He looked toward the children, took a deep breath, and asked, "Preacher, can I help ya?"

PAPAW

"To be honest, Danny, I was kinda hoping we could talk to you an' Carol," said Pastor Gamble. "Danny, this's Richard Hartley. He's an attorney."

Richard extended a hand to Danny. "Nice to meet you, sir. James' told me much about your service during the war."

Danny smiled politely at the young attorney. "That was a long time ago," Danny paused, squeezed his chin between his thumb and fingers, and stared into Hartley's eyes. "You look familiar. Am I in some kinda trouble?"

Pastor Gamble said, "Nothing like that."

Danny said, "Now, I remember. You're the attorney for the man who killed Anne."

Richard said, "Yes, I was hoping we could talk."

Pastor Gamble said, "We were hoping Carol'd be here. Maybe we can come back another time."

Danny glared at the pastor, and his voice, short of anger, took on a tense tone. "If you have somethin' to say, say it to me."

The radio crackled, and Mary said, "We need ya to shoot the cannon!"

Danny picked up his walkie-talkie. "Roger, Baker-One, you'll have to wait for artillery support. Continue to scout the woods for Jerry an' report back in fifteen minutes. Don't go past the big rock."

"Roger, Papaw, I mean White-Eagle," Mary replied. The attorney and Pastor Gamble chuckled at the adorable child wearing the black beret and carrying a toy Thompson under her arm.

"Danny, it's kind of a tough subject," said Pastor Gamble.

Danny rose to his feet and said tersely, "Cut to the chase. What 'a ya want?"

Richard jumped in. "I apologize, Danny. I can speak to you." He continued, "I still represent Jason Black."

Danny interrupted the attorney. "Yeah, we all know who you are, an' we've nothin' to talk about."

"I knew this was goin' to be tough. Please hear Richard out," said Pastor Gamble.

Richard, not wishing to upset Danny, said, "Jim, let's come back another time." Richard pulled a letter and a business card from his shirt pocket and handed them to Danny. "I do represent Jason, but today, I'm here on behalf of his mother. She asked me to deliver this letter. If you can, please read it. You may see things differently. If you change your mind and decide to speak with me, please give me a call."

Danny took the letter and card and glanced at them indifferently. "Wish I could, but I can't. Nothin' personal. I jist can't."

Pastor Gamble said, "It's okay. Just know, we love Anne. She was a true spiritual leader and a real Christian. She touched us deeply. I hope someday you can find comfort knowing she's with the Lord, and one day you'll see her again."

Pastor Gamble and Richard turned to the car, and Danny answered, "Pastor, jist wish you or your friend could tell me why. Tell me how a good woman who loved her God could die like she did. I've had too many friends who loved their God only to die, an' here I am."

Pastor Gamble paused, then turned to Danny saying, "I wish I could, but I'll never be able to completely answer that. I'm not sure anyone can. We'll never be able to make sense of it. All I can say is that if Anne were here now, she'd likely ask you to forgive him, as she would have. You see, if you really believe—I mean really believe—that Jesus is God, then you have to forgive. Forgiving even the worst things demonstrates your ultimate surrender to and trust in God. Without it, we're doomed. In the meantime, just trust in the Lord. If you do that, you'll find peace. Take care, Danny, and remember, Jesus is your God too, and you're always welcome at church." Pastor Gamble and Richard Hartley left.

Danny picked up his walkie-talkie and said, "Baker-One, this's White-Eagle-Five. Do ya read me, over?"

Tim answered, "Roger, White-Eagle-Five, this's Baker-One. We read you loud an' clear."

Danny said, "The mission's over. Jerry's on the run. Time for ice cream!"

The children shouted, "Ice cream," and ran to the house.

Carol entered the house and found Danny doling out ice cream. Surprised, Danny said, "I didn't expect ya back for a couple 'a hours."

PAPAW

Carol said, "It was slow. They said I could go home."

The children, busy enjoying ice cream, did not notice Carol making a beeline for the refrigerator. Upon opening the refrigerator door, she noticed the extra bacon missing. Puzzled, Carol rummaged through the refrigerator, unable to find it. She thought, *"Dad likely fried it. After all, there are a lot of kids."*

Carol queried her father. "Dad, looks like you have things under control, but I can't seem to find that extra pound of bacon. Did you cook it? It's okay. I can get more."

Mary, overhearing her mother, ran into the kitchen and said, "Papaw cooked it."

Carol thought for a moment. *"It's okay. The boys were hungry. I'll run an' get another pound."*

Mary, eager to tattle on Danny, blurted, "Papaw cooked it for Hunter."

With the cat out of the bag, Tim added, "Hunter ate it all."

The grandchildren's swift betrayal left Danny speechless. He turned to them with a furrowed brow. "Thanks a lot. The Gestapo would've loved you two!"

Carol glanced at the untouched fruit prepared for Hunter and asked, "Hunter, did you eat bacon?"

The boom was about to be lowered. Hunter, hesitant to rat out the man who treated him well, looked at Danny and, with pleading eyes, asked for permission to speak. Danny answered his silent plea with a nod of approval and said, "It's okay, Hunter. Answer Carol's question truthfully."

With an embarrassed smile, the child confessed, "Yes, Ms. Carol, I ate the bacon. I never ate bacon before. We've never had it. It's good. Is Mr. Shykes in twouble? It's all my fault. Are ya goin' to tell Mom?"

Carol answered in reassuring tones, "No, Hunter, you're not in trouble. I need everyone to take their ice cream outside while I speak with Papaw."

The children turned to leave. Mary, overwhelmed with guilt, got to the door, spun around, ran to her mother, and interceded on

Danny's behalf. "Is Papaw in trouble? Don't yell at 'im. He didn't mean it."

Carol said, "It's okay. Go on outside with the others." Mary, unable to face Danny and ashamed of what she had done, ran outside.

"It's okay, Mary," said Danny as the child ran by.

Carol zeroed in on her father. "What happened to the war hero with a Purple Heart an' the Silver Star an' chasing Krauts an' tracking criminals? The rescuer of lost hikers?" Danny drew a beer from his cooler, popped it open, and took a sip as Carol continued to vent. "I told ya Hunter couldn't have bacon. Did he REALLY eat a pound of bacon?"

Danny attempted to mitigate the situation. "I ate some of it."

"That's not the point. Hunter's parents trusted me with their child. Now I've let 'em down. These children need discipline. Buying toys an' ice cream's the fun stuff. Sometimes ya have to say no. Remember, like YOU did when I was little. Just practice. Say NO, N-O. Goodness, Dad, he ate a whole pound of bacon!"

Embarrassed and unable to explain how things spun out of control, Danny said, "Okay, I get it. I didn't see any harm in a little bacon. When YOU say it, it seems evil." Danny scratched his head with his hook. "I guess I'll be shovelin' coal after I die."

Danny's suggestion that he would spend eternity in hell because he fed Hunter bacon drew a laugh from Carol. "Dad, if ya end up shovelin' coal, it won't be for givin' Hunter bacon." She kissed her father on the cheek. "You're still the best papaw ever, an' the kids love ya, but you have to show 'em who's boss. Sometimes ya have to, like ya say, kick 'em in the ass. You let 'em push you around."

In an effort to alleviate the problem he created, Danny, in a childlike fashion, suggested, "Let's pretend none of this happened. Let it be our secret. I bet his mother won't even notice."

Carol found the innocence in her father's suggestion adorable. "No, Dad, I'll tell his mother tomorrow. She seems reasonable. I'm sure she'll understand."

"Are you goin' to fire me?"

"No, Dad, I'm not going to fire ya."

CHAPTER 11

The Accident

THE FOLLOWING MORNING, Carol found Danny preparing breakfast. Danny said, "I just made coffee. Why don't ya get a cup?"

Carol retrieved a mug and said, "Can I get you a cup?"

"Got one."

Carol took a seat at the kitchen table and glanced at the letter and card left by Richard Hartley. Her heart sank. In her haste, she forgot that Pastor Gamble and Richard were going to visit. She feared the unexpected visit blindsided her father. She said, "I see Pastor Gamble stopped by yesterday."

Danny tempered his anger and said, "They just showed up. I wish ya would 'a told me."

Carol said, "I know, I got busy. I meant to tell ya. Then I got called in an' forgot."

Danny stopped preparing breakfast and took a seat at the table. He stared into his mug while listening to his daughter.

Carol continued, "It's been four years, an' it seems like yesterday. I understand it's still hard. I lost Mom an' my husband. Tim an' Mary are just beginnin' to deal with not havin' a father. They're always askin' about Tom an' Mamaw. I make sure they know about 'em. You've been such a big help. What would I've done without you? I feel helpless not bein' able to help you through this. Like you, a day doesn't go by that I don't ask why. Then I ask, 'What would

Mom do?' Mom always talked about forgiveness. She told me the toughest thing to do is forgive someone who wronged you, but she also told me, as Christians, we must. It is the strongest way to tell God you have faith an' trust 'im. I think if she were here, she would forgive this man, even for this. Pastor Gamble wanted to talk with you about Jason's mother. He didn't mean to get ya upset. He felt if I were there, I could break the ice. Jason's mother just wants to meet with you, talk, an' say sorry. She's such a nice lady, an' she's carrying a burden. She's a victim too. I don't know. I just thought it might help us if you'd listen an' talk with her."

Mary and Tim entered the kitchen. Danny said, "Good morning, you two. I have some leftover batter."

Tim said, "I'll have some pancakes." Danny rose from the table and resumed preparing breakfast.

Carol admonished her children, "Hurry, we have to get ready for church."

Mary protested, "Me an' Tim're goin' to stay with Papaw."

Carol scowled at her children. "I don't think so."

In vain, Tim backed up his sister, asking rhetorically, "Why can't we stay? Papaw doesn't have to go."

Carol shut down all discussion. "Okay, tell ya what. When you two're sixty, ya don't have to go to church. For now, ya gotta go. Got it!" The cause was lost, and they resumed eating.

Danny told his daughter, "We'll discuss this later."

Mary asked, "Discuss what, Papaw?"

Danny snapped, "Nothin' that concerns you. Listen to your mother," and busied himself cleaning the kitchen.

Hurt by her grandfather's terse reply, Mary said, "Sorry, Papaw."

Tim and Mary rushed to the car. When Carol reached the door, she looked at her father. "Dad, I hope you can go to church again. Everyone asks about ya."

Danny said nothing. He found himself alone and refilled his mug. Carol's pleas crowded his thoughts; the letter from Jason's mother beckoned him. Danny returned to the table and picked it up. He smacked it against his hook several times, then returned it to the

PAPAW

table, leaving it unopened. While sipping coffee, his mind slipped back to the dark and rainy evening of March 28, 1975.

* * * * *

It rained for days and looked as if it would never stop. The creek running through Danny's property had swollen beyond its banks but did not threaten the house. Anne, just five miles away, was at Carol's house watching Tim and Mary. He cracked the front door and listened to the water crashing over the small boulders that lined the stream. In spite of Anne's assurances, dread ate at Danny. He thought, *"I don't like it. I better check on her,"* and Danny called Anne.

Anne answered, "Hello."

Danny replied, "It's raining hard. Why don't I come an' get ya?"

Anne answered, "It's letting up. Carol just got in an' said Tom'll be home directly. He'd bring me home. No need for ya to get out."

Danny pressed the issue. "Yes, it's letting up, but the roads are slick. I'll get ya."

"No, it's okay, I'll be fine. Just relax. I'll be home shortly."

Reluctantly, Danny replied, "Okay, I love you."

Anne said, "I love you more."

Danny hung up the phone. It was their last conversation.

After an hour passed, Danny's concern intensified. He thought, *"Maybe they slid off the road and needed help. It's not like Anne to run late. Perhaps she and Carol are visiting."* Danny decided to call Carol and confirm his suspicions and put his mind at ease.

Carol answered, "Hello."

"Hello, Carol."

"What's up, Dad? Mom forgot her reading glasses. I was about to call ya when the phone rang. Tom took her home thirty minutes ago."

Screaming sirens turned concern into fear. Danny said, "She's not here. Let me call ya back. I'll go out an' see if they had car trouble."

As Danny hung up, he heard an unsettling knock at the door; the screaming sirens had silenced. Upon opening the door, Sevier County Deputy Neal Thomas and a state trooper whom he had never met greeted him. The sight of the two officers caused Danny to become lightheaded. He gripped the door frame to steady himself. "Come in. I was just about to go out."

Neal supported his friend. "Danny, let's go inside."

The three made their way into the living room. Danny collapsed onto his recliner and asked, "What's goin' on?"

"There's been an accident." Neal put his hand on Danny's shoulder. "I don't know how to tell ya except to come out with it. Anne died at the scene. Tom's on his way to the hospital. I'm not sure he's goin' to make it."

In a state of shock, Danny stared at the floor and murmured, half to himself and half to his friend Neal, "I don't understand. How can this be? I talked to her not even an hour ago. She was fine. She can't be dead."

Neal said, "It happened fast. They were hit head-on. There was nothing they could've done. The other driver may have been drunk. He lost control on the wet road."

Unable to comprehend his friend's statement, Danny asked, "What about the other driver? Was he hurt?"

"No, he had no injuries an' was taken into custody."

"What's his name? Is he from around here?"

Neal answered, "His name's Jason Black. He lives in Knoxville an' will likely be booked with DUI and vehicular homicide."

Quiet tears tracked down Danny's face. Neal said to the state trooper, "I'm goin' to stay with Danny. Can you go to the hospital an' check on Tom? We'll notify his wife."

The trooper replied, "I'll get down there," and looked at Danny and said, "Sorry for your loss, Mr. Shykes." Danny acknowledged the trooper with a nod.

After he regained his composure, Danny slipped on a windbreaker and followed Neal to the patrol car. Danny mumbled, "I don't get it. She made sure I made it home. All those years fighting a war, she was there. When she needed me, I let her down. I've nothin' to live for."

* * * * *

PAPAW

Danny's mind returned to the kitchen table and coffee. The death of his wife defied logic. He would never see her again, and their plans would remain unfulfilled. The horror of that fateful night choked out all pleasant thoughts. Danny's mind never relented.

He stared into his cup, deep in thought, asking, *"Why do I keep living? Where's God?"* Danny, climbing a mountain of insanity, could not reach the summit of reason. *"Why was I not with her?"* He thought, *"Five minutes, sooner or later, thirty seconds sooner, or thirty seconds later, Anne and Tom would be alive. What device could God employ that would allow the death of this wonderful woman? A woman who immersed her entire life in Jesus and his word. Why did Smitty and the Captain have to die?"* Danny could not find answers.

Carol returned from church and found Danny asleep on the recliner. Mary and Tim rushed in behind her, carrying a bucket of chicken and fixings. She admonished them, "Quiet, let Papaw sleep. He'll eat when he wakes up." The children went to work filling their plates. Carol returned to her car to retrieve her purse.

Carol stepped onto the porch only to find Hunter's mother storming her way with quick and determined steps. She paused to wait on the angry woman. She greeted Hunter's mother. "Hello, Mrs. Carlson. I was goin' to call ya. Won't ya come in?"

"You can call me Candice, and I don't have time to come in. This will only take a few minutes."

Surprised by Candice's seething anger, Carol contemplated ways to defuse the situation before it erupted. She replied nervously, "Okay, Candice, I'm glad ya came by. I wanna explain what happened yesterday." Tim and Mary came to the door.

Tim asked, "Hello, Mrs. Carlson. Did ya bring Hunter?"

Carol dismissed the children, saying, "Go an' eat your lunch. I'll be in shortly. Hunter's mother an' I need to talk." Tim and Mary left with no reply.

Carol attempted to explain the bacon, and Hunter's mother cut her off. "You don't need to explain, Carol. You were given clear instructions regarding Hunter. I explained how important it was."

Carol jumped in, "Candice! I'm sorry. I knew, but I got called in unexpectedly to work and—"

Anger and condescension churned within the enraged woman; she cut Carol off and took the initiative. "We're vegetarians! You fed Hunter BACON. Mr. Carlson and I don't eat bacon. We've never allowed Hunter to eat any kind of meat, let alone bacon. Bacon is an indulgence of the uneducated. Now he's demanding we start FRYING BACON! WE DON'T EAT MEAT AT OUR HOUSE! The thought that Hunter ate bacon makes our blood run cold. Mr. Carlson fears Hunter has succumbed to a bacon-induced psychosis and is beside himself with worry. He scheduled an emergency session for Hunter next week with his therapist."

Carol, through laughs, asked rhetorically, "Psychosis? Goodness, Candice, do ya really think Hunter eating bacon triggered a psychotic event?"

Candice's indignation escalated, and she ruthlessly patronized Carol. "Yes, Carol! Actually, I do. This is no laughing matter. I thought you were a nurse. You should know. It's like PTSD, the same thing soldiers suffer from after returning from a war zone. It could take years to reverse the damage caused by your father. Did you not learn anything in nursing school?"

It took all the self-discipline she could muster, but Carol managed to control the boiling anger within her. She thought, *"It won't do any good to say anything. She's out of control."*

Carol nodded while Hunter's mother continued her tirade. "Furthermore, because there was no one for Hunter to play with and against my better judgment, I tolerated the toy guns and pretend army battles, but now he comes home talking about shredded bodies and killing Krauts. Mr. Carlson and I are pacifists. Thanks to the influence of your father, Hunter may be in therapy for years. I'll have you know my husband turned down a tenured position at Berkley before moving to this hillbilly hellhole. But he convinced me that moving here was the right thing to do. He, with all his good but misguided intentions, felt he could use his knowledge to establish an enclave of enlightenment in this vast pit of intellectual darkness. He and I were willing to make sacrifices when we gave up good positions to move here. A decision we regret. Now we're surrounded by uneducated rednecks and hillbillies who know nothing but Jesus and guns. As far as we're concerned, you can keep 'em both."

Carol, amused at the bacon and guns, loved Hunter, and for everyone's sake, in the Christian spirit of turning the other cheek, Carol overlooked Candice's insults. But insulting her father and friends went too far. The condescension and arrogance were too much, and she stepped back and pulled the door shut behind her. The last thread of civility within her snapped.

Carol exploded onto Hunter's mother. "Okay, Candice. I've taken all the shit from you I'm goin' to. Let me tell ya something, you arrogant, pompous twit. The man in there's a saint—an absolute saint! It was guys like him an' kids today fighting in far-off lands who made it possible for fools like you an' your husband to teach nonsense an' pollute the minds of our children. I love Hunter. He's a good kid, an' that's why we've tolerated your ignorance an' arrogance since ya moved here. Yes, Hunter ate some bacon, SO WHAT, an' he played army, SO WHAT. If anything, you should get down an' kiss my father's feet because he saved that boy's life. What Hunter needs is a REAL man in his life before he becomes totally emasculated an' dies a WIMP before he's twenty. Now, after I throw your ASS off this porch, I want ya to know I'll say a prayer an' ask forgiveness for myself an' a prayer for you an' your family. I'll make this prayer in the name of Jesus, the God you have such disdain for. I'll pray that God may grant you an' Mr. Carlson wisdom an' common sense, two things you're in desperate need. DON'T say another word. Just leave."

Candice turned on her heel and left. Carol watched her leave and did as she said. She offered a sincere prayer, asking for forgiveness. Shaken by the incident, Carol took a moment, stood on the porch, and took in the beauty of God's hand. She contemplated how her own mother and father filled her life with joy. The following week, Hunter's family moved, and the children never saw Hunter again.

Carol returned from the porch and found her father still asleep on the recliner and unaware of the commotion. A can of beer fell to the floor, spilling its contents. His hook lay across his chest. Danny awakened, yawned, and asked, "Was that Hunter's mother? Did ya get that whole bacon thing straightened out?" He scratched his chin. "I'm sorry to cause ya trouble. You're right. I guess I let things get outta hand."

Carol bent over, kissed her father on the forehead, and said, "Yes, Dad, it's taken care of. You never cause me any trouble. Everything's fine. I love you. Lunch is ready. C'mon an' eat."

CHAPTER 12

Prolotype

MONDAY MORNING, AS Danny and the children ate breakfast, Carol grabbed her purse, blew by the table, and headed for the door.

Danny asked, "Don't ya want breakfast? I have bacon, eggs, an' hash browns." Danny paused and thought of the commotion caused by the bacon, adding, "Forgot, bacon may be a sore subject."

Carol laughed. "Nothin' like that. Just running late." She glanced at Mary and Tim and asked, "What're you two goin' to do?"

Tim looked at Mary and said, "There's nothin' to do. Maybe play by the stream."

Danny suggested, "It'd be a good day to take Torch for a ride." Danny got a Shetland pony for the children the previous summer and named him Torch after the Allied invasion of North Africa, where he first saw action.

Mary looked at Tim and said, "I'm first."

Danny said, "Don't worry. You'll get to ride 'im."

Carol turned her attention to Danny and said, "By the way, Mike's goin' to have a couple a engineers come around ten or so an' install the prototype toilet I told ya about."

Danny asked skeptically, "Engineer! Why not a plumber?" Danny continued, "They're not building the Great Pyramid of Giza."

Carol said, "Don't know. It's a prototype an' has a special box to collect data, kinda like a computer."

Danny looked at Tim and Mary, furrowed his brow, and squinted his eyes until they were slits. "They got computers everywhere these days. What exactly are they goin' to do with all that data? Give it to FBI or the CIA. Damn government. They got their nose in everything. I don't trust 'em. I tell ya I just don't trust those bastards."

Carol and the children laughed. She replied, "I bet they're lookin' for commies. I hope they don't find any there."

Tim perked up and asked, "Is it the toilet they're goin' to use on the submarine?"

Carol said, "You can ask Mike this evenin'. He's comin' over for dinner an' wants to make sure it's set up properly."

Danny looked at the children and rolled his eyes. "In my day, I'd send your mamaw flowers." He looked at his daughter and said, "Don't worry. I got everything ready for 'em."

Carol said, "Don't forget. We'll be havin' dinner around 6:30. I'll take care of it. Youins be good for Papaw."

Mary said, "Okay, we'll be good."

Upon finishing breakfast, Danny threw a few apples and carrots into a bag, then handed it to Mary. "Here, you can feed this to Torch." He grabbed a thermos filled with coffee, turned toward the door, and said, "I'm goin outside."

The children cleaned the table and bolted for the door with Ike at their heels. Mary had the bag Danny gave her clutched in her hand. The dog, vying for attention, barked and playfully lunged at their heels. Danny, reclined comfortably under his favorite shade tree, watched Anne's palomino Goldie grazing, and lost track of time. Soon, 9:00 a.m. turned into 10:00 a.m. A white van pulled into the driveway.

Mary stopped and shouted, "Papaw, look! Is that them?"

Tim shouted, "They're bringin' the toilet!" And he ran toward the house.

Mary let Torch go, dropped the bag of carrots, and followed Tim, with Ike at her heels. The agitated dog barked as if he were tracking a desperate rat. Mary shouted, "Wait for me!"

Danny, disappointed, focused on the Hydro-Dyne logo. He entertained hope that they would run late. He arose from his shady spot and admonished the children, "Goodness, hold on, you two. For cryin' out loud, it's just a toilet."

Tim said, "But it's a submarine toilet."

Danny walked to the house and met the driver, who asked, "Sir, are you Jerome Shykes?"

Danny answered, "Yes, but call me Danny. Just back your van to the front door. It'll be easier to get it in."

The man did as requested, then he and an associate got out. The driver approached Danny, handed him a business card, and introduced himself. "Danny, my name's Roger, an' my friend's Jack. Looks like you're signed up for a field trial. We're engineers from Hydro-Dyne, an' we've come to install a prototype Hydro-Dyne 600. If you'd be kind enough to show me where it goes, I'll let ya get back to what ya were doin'."

"Come with me," replied Danny. The children, with Ike close behind, followed. He showed them through the front door, and like a small parade, they made their way to the end of the hall. Danny pointed and said, "There. Have at it."

Roger said, "Thanks, Danny. We'll take it from here." They turned and headed to the van.

Mary and Tim went with the men. The children stood spellbound, with Ike panting at their feet, watching the engineers unload the mysterious box. Wielding a box cutter, Jack carefully sliced through the cardboard until each side of the container fell away. Freed from its confinement, it glistened in the sunshine.

Mary anticipated a grand spectacle, but instead, she saw a toilet, not much different than what they had. She whispered to Tim, "Looks like a regular toilet to me."

Annoyed with Mary, Tim snapped, "Can't ya see it's a PROTOTYPE!"

Mary, confused, asked, "What's a PROLOTYPE? What's it do?"

With an air of sophistication, Tim replied, "Goodness, Mary! Don't ya know nothin'? That's PROTOTYPE. Can't ya tell?"

Mary repeated her query, "But what does a prolotype do?"

Tim, annoyed with Mary's mispronunciation, said, "THAT'S PRO-TO-TYPE!" Unable to provide an answer and not wanting to expose his ignorance, Tim said, "Ask 'em. They can explain it to ya better than me."

"You ask 'em," replied Mary. The men snickered while listening to the children.

Tim's curiosity got the best of him. He approached the men and peppered them with questions. "What's a PROTOTYPE? Will it really go on a submarine? Is it like the ones they use in submarines? It looks like a regular toilet. Can ya 'splain it to my sister?"

Roger became serious. "Engineers make a few prototypes to see if there are design flaws an' how they'll work under normal operating conditions. We build the prototypes like the ones we intend to use. We install 'em in houses like yours for testing. If there are problems, we can change the design before we make a bunch of 'em. If the trial goes well an' we get a contract, they'll be used on submarines."

Mary asked, "Why do they need a *prolotype* toilet? Can't they use a normal toilet?"

Danny stepped onto the porch and said, "Okay, you two. Leave these men alone. You need to go out an' play." Danny looked at Ike. "An' take that mangy mutt with ya."

"Awe, Papaw, please let us watch," Mary pleaded.

Roger said, "It'll be okay."

Danny gave Tim and Mary a terse warning, saying, "Okay, for now, but ya gotta stay outta their way. I catch ya pesterin' 'em I'll make ya muck the barn."

Mary and Tim replied in unison, "Okay, we'll be good."

Danny looked down at Ike and asked, "You goin' to come with me?" Ike looked at Danny, turned, and followed the children.

Danny reclaimed his seat under the shade tree, watching Anne's palomino graze on the hilltop; its golden coat and white mane struck a beautiful contrast against the clear blue sky and green pasture. He got the mare for Anne five years earlier; she named the palomino Goldie after the horse that brought them together. Danny remembered when Anne broke the spirited horse everyone gave up on.

A gentle breeze and unusually mild temperatures for July brought back memories of June 1941, six months before the attack on Pearl Harbor. Danny surrendered to his memory of the summer when he met Anne, and she broke Goldie, and they fell in love.

CHAPTER 13

June 1941, Benny's

On Friday, June 13, 1941, Danny entered Benny's, a honky-tonk favored by young people in the Maryville and Knoxville area. The proprietor, Benny, an accomplished guitarist and singer, started playing bluegrass but quickly developed a taste for country music. He formed a four-piece band, and in spite of his talent, Benny's dream of playing the Grand Ole Opry went unfulfilled. In order to continue playing, he found five acres well situated just outside of Maryville and built a honky-tonk. The luck that eluded Benny in his search for stardom found him in the realm of business.

Benny's timing could not have been better. He opened Benny's in 1935, just two years after the ratification of the Twenty-First Amendment, which permitted the sale of alcohol in the United States. While most counties and townships in east Tennessee were dry, he was able, after considerable effort, to acquire a license to sell beer. Benny's license, however, did not allow him to serve distilled spirits like whiskey.

Customers brought their own whiskey. Benny sold setups consisting of empty glasses, water, ice, and, for a little extra, a mixer. Benny employed two large off-duty police officers as bouncers. His establishment had a good reputation as a safe place where people could enjoy his music and have a good time.

Jan, Benny's wife, wanted to add a restaurant, but Benny wanted no part of anything that kept him from playing. He compromised and added chicken wings and fried shrimp to the standard offering of peanuts and pretzels. Benny agreed to let her manage the place however she saw fit as long as he could play country music.

Jan tended the bar and kept the books. He wanted to play music and make enough money to be comfortable. His honky-tonk became the most popular nightspot in the area. It grew faster than anticipated. By June 1941, he had three bartenders and five waitresses.

When Danny entered Benny's, the band was on break. After weaving through patrons standing and sipping beer, he made it to the bar. Tables, filled with young adults, were scattered between the bar and dance floor. Beyond the dance floor was a small stage where Benny and his band played. Danny ordered a beer and turned to a familiar voice.

"Hey, Danny, be careful. It's Friday the thirteenth." The friendly voice belonged to Danny's friend Brian Atwater, or Bry to his friends, who, beer in hand, stood alone at the bar. Bry's father, known to locals as Vern, built houses. When Danny graduated from high school four years earlier, Vern hired him to work alongside Bry. He taught the two how to build houses. From foundation to roof, Bry and Danny knew everything about building houses.

Bry, unlike Danny, was a large and scruffy man. While he adhered to basic cleanliness, he would go days without shaving and rarely comb his long red hair. He wore his shirt untucked, which added to his slovenly appearance. Bry, neither shy nor unintelligent, was a confident and smart man; he just did not care how he looked.

On the other hand, Danny, of average height and weight, with thick black hair and a dark complexion, maintained a neat, well-groomed appearance. He had a square jaw, a cleft chin, straight white teeth, and dimples that popped when he smiled, making him a natural draw for the ladies. Along with good looks came a gregarious personality that radiated confidence. His large ordinary brown eyes captivated those with whom he engaged in conversation; he possessed an abundance of charm and never found himself without friends.

PAPAW

Danny made his way to his friend and replied, "Bry! It's been a good day so far. What're ya worried about?"

"There's still four hours left." Bry took a sip of beer. "Looks like Benny has a good crowd tonight. Not many ladies."

"You'll find one," replied Danny.

Bry, while ready to get married, refused to accept that his slovenly appearance thwarted his efforts to find a wife. Danny, on the other hand, enjoyed single life, never expressing an interest in marriage.

Bry looked to his right, nodded, and said, "Now just wait a minute. Look over there."

There were three attractive young ladies, in their twenties, dressed in western attire. One beautiful young lady with blond hair caught Danny's eye. "Look at the blond. What a dish! I've never seen her here. Do ya know 'er?"

Bry laughed. "Yeah, I know 'er. She's a real dish all right. That's Anne Miller. She comes here now and then. Her father breeds walking horses an' made lots of money in real estate in the '20s. When the crash hit, everyone went belly up. He come out good. There are people that, ya know, always land on their feet." Bry took a sip of beer. "We built a house for 'em several years ago, not long before ya come to work for us."

Danny, smitten with Anne, said, "Ya say she's been here before. How could I miss a dame like that? Tell me about 'er."

"Anne's into horses. Ya know, rodeos. I think she's a barrel racer. I hate to tell ya, but she's way outta your league. Even for you." Bry took a sip of beer, laughed, and continued, "She's a holy roller. You'd have to go to church. You, walk into a church. You'll burst into flames."

Danny did not like to be told he was not good enough for anyone and, determined to prove a point, improvised a plan to get to know Anne. Danny asked, "Ya say she knows a lot about horses, do ya?"

"As far as I know, that's all she does."

"Bry, ole buddy, ya just gave me an idea. Just watch. I'll have that dame eating outta my hand." Danny started for Anne's table, then stopped in his tracks. A large good-looking man around thirty years old approached Anne. He wore jeans and a tightly fitted light blue denim shirt that complimented his broad shoulders and, adorning his head, a large white Stetson.

Bry laughed hysterically at Danny. "You're too slow!"

"Do ya know that clodhopper?"

Bry replied, "No, I don't. I've never seen 'im around here, but that joker just shot ya outta the saddle. Don't worry, the night's young. There'll be others."

Danny took note, watching the man like a cat ready to pounce on an unsuspecting bird, and bided his time, waiting for the right opening. Anne, doing the talking, made wide gesticulations as she spoke, and the man nodded politely without saying a word. After a few minutes, he tipped his hat, turned, headed straight for Danny, rested his arms on the bar, and ordered a beer.

After taking a large swallow of beer, he turned to Danny and said, "That gal sure's purty." He turned toward the stage and propped his back against the bar. "I'd rather ya hit me in the head with a ball-peen hammer than talk to her. Good luck. You can have her."

Danny's time came, and he turned to Bry and said, "I'll be back."

Brian laughed and replied, "Good luck. You'll need it."

With beer in hand, Danny made a beeline to Anne's table and thought, *"Step aside, clodhopper, an' let ole Danny Shykes work his magic. I'll show ya how it's done."* Anne watched Danny approach her table. Impressed with his good looks and crisp white cotton shirt, she smiled invitingly.

Danny broke the ice and introduced himself. "Hello, you must be Anne Miller. My name's Jerome Shykes. But my friends call me Danny."

Anne, with a puzzled look, asked, "Danny? Danny Shykes? Are you the Shykes with the cattle farm on Owl Creek just outside of Townsend?"

"Yes, kind of a sideline. We have about a hundred head," replied Danny, pleased she knew his family.

PAPAW

Anne squinted her eyes and furrowed her brow. "An' just how do ya know my name?"

Danny pointed to his friend. Bry raised his beer as if to offer a salute, smiled, and nodded his head.

"Oh! Brian Atwater. I remember Brian," said Anne. "He an' his father built a house for us several years ago." She continued, "They do good work. Ya need to tell Brian to clean up a little. He'd look really good. He's a nice guy an' very smart. But I'm not telling ya anything ya don't already know."

Danny laughed and said, "Yes. I've known Bry for some time. I went to work for his father a few years ago." He pointed to an empty seat. "Uh, ya mind if I sit here?"

"Sure, have a seat," said Anne. Danny sat down next to Anne and put his beer on the table. Anne snatched it, took a sip, and set it in front of her, drawing laughter from her friends. "That's my favorite. What're ya drinking?"

Danny, bested by the beautiful young woman, did not intend to give up his seat. "I'm not all that thirsty. Are ya here with anyone?"

Holding her newly acquired beer, she made a slow arcing motion toward her friends and replied, "No, just my friends." Adding nonchalantly, "I suppose you're goin' to ask me to dance."

Danny, amazed at her apparent ego, said, "Ya sure think a lot of yourself, don't ya?"

"Well," said Anne. She used the beer bottle to push her cowboy hat back, exposing her large blue eyes. "Ya see, women are the gatekeepers of civilization. It's a great responsibility, an' I can tell ya after looking around here that some of these ladies aren't doin' a very good job."

Anne paused and looked into Danny's eyes. "I have to cull out the wolves an' losers. Why, Danny, did ya know the queen bee flies as fast an' as high as she can while all the guy bees try to catch 'er? Only the strongest an' best bee can mate with her. Like I said, there are wolves an' losers out there. Which is it, Danny? Are ya a wolf or a loser?" Anne's friends laughed; they have seen her perform this routine many times, and they wondered how long it would take Danny to grow weary and give up.

Danny sensed the frustration the man felt. But the more Danny watched and listened to Anne, the more he wanted to get to know her. Danny said, "Why hell, Anne, NEITHER! All I wanted to do was talk to ya about a damn horse, not bees, civilization gatekeepers, mating, an' such. Bry said you were some kinda hotshot rodeo rider."

Anne grinned innocently and shot Danny a puzzled look. "Why didn't ya say so in the first place? I'd hate for ya to waste your time. It's a sin to waste time. Ya know, no one even knows what time is, but we don't need to waste it." Anne shook her head in the negative, sighed, and said, "Ya never get time back."

Danny glanced at Bry while rolling his eyes. Bry, in turn, laughed hysterically as Anne continued, "Danny, there's this fella who tried to figure out what time is but couldn't. I read 'bout 'im in one of my father's *Popular Mechanics* magazines. His name's Einstein, or somethin' like that. Ya ever hear of 'im?"

Before Danny could respond, Anne continued. "Why, they say he's the smartest man to ever live, an' even HE can't figure it out. If a smart guy like that can't find the answer, what're we to do? But it's simple for me 'cause I believe in Jesus. That way I don't have to worry 'bout all that stuff, an' when I die, I inherit paradise."

Danny thought, *"This gal's a real pistol."* He smiled patiently and listened.

"Are ya a heathen? I hope not. You're kinda cute, an' ya seem like a nice guy. I hope you're not a heathen, Danny. Ya don't need to spend eternity shovelin' coal. Now, don't get me wrong. I have nothin' agin shovelin' coal. I don't want ya to think I'm uppity. I've mucked horse stalls more times than I can count, an' if ya shoveled as much horse shit as I have, coal's no big deal. But we don't wanna go to hell. Are ya saved, Danny? I mean, do ya love Jesus?" Anne became silent and smiled adoringly while looking into Danny's eyes.

Danny, wishing to avoid a protracted religious discussion, said, "I'm not a heathen. I'm a Christian like you. I was baptized an' all that. Uh, do ya always talk this much? I mean, all I want is to ask ya about my horse."

Anne perked up and asked, "Are ya sayin' I talk too much? We just met. I just wanna get to know ya. I can tell already ya don't do much fishin'." Anne shook her head in the negative. "No. I don't think ya fish much."

Danny's voice became tense. "I fish all the time. An' what the hell does that have anythin' to do with what we're talkin' about?"

Anne continued, "Ya mustn't be very good. I fish with my brothers all the time. I catch lots of fish."

Indignant, Danny said, "I'm a good fisherman. I'd catch more than you."

Anne smiled and said, "Oh, no, Danny. Ya have no patience. Ya have to have LOTS AND LOTS of patience to catch the big ones." Danny shook his head in frustration and tried to take the initiative.

"Bry told me ya know a lot 'bout horses." Danny, seeking an opportunity to score points with Anne, said, "Maybe YOU can help me with my horse?"

"Why, I'd be delighted to help ya. I already see why you're having trouble."

Danny was making headway. "How can ya say that? Ya haven't even seen my horse."

"Ya have no patience. Like fishin', ya have to have patience when tryin' to break a horse."

Danny, wearing down, wanted to end the conversation and said, "Oh, she's a beauty like you. Her name's Goldie." Anne's furrowed brow indicated her displeasure with his pronouncement. Danny, attempting to recover his misspeak, did not give Anne a chance to reply and attempted to clarify what he said. "What I mean is, she's the most beautiful horse around these parts. She's spirited, full 'a fire, an' has a golden coat an' blond hair, but not your pretty blue eyes."

Anne rolled her eyes. "I bet you're a hit with the ladies. Do ya tell all the ladies they look like horses an' TALK too much? My father told me a long time ago that if you're digging yourself into a hole, the first thing ya need to do is PUT THE SHOVEL DOWN."

Danny, on to Anne's little game, thought, *"Maybe Anne's right. Maybe I'm not patient."* He, nevertheless, concluded Anne would be his wife and would move heaven and earth to make that a reality. For now, worn out, he wanted to get out of there.

Danny said, "I'm tryin' to break 'er, but this horse's a tough one. No one can break her."

Curiosity drove away Anne's indifferent attitude. "Really! No ONE! Your horse's a palomino. You're right. They're pretty an' smart too."

Finally, Danny was gaining ground. "No ONE can break this horse."

Not able to resist a challenge, Anne said, "All horses can be broke. I've grown up on horses. I'm a champion barrel racer, an' I've been breakin' horses since I was fourteen. There's not a horse I can't break. Not one!"

Danny pounced on her ego. "I'm not so sure ya can. I don't care if ya broke a thousand horses or run barrels to the moon an' back, ya can't break this horse."

Anne took on a skeptical tone. "Then why are ya sittin' here? Are ya tryin' to part my loins?"

Danny, both stunned and amused by her shocking candor, laughed and asked, "Part your loins? What're on earth are ya talkin' about?"

Anne said, "Well, if ya don't think I can break 'er, why are ya talkin' to me? That's what that other fella was after. Ya know, my loins. PROCREATE."

Danny snickered and replied, "I'm not here to PART your loins. Bry suggested I talk to ya, so I'm here."

Anne, playing her cards close to the vest, wanted to get to know Danny and, at the same time, keep him at arm's length. "So, Danny, do ya want me to look at your horse? Goodness don't beat 'bout the bush. A simple yes or no."

Danny, exhausted and excited with the outcome of his encounter with Anne, said, "Yes."

"See that wasn't so hard. Can I come by an' meet Goldie tomorrow?"

"Sure, is two good?" Danny added, "I keep her at my father's farm. Ya need directions?"

Anne replied, "I know where it is. I'll be there at two." Benny's band started toward the stage. Danny got up from his seat. Anne

PAPAW

asked, "The band's gettin' ready to start. Are ya goin' to ask me for a dance?"

Danny wanted to but after their tedious conversation, said, "No, I'll pass. See ya tomorrow." Danny returned to his friend.

Bry asked, "How'd it go? Where's your beer?"

"I wasn't all that thirsty. I let her have it. She's goin' to look at Goldie. Ya know, Bry, she don't know it, but she'll be my wife someday."

Incredulously, Bry asked, "Are ya telling me you're goin' to let her on that horse? Isn't that how your uncle John broke his arm? Do ya really think that's a good idea? Look at her. She's too pretty to get all busted up."

"One time on that horse an' she'll give up an' be so busy fallin' in love with me, she'll forget about it. Besides, she's an expert. She's been breakin' horses for years. Bry, I think I'm goin' to call it a night."

As promised, the next day, precisely at 2:00 p.m., Anne pulled her father's 1930 Ford pickup truck onto the Shykes' gravel driveway. The driveway evenly divided a small, twenty-acre pasture framed by plain, rugged, ranch-style fencing, where cattle were grazing.

She idled the truck by a well-maintained, single-story white farmhouse before stopping next to a large red barn. A canopy formed by large hickory and maple trees provided welcome shade for the barn and house. Next to the barn sat a small John Deere tractor and a hay rake. Two cats, one a tuxedo and the other a calico, tumbled and played, darting in and out of overgrown Johnson grass that camouflaged derelict farm equipment. Anne sprang from the truck with her shoulders back and her head erect. She briefly hung onto the open door and scanned the terrain until she found Danny and his father. Her eyes met Danny's, and they exchanged smiles. She turned to Danny's father, smiled, nodded, then slammed the door and, taking long, quick strides, made her way to greet them. With horses, she was in her element, and everything about her exemplified horsemanship. She looked forward to working with Goldie and did not want to miss an opportunity to learn more about Danny.

Danny eagerly watched her approach; she was more beautiful now than at Benny's, and he thought, *"Can I be this lucky? Could I be the one to capture her heart?"*

Like Danny, Anne found herself in unfamiliar territory. She had never felt this way about a man. He passed the first test at Benny's. She contemplated, *"Is there more to this man than good looks?"*

"Dad, I want ya to meet Anne Miller. She can break Goldie."

Anne, ready for work, came dressed in snug-fitting blue jeans and bronze cowboy boots decorated with rows of intricate stitching. An open light suede shirt, with sleeves rolled to the elbows, hung loosely over a navy-blue cotton T-shirt. On her head, matching her boots, was a bronze leather Stetson, cocked slightly back and trimmed with a scalloped concho knot hat band. The hat contrasted her shirt, framing her deep blue eyes, high cheekbones, and bright smile. Anne's petite size masked the toughness she acquired growing up as the only female and youngest sibling among five boys. Along with a love of horses, Anne regularly hunted and fished with her father and brothers. She wore her blond hair pulled into a ponytail that fell between her shoulders. Anne looked every bit the horse expert, and the beautiful tomboy left a favorable impression on Danny's father.

Anne extended her hand toward Danny's father and said, "Hello, Mr. Shykes. Danny says ya have a horse that can't be broke. Maybe I can help. Don't like to brag, but I'm pretty good with horses." When Danny heard "don't like to brag" roll from Anne's lips, he rolled his eyes, thinking of their encounter at Benny's.

Danny's father had no interest in breaking Goldie. One look at Anne, however, betrayed where his son's interest lay. He smiled and took Anne's hand, looked her square in the eye, and gave her a firm handshake. "Lil' lady, call me Buddy. That's what all my friends call me." He pointed to a palomino grazing. "That's Goldie, an' she can't be broke. Everyone here tried. No one can, an' I really don't wanna waste any more time. I certainly don't want ya to git all busted up. Just ain't worth it. I think I'll jist give 'er away."

"Buddy, ya said everyone. That's everyone except me. I can break 'er. Just let me see 'er. I already see from here Goldie's worth it."

Danny shrugged his shoulders. "What 'a ya gotta lose?"

PAPAW

"Okay, Anne, I reckon it won't hurt for ya to look at 'er," replied Buddy, and the three headed to see Goldie.

They walked one hundred feet to a small corral and found Goldie. The horse stopped grazing long enough to cast an indifferent glance at the approaching trio, then resumed grazing as if it saw nothing. Anne, impressed with Goldie, turned to Danny and said, "She looks big—at least sixteen hands, maybe seventeen."

"Smart too," Danny added.

Buddy said, "My brother John broke his arm tryin' to break 'er."

"Don't worry. I know what I'm doin'. Been breakin' horses since I was fourteen an' broke my right arm once."

Buddy needed to be convinced. "This is no ordinary horse. I don't think she's worth the trouble."

Anne pulled an apple from her pocket and held it out. Goldie saw the treat and trotted toward Anne. She fell in love with the beautiful palomino and gave her the apple while rubbing the horse's muzzle. "She's beautiful. Give me three weeks. If I can't break her, let 'er go."

Eager to spend time with Anne, Danny said, "I'll be nearby. What 'a ya think? Don't worry. It'll be fine."

Buddy scratched his chin. "Don't seem like much time." The obvious attraction between Anne and Danny compelled Buddy to relent. "It's okay with me. Give it a try. It'll make your mother happy to see ya around here more."

Anne extended her hand to Buddy. "We have a deal. I'll start tomorrow at five. If I can't break her, no one can."

Buddy, charmed by Anne, took her hand. "Okay, lil' lady, ya got yourself a deal."

* * * * *

A nicker pulled Danny from his pleasant daydream. Goldie, with its ears perked up, stared at Danny from the other side of the fence. The horse made its way from the hilltop, seeking a treat. Danny walked to the horse and pulled an apple from the bag left by the children. Holding the apple out for the horse, he whispered, "Goldie, are ya hungry? Take this."

Goldie took the apple while Danny gently rubbed behind her ears, saying, "Do ya miss Anne? I understand. I miss 'er too. Just not the same around here without 'er, is it?" Danny returned to his seat under the tree. He looked at his house and the Hydro-Dyne van as Tim, Mary, and Ike played, then turned his gaze to Goldie.

His mind resumed the pleasant daydream, and Danny returned to the summer of 1941. To the happy moments before World War II. A time when another palomino named Goldie allowed him to find the mother of his only child and his one true love that would endure a lifetime, Anne.

CHAPTER 14

Goldie

THE FOLLOWING DAY, Anne parked her truck next to the corral, jumped out, and grabbed a bridle and burlap sack from the truck bed.

Danny greeted Anne, saying, "Bein' the first day an' all, I figured ya might need a little help gettin' started." Anne, with the bridle dangling over her left shoulder, blew by Danny with quick, deliberate steps. She tossed the burlap sack at Danny, who in turn bobbled the sack, nearly spilling its contents.

He peeked into the bag and found apples and carrots. Anne watched as Danny fumbled with the sack, and she snapped, "Come now, we ain't got all day while you fiddle with that sack. Let's get this bridle on 'er." Danny closed the bag as she continued her playful tirade, then sprinted to catch up.

"Sure, whatever ya need."

"It's not magic. Just hard work an' PATIENCE. Can't do a thing till we get a bridle on 'er. Just let me deal with Goldie. You can help by doin' what I ask an' when I ask."

"Sure, let's get that bridle on 'er. Uh, maybe we should move her away from the fence. She don't like bridles."

"She don't," replied Anne. "Can't break 'er let alone ride 'er till we get that bridle on 'er. Let's try." Anne squinted her eyes skeptically. "Uh, do ya know anything about horses?" Danny had no answer, and

Anne got snarky. "Duh is not a good answer. Here, take this." Anne handed the bridle to Danny.

Danny took the bridle from Anne as they moved toward Goldie. Anne asked, "Ya do know how to put one on, don't ya?"

Danny shook his head from side to side while rolling his eyes. "Yeah, boss, reckon I do."

Anne rubbed the side of Goldie's neck as she spoke in soothing tones. "Okay, Goldie, let's slip this on, ole girl."

Danny worked the bridle on Goldie while Anne stroked the horse's neck. Goldie backed away, snorting and shaking her head.

"See!"

Anne looked at Goldie and thought, *"Could she have a bad tooth?"* She ran her hand along Goldie's jowl and said, "Get me a stick."

Danny ran to the barn and returned with an old tobacco stick, which he handed to Anne. "Will this do?"

"Yes."

She poked the stick deep into the horse's mouth and pressed it on the horse's back bottom teeth. Goldie jumped and neighed. Anne said, "What I thought. I'm certain she has an abscess. We gotta get a vet out here tomorrow an' get a tooth out. We're done for the day."

"How do ya pull a horse's tooth?"

"The vet can do it. I'll call 'im an' have 'im come out tomorrow."

Danny scratched his head. "A tooth! None of us thought of that."

The vet arrived the following morning, confirmed Anne's suspicion, and pulled the tooth. The next afternoon, much to Danny's delight, Anne began taming Goldie. After three days of working with Goldie, Anne was able to mount the beautiful horse.

During the next three weeks, Anne worked with Goldie, hoping to turn her into the riding horse Buddy wanted. Danny enjoyed spending time watching and helping Anne in any way he could. He used the time wisely and allowed Anne to get to know him. After three weeks, Anne called Danny's father, so he could see what she accomplished. She proudly rode the horse and showed Buddy how easy the horse was to control.

PAPAW

"Here, Buddy. Give 'er a try." Anne dismounted Goldie and held the reins.

Danny said, "Go ahead. She's a different horse. Ya won't have any trouble." He turned to Anne, adding, "Anne did a good job."

Anne said, "Go on, Mr. Shykes. I think you'll like 'er." Buddy took the reins and climbed onto Goldie. He sat in the saddle amazed.

Anne cautioned Danny's father, "Buddy, she's easy. No need to tug on the reins. If ya lay the reins on the right side of her neck, she'll turn to the right. Lay 'em on the left, an' she'll go left. To go backward, just pull on the reins gently with both hands. Just a gentle nudge with the heels will get 'er goin'."

Buddy did as Anne instructed and walked her around the pasture then opened her to a trot. When he got back, he said, "I'll be. Almost like drivin' a car." Buddy dismounted Goldie. "Lil' lady, ya did what ya said. I admire that. Ya certainly know horses. Tell ya what. Why don't ya keep 'er? I was goin' to give her away. That horse suits ya."

Anne replied, "Buddy, I love Goldie. She's a great horse. But I'm not going to take her. Tell ya what. I've got a gelding I'll trade. He's a little older but a good horse." She smiled at Danny. "Easier to ride than Goldie. Why even Danny can handle 'im"

Danny laughed at the little dig. Seizing an opportunity to ride with Anne, he said, "Sounds like a fair trade to me."

Buddy could not deny the chemistry between Danny and Anne. "Okay, ya gotta deal."

Anne said, "Good, I'll bring 'im by tomorrow."

CHAPTER 15

Anne and Danny Fall in Love

ANNE ARRIVED AT the farm the next morning with a small horse trailer in tow.

Danny greeted Anne. "Hello, Anne. Ya bring me a horse?"

Anne jumped out of the truck and made a beeline to the trailer, with Danny at her heels. She lowered the ramp and guided the horse from the trailer. The beautiful horse, similar in size to Goldie, had a solid black coat, tail, and mane. Anne said, "Here. You'll like 'im. His name's Black Jack."

Danny rubbed the horse's neck. "Handsome horse. Black Jack makes sense."

Anne said, "Dad served in the Great War. You know, fighting the Kaiser. He fought in Pershing's army. So he named his horse after 'im. Pershing was known by the nickname Black Jack. My father met Pershing. Said he was a good man."

"Horrible war. Some say it was the war to end all wars," replied Danny.

Anne sighed and said, "I'm afraid there'll always be war. We'll be in this one before long. Hitler conquered France an' is about to conquer Russia. Only a matter a time."

Danny replied, "Roosevelt'll keep us out. He's committed to keeping us out. It's Europe's problem.

PAPAW

Anne loved Danny's innocence. "Ya have more faith in politicians than me."

Danny did not wish to ruin the day talking politics. "God won't allow it."

For the first time since they met, Danny invoked God. Anne, not wishing to let politics ruin the day, said, "I DO hope you're right. No need to borrow problems." She changed the subject. "How about a ride? I mean, I want to make sure ya like Black Jack. He's a great horse, but ya never know. You may not like 'im."

When they met at Benny's, Anne subjected Danny to a barrage of chatter in an effort to drive him away. Danny, however, had proven himself a gentleman of the highest order. Now ready to draw him near, in a nonchalant tone she said, "I think ya should try 'im out. Besides, it's a nice day for a ride. Give ya a chance to get to know 'im."

Danny's good fortune sent him over the moon with joy. He thought, *"She's interested in me."*

He replied, "I don't see any reason why I wouldn't like Black Jack. But let's take 'im out."

"Good because I packed lunch. Nothing fancy, ya know, just some fried chicken, potato salad, an' lemonade. Do ya care to get those saddlebags outta the truck?"

Flying high with excitement, Danny got the saddlebags. Everything was falling into place just as he hoped. He thought, *"All this work, she's got to care. If I don't do anything stupid, I'm home free."*

After they saddled the horses, Anne said, "I know a good place we can go. It's a safe place to ride, an' I'll have ya back before dark."

Danny thought, *"This's her show. I'll do whatever she wants."*

He replied, "I'm sure I'm in good hands. We're starting here?"

Anne pointed to a hill. "Yes, we'll cut through that pasture." They mounted the horses and headed to the foothills of the Great Smoky Mountains.

Danny fell in behind Anne, and they made their way through the open pasture under clear blue skies. A gentle breeze and the warm morning sun fueled Danny's optimism. Concerns of political leaders over an escalating war in Europe, which would soon wreck Danny's plans, were not going to ruin his day, the happiest day of his young life. In his mind, they would solve the problems, and America would stay out of Europe's war. For now, he had Anne, and nothing else mattered. Danny learned patience and had the time he needed to make Anne his. Danny nudged Black Jack and pulled alongside her.

Anne said, "Black Jack's been on this trail more times than I can count. He knows the way. He gets a little lazy. If he sees something he wants to eat, he may stop an' graze. Just give 'im a gentle nudge in the belly."

"I've noticed that."

Before they knew it, they arrived at the trail leading into the forest. Anne said, "Dad used to take me an' my brothers campin' here. The trail leads to the top of this hill an' a spectacular view of the valley. From there, you can see Owl Creek an' your house. Some good hunting up there too." Anne pointed to the narrow trail. "Why don't ya lead the way? Black Jack knows where to go." Danny nudged Black Jack, and he entered the forest.

The sun disappeared, and Danny felt a rush of cool air. His nostrils filled with the aroma of moist earth and pine. The trail wound through firs, dogwoods, and maples. Rhododendrons crowded the trail, providing a dense covering of shade. Danny rocked in the saddle, while Black Jack walked along, with Goldie following.

Anne said, "Hope you're not in a hurry."

A different side of Anne emerged, and time became a welcome friend to Danny. While riding Goldie, the impenetrable shroud of confidence he saw in Anne at Benny's gave way to a gossamer veil of vulnerability. Danny, on the verge of acquiring his most cherished gift, Anne's love, found himself in a position to gently lift the veil. Today, a make-or-break moment would become the most memorable of his life.

Danny replied, "I got all day."

The trail took them through multiple switchbacks while ascending to a flat area lined with boulders of varying sizes. The darkness gave way to a sudden burst of sunshine. A gentle breeze broke the silence and blew through Danny's hair. Moved by the splendor, he remarked, "This's the most beautiful place I've been. Thanks for bringin' me."

Anne answered, "It is. I figured you'd like it here. You get the saddlebags with our lunch. I'll spread the blanket."

Danny set the saddlebags on the ground and removed items while noting the effort Anne put into the picnic. Each item indicated her interest in a future together, and his confidence intensified.

"I'm impressed. You do all this?"

"Why yes, Danny, I did. It's just fried chicken. Everyone likes fried chicken. You DO like fried chicken, don't ya?"

"Of course. Look at those fresh rolls! Did ya make those too?"

"Yes, I did. Mama taught me how to cook. Dad taught me how to fish, hunt, an' field dress a deer. He taught me to ride too." Anne made a fist and playfully shook it at Danny. "My brothers taught me how to fight. So ya better be careful, Mac."

Danny poured lemonade. "You're just a jack-of-all-trades."

"I know, an' I can catch more fish than you."

"As for fishing, we'll have to see 'bout that. You're not goin' to go on about patience, are ya?"

Anne replied, "I'd hate to embarrass ya. Lucky for you, I'm too hungry to talk about it. I need to eat."

After they ate, Danny touched Anne's hand. During the three weeks he and Anne trained Goldie, he showed no affection. She welcomed the touch of his hand with a smile and allowed Danny to take the lead.

Danny said, "That was good. Care to go for a walk an' show me around?"

Anne, while determined to impress Danny, remained coy, waiting for him to express his feelings, and said, "Sure." They rose to their feet. "Let's go this way."

Danny took Anne's hand; she led him down a short trail to a rocky bluff where they could take in the view and feel the welcoming breeze that brought a burst of warm air from the valley below.

They stepped onto the overlook and admired the panorama. The beautiful expanse of Wears Valley, dotted with houses and farms, came into view. A breeze tossed their hair and brought the aroma of summer. Anne turned to Danny, and instantly he pulled her into his arms and gently kissed her. His swiftness caused her to instinctively pull back. Anne's eyes widened, and her mouth opened slightly, exposing her surprise.

Danny thought, *"Why did I do that? I just ruined everything."* Danny said, "I'm sorry. I don't know what came over me."

Danny's kiss liberated Anne. She found the man to whom she could give her earthly love. After regaining her composure, her eyes softened, and she looked at Danny, whose eyes were now wide. An impulsive smile replaced her surprise, and she said, "Who are YOU kidding? You knew exactly what came over you. You wanted to kiss me. Goodness, what took ya so long?" She pulled herself into Danny's arms. "One'll get ya two." Anne reached around, grabbed Danny behind his neck, and kissed him.

Danny ran his fingers through her hair and asked, "Ya think it's too fast to say I love you?"

Anne replied, "After a kiss like that, you better. What took ya so long? I loved you from the first moment I saw you at Benny's. I felt like I've known ya my whole life. You walked right up to me like ya owned the whole world."

With his confidence restored, he said, "I love you." He thought, *"Someday you'll be my wife."*

Danny had no way of knowing their carefree time together would be brief. They were young, and he wanted to make memories. He found the patience Anne often talked about, and he cherished their days. The talk of war and fighting in Europe did not cause Danny concern. He never thought America would enter the war. However, if drafted, he would serve his time and return to life with Anne.

Anne's intuition, however, told her otherwise.

America would soon be at war.

CHAPTER 16

December 7, 1941

DANNY AND ANNE became inseparable during the summer of 1941, making good use of their time. They spent every free moment riding Goldie and Black Jack along the many trails in Wears Valley and the foothills of the Smoky Mountains. Meanwhile, Anne kept up with the turmoil in Europe. Not far from her mind were stories her father told of the Great War. Most of them were horror stories of death and destruction on a scale beyond imagination. And even as storm clouds of war in Europe were closing in on their little community, Anne never spoke of her concern, fearing Danny would face the same nightmare. For now, Anne wanted to create cherished memories they could share. Danny, on the other hand, believed President Roosevelt's promise—he would keep America out of the war. The escalating war in Europe did not concern him, and Anne would not poison his optimism. Her fears, however, came to fruition.

December 7 was a nice Sunday morning, especially for Anne, because she persuaded Danny to go with her to church. Danny, baptized a Methodist, drifted away from active fellowship. Anne found herself at the beginning of a journey that would one day see Danny fully embrace the teachings of Jesus. However, she wanted him to find his own way. Hopefully, through her example, he would acquire a deep commitment to Christ. For now, like she advised Danny, she would have to be patient.

Danny and Anne greeted the pastor as they exited the church. Anne said, "Pastor Kirby, I'd like ya to meet Jerome Shykes, but everyone calls 'im Danny."

The pastor of Owl Creek Baptist Church, sixty-year-old Matthew Kirby, extended his hand and welcomed Danny. "Welcome to Owl Creek Baptist Church. I know your father, Buddy. How's he doing?"

Danny took the pastor's hand and replied, "I enjoyed the sermon. Dad's doin' good. Today's his birthday. Me an' Anne're headed to see 'im an' have dinner."

"Today's my anniversary. Jane and I've been married for forty years. We were married on December 7, 1901," replied Pastor Kirby. "I hope to see ya around here, even if you're a Methodist," laughed the pastor.

Anne and Danny entered Danny's father's house and were greeted by Florence, Danny's mother. In a state of high agitation, Florence said, "We've been attacked!"

Danny peered into the living room, and several members of his family were gathered around the radio, which included his father, Uncle John, and John's wife, Aunt Nell. Danny returned his gaze to Florence and asked, "Mom, what're ya talkin' about? Attacked?"

Buddy shouted, "JAPAN'S ATTACKING US. SOME PLACE CALLED PEARL HARBOR."

Anne followed Danny to the radio. The stark realization of her worst fears came to pass. Instead of the rage felt by the others, Anne felt a sense of loss. She witnessed the last vestige of Danny's innocence be ripped from his soul, and only she could see it. She thought, *"I'm going to lose Danny."*

"Thousands of our boys're bein' killed. This's war," said Danny's Uncle John.

"I can't believe it. Horrible, just horrible," said Nell.

Danny turned to Anne and said, "Looks like you were right."

Anne kissed Danny on the cheek and held him. Her thoughts turned to the mothers, fathers, brothers, and sisters of the men whose lives were cut short in their prime, many of whom were boys still in their teens. She prayed as she held Danny, *"Dear heavenly Father, comfort those who lost loved ones and guide us during this troubled time. I ask in the name of Jesus, amen."*

On Monday, December 8, shortly after noon, Danny and Anne, along with Buddy and Florence, were sitting in the Shykes's living room waiting for President Roosevelt to address Congress and the nation.

President Roosevelt Infamy Speech

Mr. Vice President, and Mr. Speaker, and Members of the Senate and House of Representatives:

YESTERDAY, December 7, 1941, a date which will live in infamy the United States of America was suddenly and deliberately attacked by naval and air forces of the Empire of Japan.

The United States was at peace with that Nation and, at the solicitation of Japan, was still in conversation with its Government and its Emperor looking toward the maintenance of peace in the Pacific. Indeed, one hour after Japanese air squadrons had commenced bombing in the American Island of Oahu, the Japanese Ambassador to the United States and his colleague delivered to our Secretary of State a formal reply to a recent American message. And while this reply stated that it seemed useless to continue the existing diplomatic negotiations, it contained no threat or hint of war or of armed attack.

It will be recorded that the distance of Hawaii from Japan makes it obvious that the attack was deliberately planned many days or even weeks ago. During the intervening time the Japanese Government has deliberately sought to deceive the United States by false statements and expressions of hope for continued peace.

The attack yesterday on the Hawaiian Islands has caused severe damage to American naval and military forces. I regret to tell you that very many American lives have been lost. In addition, American ships have been reported torpedoed on the high seas between San Francisco and Honolulu.

Yesterday the Japanese Government also launched an attack against Malaya. Last night Japanese forces attacked Hong Kong:

Last night Japanese forces attacked Guam. Last night Japanese forces attacked the Philippine Islands. Last night the Japanese attacked Wake Island. And this morning the Japanese attacked Midway Island.

Japan has, therefore, undertaken a surprise offensive extending throughout the Pacific area. The facts of yesterday and today speak for themselves. The people of the United States have already formed their opinions and well understand the implications to the very life and safety of our Nation.

As Commander in Chief of the Army and Navy I have directed that all measures be taken for our defense.

But always will our whole Nation remember the character of the onslaught against us.

No matter how long it may take us to overcome this premeditated invasion, the American people in their righteous might will win through to absolute victory.

I believe that I interpret the will of the Congress and of the people when I assert that we will not only defend ourselves to the uttermost but will make it very certain that this form of treachery shall never again endanger us.

Hostilities exist. There is no blinking at the fact that our people, our territory, and our interests are in grave danger.

With confidence in our armed forces with the unbounding determination of our people we will gain the inevitable triumph so help us God.

I ask that the Congress declare that since the unprovoked and dastardly attack by Japan on Sunday, December 7, 1941, a state of war has existed between the United States and the Japanese Empire.

CHAPTER 17

Danny Goes to War

LIKE MANY, SHORTLY after the attack on Pearl Harbor, Danny enlisted in the Army. He reported to Fort Dix, New Jersey for thirteen weeks basic training. Upon completion, he returned for a one-week furlough before shipping out. Anne wanted to get married, but Danny, fearful he would die in combat, insisted they wait until his return. Anne, deeply hurt, acceded to his wishes and made the most of their final week together. The week flew by.

Anne parked her truck across from the bus stop. She went all out, wearing a simple, sleeveless white cotton dress with navy blue polka dots and trimmed with a navy blue notched neck. She wore matching navy blue shoes, and her hair was pulled into a ponytail secured with a navy blue ribbon. Danny wore his Army dress uniform, which consisted of a green tunic over lighter green trousers. He fidgeted with his hat silently, beholding Anne. "You're so beautiful. I'll miss you," said Danny with a bittersweet smile.

"Goodness, there ya go, smilin'. I love your smile. Even a sad one. Those dimples of yours," Anne replied.

Danny, wishing to set Anne free, reluctantly said, "Ya know, from this moment you should consider me dead. If ya meet someone, a fella, an' want to, you know, get on with your life, I'll understand. As beautiful as you are…"

Shocked and hurt by Danny's words, Anne cut him off. "Don't say another word, Danny! Don't talk like that. I'm upset enough as it is. Two things'll happen. One, you're coming home. Two, I'll be waitin' for ya. No matter how long it takes, even if it's fifty years."

The bus turned the corner, and Danny wiped away a tear. "It's time. I see the bus. This's goin' to be tougher than I thought." Anne's tears flowed, bringing mascara with them. Danny pulled a handkerchief from his pocket and dabbed her face carefully, saying, "I guess ya really do love me. We better go."

"Okay."

They slowly got out of the truck. Danny grabbed his duffle bag from the bed, and they scampered across the street. Upon reaching the bus stop, Danny dropped his duffle bag, took Anne in his arms, and kissed her passionately, showing no concern for his surroundings. The bus rolled to a stop; the hissing of air brakes and the door slamming open announced its arrival.

Danny threw his duffle bag in and returned to Anne. "Thanks for the greatest summer I ever had. I love you."

Anne looked into Danny's eyes. "I don't want ya to go."

Mildred, an elderly woman in the bus, captivated by the scene and swathed in emotion, watched them from the window. She turned to her friend in the next seat and said, "Look, Madge, isn't he handsome? Looks a little like Gary Cooper."

Madge craned her neck and looked through the window at the young couple. "Well, he sure is. I think he's better looking than Gary Cooper. I just saw 'im in *Sergeant York*. I declare that young lady looks just like Ginger Rogers."

"Yes, she does look like Giger Rogers. Just look at 'em. Like watchin' Gary Cooper say goodbye to Ginger Rogers. Such a beautiful couple, and he's going off to war. Just like in the movies," said Mildred as she wiped tears from her eyes.

The bus driver laid on the horn and yelled at Danny. "Hey, Mac, I ain't got all day!"

Enraged, Madge shot up from her seat, grabbed her cane, and shuffled to the driver, who was rolling his fingers on the steering wheel impatiently while gazing out his window. The short, old woman,

PAPAW

trembling with rage, raised the cane as high as she could and, with all her might, slammed it on his head. The blow sent his hat tumbling to the floor and the other passengers roaring with laughter.

The driver shouted, "WHAT THE HELL!" While turning toward the assaulting party, he shouted, "I'LL BEAT YA TO NEXT SUNDAY YOU SON OF A..." After realizing the assaulting party was an old woman, he said, "Mam, are ya crazy? What's the big idea?"

The old woman shouted, "LISTEN HERE, BUSTER. I'LL CONK YA AGIN IF'N YA DON'T SHUT UP. LET THAT YOUNG FELLA SAY GOODBYE TO HIS SWEETHEART!" She stood motionless with the cane raised high, ready to administer the beating she just promised.

"Okay, toots, just slowly put the cane down, and go back to your seat." He looked through the door at Anne and Danny and, with a sarcastic tone, said, "You two take all the time ya need. We got ALL DAY LONG."

The driver glared at the old woman as she reclaimed her seat and thought, "*They need to put her in a uniform an' send her to France and fight the Germans. One look at her, and they'll surrender.*"

Madge shuffled to her seat. Mildred said, "Good job." The two old women resumed watching Anne and Danny say goodbye.

Danny smiled and nodded at the driver, then returned his gaze to Anne and said, "Sayin' goodbye's hard. I'm not sure I'll be back. I want ya to know how much our time together meant. I guess I'm not good with words like you. Just know, I love you so much."

Fighting tears, Anne said, "Don't think like that. I promise, you'll return, an' I'll be waitin'. I love you. I'll pray every day an' remind God how important you are to me. You'll come home. To ME. When ya do, I'll be wearin' this very dress."

Tears fell from Danny's eyes. "I love you. I gotta go." Danny took Anne in his arms and kissed her for the last time.

As Danny pulled back, Anne grabbed him and said, "One'll get ya two." Anne returned his kiss with equal passion.

Danny handed Anne his handkerchief. "I love you. Goodbye."

Anne said, "I love you, Danny."

She stood by the bus and watched him take a seat behind the two old women, who were overcome with emotion. Several passengers who witnessed the goodbye became emotional. The driver released the brake and slammed the door shut. The hissing brakes drove reality into Anne's heart like a nail and drained her remaining strength; she wept bitterly, their fate in God's hands.

Danny waved at Anne as the bus pulled out and wondered if he would ever see her again. He would carry with him the image of her—the dress, her hair, and her promise. Above all, the promise that he would return to her would sustain him during his darkest hours.

The engine roared to life. Danny jumped from his seat, ran to the back of the bus, and looked out the rear window. The bus picked up speed, and Anne stood stoically, growing smaller in the distance, until she disappeared from Danny's view. He reclaimed his seat, and Anne went home. She changed out of the dress, removed her shoes and ribbon, and carefully packed them in a suitcase along with her small clutch. She shoved them under her bed. They would stay there until Danny's return.

Instantly, the waiting began. Like a mother sitting by her sick child's bed, she waited. Instead of hours or days, it would be years. Anne found things to do and stayed busy, but Danny would always remain in her thoughts. She wondered where he was or what peril would come his way. Her heart told her one day she would wear the dress for Danny's return.

* * * * *

"Hear ye, hear ye, all rise. The honorable Judge Nelson B. Samuelsson presiding," announced the bailiff. Judge Samuelsson, an enormous man with silver hair and a pocked face, was sixty-five. Considered firm and fair, he understood the rule of law and the constitution.

Samuelsson took his place, slammed the gavel, and said, "Court's in session. Please be seated."

Judge Samuelsson looked at the defense table and said, "Will the defendant please rise."

The defendant, Jason Black, and his attorney, Richard Hartley, stood and faced the judge.

"I see we have Case 3115, *State of Tennessee vs. Jason Black*. Mr. Black has been indicted on two counts of vehicular homicide. Is this correct?"

"Yes, Your Honor," said Hartley.

"It is also my understanding that Mr. Black wishes to enter a plea of guilty on both counts. Is this also, correct?" asked Judge Samuelsson.

"Yes, Your Honor."

Judge Samuelsson, puzzled, squinted his eyes and pursed his lips tightly. After a brief pause, he turned to the prosecutor. "Gentlemen, please approach the bench."

Jason Black observed the three men discussing his case. The judge fiddled with his gavel as Hartley spoke to the prosecutor. The cold reality of that fateful night and the full burden of the families victimized by his thoughtless conduct came crashing down on the young defendant. He wanted to end his life, but his mother, sitting in the gallery and feeling the same shame and guilt as him, kept him alive. Jason was her only living son, and she loved him without condition. He had to stay alive and somehow do the impossible—right an unforgivable wrong. But how?

Judge Samuelsson probed Hartley. "Richard, this is highly unusual. I've read the case. Are you going to present any mitigating factors?" Judge Samuelsson glanced at Jason. "Your client desires to go straight to sentencing?"

Hartley replied, "Your Honor, my client wishes to dispose of this quickly. He feels true remorse and doesn't want to cause the family any more grief. He's taken complete responsibility and is prepared for whatever sentence you hand down."

Judge Samuelsson turned his attention to the prosecutor and said, "I see no sentence recommendations from you," then looked at Hartley and said, "nor from you."

"Your honor, the state, and I agreed to let you sentence Mr. Black as you see fit based on the facts before you," replied Hartley.

The prosecutor replied, "I've discussed this with the families. It's their wish to let you settle it today, your honor."

"Okay, Richard, I don't have anything else to say except that I need to speak with your client. Please bring him to me," said the judge. Hartley turned to Jason and, with a wave of his hand, summoned Jason to the bench. Judge Samuelsson turned his attention to the defendant, standing before him flanked by his attorney and the prosecutor.

Jason Black, thirty-five years old and of slight stature, had, as a result of alcohol addiction, aged prematurely. He enjoyed the benefits of a solid middle-class upbringing with a loving mother. In spite of his father's battle with alcoholism, Jason graduated cum laude, with a degree in engineering. He showed considerable promise, and after graduation, a prestigious engineering firm in Knoxville hired him. However, like his father, he descended into the unforgiving depths of alcohol dependency. After the tragic accident, with his career and life over, he wanted to bury himself in his cell.

Jason turned and looked at his mother. The small, frail woman of quiet beauty appeared older than her sixty years. She wore her once auburn hair, now white, in a tight bun and returned her son's glance with a humble smile while remaining dignified and stoic.

Judge Samuelson addressed Jason Black, "Are you Jason Black?"

Since the accident and subsequent arrest, Jason spent his time preparing for this moment, but the simple question hit him hard. The mechanical indifference in the judge's voice brought home reality, and Jason trembled. Gripped with shame, he wished to relive his life, but it mattered little now. He raised his head and looked the judge in the eye.

"Yes, sir, Your Honor," came Jason's soft reply.

"Please speak a little louder," admonished the judge. "Are you Jason Black?"

Jason spoke up. "Sorry, Your Honor, I'm Jason Black."

"Do you reside at 1525 White Avenue, Knoxville, 37916?"

"Yes, your honor."

"Mr. Black, your attorney has informed me that you wish to enter a guilty plea to both counts of vehicular homicide. Is that correct?"

"Yes, Your Honor."

"Have you been advised that by entering a plea of guilty, you waive all rights to appeal?"

"Yes, Your Honor."

"Mr. Black, do you fully understand what I explained, and do you now wish to enter your plea?"

Jason turned to his attorney and whispered a question. Hartley acknowledged his answer with an affirmative nod. Jason turned his attention to the judge and said, "Your honor, I fully understand, and I wish to enter a plea of guilty on both counts."

Hartley added, "We wish to move to sentencing immediately, Your Honor."

"Very well," replied Judge Samuelsson as he turned to the prosecutor. "Does the State have any issues? Do any family members wish to make a victim impact statement?"

The prosecutor said, "No, your honor. I have spoken with the families of the victims, and they wish to proceed."

Judge Samuelsson turned his attention to Jason Black and said, "Mr. Black, before I impose sentence, do you wish to address the court?"

Jason looked to Danny, Danny's daughter Carol, and the parents of Carol's late husband. He briefly turned to his mother and said, "I know it's little comfort to the families, but I wish to apologize." Danny looked straight ahead and did not acknowledge Jason's apology. Jason's mother quietly wept.

Judge Samuelsson rendered his opinion and handed down the sentence.

"Sadly, sorry is something I hear too often in this court. I have no doubt Jason Black and, unfortunately, those who come before me in the future, are sorry for what they have done. However, like you said, Mr. Black, saying sorry is little comfort to the families of those whose lives were taken by your careless actions. If it were possible that one would consider the consequences of their actions before they acted, there would never be a need for courts. Unfortunately, that will never happen, and unfortunately, society has no real understanding of or remedy for this. The law can only mete out justice after the fact. And justice by the only means available to it. It cannot undo or provide a remedy for your actions. It cannot restore lives lost or make survivors whole. Only God can deliver a remedy. Mr. Black, I find it remarkable that you conducted yourself well during your college years and had a successful career thus far. Yet in the past three years, you have been convicted twice of driving under the influence and have been shown a considerable degree of mercy by society, and yet here you stand before society again. This time, however, two people lost their lives at your hands. Two people who had full and meaningful lives before them and their families will have to deal with this tragic event. You handed them a life sentence and took their joy. I therefore sentence you to fifteen years imprisonment for each count, to be served consecutively. You will be remanded to Brushy Mountain State Prison and serve your sentence. Mr. Black, it is the hope of this court that you will use this time to reflect and rehabilitate yourself so that when you reenter society, you will be a productive part of that society."

Judge Samuelsson slammed his gavel and said, "Court adjourned."

* * * * *

A nicker roused Danny from his thoughts. Goldie stood with her eyes blinking and her neck stretched over the fence, seeking a treat. In despair, Danny spoke to God, *"Why must I suffer! This torment is too great to bear. Must every good memory be overcome by my nightmare? Tell me, God, what I must do to stop this."*

CHAPTER 18

Inmate 22525

"Papaw, Papaw," cried Tim. "They're done. They told me to get ya."

The sight of Tim, Mary, and his dog pulled Danny from the brink of despair. They looked as if they won the grand prize at the county fair. The times were too numerous to count when his grandchildren saved Danny from sinking into depression and his tormented mind. Danny snapped free of his nightmare and asked Tim, "Done with what?"

Mary answered, "The new toilet, Papaw. The prolotype."

Danny glanced at his watch. "Oh, okay, let's go check it out."

Tim said, "It's got a fancy box that beeps when ya flush it."

Danny got up, stepped next to Goldie, and ran his hand through her mane, then turned and headed for his house. Tim, Mary, and Ike followed.

Roger, waiting at the front door, said, "Sorry, it took so long, but when we pulled the old unit up, we found the seal was not properly set, an' the subfloor rotted. It had to be replaced. Whoever installed the old toilet should have used an extra seal. You were lucky. The floor joist looked good."

Danny, who installed the toilet, said sheepishly, "Glad ya fixed it. Thanks." He looked at Tim and Mary. "You two take that mangy mutt out until we get done."

Mary, disappointed, said, "Let's go, Ike." Mary and Tim left with the dog.

Danny said, "Let's look at this thing," and fell in behind Roger. When they reached the end of the hall, they found Jack cleaning up. The small toilet looked ordinary, and instead of a flush handle, there was a small black box with three lights and two buttons. Danny turned to Roger and asked, "Goodness, what's with this contraption?"

Roger laughed. "Danny, that's a small computer. It'll collect data, so we can evaluate flushing efficiency."

Puzzled, Danny asked, "Just exactly what kind of data does THAT thing collect? I mean, it don't take pictures or record sounds, does it? All I need is some joker at the CIA watchin' me wipin' my ass."

Jack laughed hysterically while Roger reassured Danny. "Nothing like that. It'll track water consumption, flushing force, and how much fecal matter's moved through the system." Roger paused and, with a laugh, said, "I need ya to give me your best. If ya know what I mean?"

Danny grumbled, "Don't worry. I'll give it a run for the money. How the hell do I flush the damn thing?"

Roger chuckled and shot a glance at Jack, who responded, "All ya have to do is push the green button like this." Jack reached down and pushed the green button. The toilet went through its flush cycle, and when finished, the box emitted a series of chimes followed by a beep.

Do, do doodle lee dee, beeeeeeeeeeep.

Danny stood, astonished. "I'll be. Sure's quiet."

Roger replied, "That's the idea."

"Can't even hear the water goin' down," said Danny, scratching his head with his hook.

"Mr. Shykes, I mean Danny, if ya have no further questions, we'll be on our way."

Danny answered, "I think I can handle it." Roger and Jack turned to leave.

Roger reached the front door, stopped, and reminded Danny, "Ya shouldn't have any problems. But if ya do, just call me. My number's on the card. Remember, this's top secret. Thank you for your help."

Danny rolled his eyes. "Anything to help my country." He stood for a moment, studying the toilet, and thought, *"I guess now's as good a time as any to see what this thing can do."* Danny locked the door and picked up a book he had been reading.

Tim and Mary followed Roger and Jack. Tim asked, "Are ya done?"

Roger said, "Yes." He lowered himself on his haunches, looked into Tim's eyes, and admonished him. "You guys can't tell anyone, okay?" He made a motion as if he were closing his mouth with a zipper and climbed into the van.

Mary shouted, "LET'S TRY IT OUT!"

Tim shouted, "ME FIRST!"

Tim, Mary, and Ike rushed into the house, thundering down the hall. Tim turned the knob. "No use. It's locked," said Tim. The excited dog barked wildly at the door.

"Let me try," said Mary.

Ike morphed into a rat-hunting monster, barking and scratching. Tim continued, turning and pushing on the doorknob. "Papaw, you in there?"

Danny looked over the top of his book. The doorknob twisted about, and the door shook under the force of the frantic dog trying to get in. Danny felt as if ice water had been dumped on his head. "Hell, yes, it's Papaw. Who the hell do ya think's in here? The pope! I'm tryin' to SHIT. Now go out an' play, an' take that dog with ya."

Tim said, "Tell me when you're done! I wanna push the button."

Mary pleaded with Danny, "Papaw, tell Tim I get to push the button."

Danny shouted, "YOU TWO, GET OUTSIDE AN' LEAVE ME ALONE, AN' TAKE THAT DAMN DOG WITH YA."

Carol walked through the front door and heard her father yelling.

She found Tim and Mary arguing outside the bathroom, with Ike barking and scratching at the door. "HEY, HEY, HEY, what's goin' on here?" Carol demanded.

"I'll tell ya what the HELL's goin' on. I'm trying to shit for cryin' out loud. Can't I have some peace an' quiet? I'm on a top-secret mission here!"

The children loved to get their grandfather going on a profanity-laced tirade and would often needle him. Carol scolded the giggling children. "Youins, leave Papaw alone. Go out an' play, an' take Ike with ya."

"Awe, Mom," protested Mary. "I wanted to push the button."

From inside the bathroom, Danny said, "I'm goin' to push the damn button. Now git." From behind the door, Danny complained to Carol, "Carol, this's like being in North Africa. Those two kids are worse than the Krauts!"

Carol laughed and said, "Okay, Dad, we'll leave ya alone."

Do, do doodle lee dee, beeeeeeeeeep.

"What was that?" asked Carol.

Danny emerged from the bathroom, drying his hands. "'I'll tell ya what that was. This thing has a music box. Some kinda computer tells ya how big a turd ya have an' how fast it goes. All kinds of lights a flickerin'. You'd think I was one a them NASA astronauts flying to the moon."

With a grand sweeping gesture of his hand and a bow, Danny said, "Your turn, Carol. Maybe we can have a competition. Your new beau can keep score."

Carol laughed. "Not now, Dad. I'll try it later. My beau's comin' over for dinner. He wants to make sure your toilet is set up properly."

Danny smiled and said, "Good. We can all take turns. Make a game of it instead of monopoly." Carol laughed as Danny continued, "You two must be gettin' along. I mean a new toilet an' dinner. I'll do my part."

Carol handed Danny a letter and said, "Here, Dad, I got the mail for ya. Just this letter."

Danny took the letter from his daughter and asked, "This all I got?"

"Yes, that's it."

PAPAW

The return address read, "Inmate 22525, Brushy Mountain State Penitentiary, Wartburg, TN 37887." Danny stared at the letter without saying a word.

Carol asked, "What's wrong, Dad? Ya look like ya saw a ghost."

Danny tapped the letter against his hook. "Maybe I did."

Carol asked, "Who's it from?" Danny returned the letter to Carol. She, like Danny, instantly knew who sent it.

Carol handed the letter to her father and pleaded, "I know it's not easy, but why don't ya read it, an' see what he has to say?" Danny said nothing. Carol added, "There's no hurry. Put it in a safe spot, an' don't be afraid to pray over it. I'm goin' to work on dinner. Mike'll be here at six. He wants to check on the installation."

Danny took the letter, put it on the kitchen table with the letter from Jason Black's mother, and went downstairs to his apartment.

CHAPTER 19

Monsters, Ghosts, and a Conversation with Tim

Danny watched TV while reclining in his chair when he heard a knock at the door. He set his beer down and glanced at his watch; it read 6:05. Tim and Mary ran to the door and looked through the window.

Tim said, "Look, it's Mike. He brought Mary a giant teddy bear. I wonder what I got."

"Hey, open the door, an' let 'im in," Danny yelled.

Mary pushed Tim to the side and pulled the door open. "Let me see!"

Mike stepped in and greeted the children. "Hello, Mary, would ya be kind enough to take this guy off my hands?"

Overjoyed at the unexpected gift, Mary grabbed the stuffed bear, nearly as large as her, hugged it, and asked, "What's his name?"

Mike looked warmly into Mary's eyes and said, "He doesn't have a name. When ya get to know 'im, you can give 'im a name." Tim, fidgeting with anticipation, kept his eyes locked on Mike. "Hey, wait, I forgot somethin'." Mike stepped through the door and returned with a bag. From the bag, he retrieved a small plastic model plane kit, a P51D Mustang fighter. Along with it came the paint and glue needed to complete the model. Tim took the box and carefully scrutinized the picture depicting the legendary aircraft with its guns blazing away, chasing an ME109.

"Cool!"

"I had one just like it when I was your age. I still have it."

"Can ya help me with it?"

"Sure, that's what I had in mind."

Carol entered the room. "Now youins thank Mike."

"Thanks," said the children in unison, and they ran off with their gifts.

Mike approached Carol, kissed her on the cheek, and, from the same bag, he produced a bottle of red wine. "Hello. Can I help you?"

Carol took the wine and said, "Napa Valley, good."

Mike said, "Mother told me what to buy. She knows about that stuff."

The bottle of wine rekindled, within Carol, a recent memory. "We had a director at the hospital. He liked to brag about bein' a wine connoisseur. He invited us to a wine tastin' at his house." Carol continued, "He said he'd be happy to rate any wine we'd bring. He's a bit on the snooty side. Well, one of our lab techs took 'im a bottle a Boones Farm. Kinda as a joke. The ER shift supervisor took a bottle of Mad Dog. They asked 'im to settle a long-standin' debate."

"Oh no!" laughed Mike.

"Yes, they asked 'im to determine which was better. He wasn't pleased to say the least. He told 'em he wouldn't use either to clean his toilet." Mike laughed hysterically. Carol sighed, shook her head in the negative, and said, "Some folks have no sense of humor."

Mike said, "I wish I could 'a seen that."

"Make yourself at home. Dad's in the living room. You two can visit while I finish dinner."

Danny started to rise from his seat to greet Mike. Mike said, "No need to get up. How'd the installation go? Ya mind if I look?"

"It went swimmingly."

Mike laughed and said, "I'll go an' look." Danny got up from his seat and followed him with the children behind.

Tim jumped in. "Papaw tried it out as soon as they got done."

Mike entered the bathroom and flushed the toilet. He watched it silently run through its cycle. The lights blinked with no discernible pattern. When the cycle came to an end, the box emitted *do, do doodle lee dee, beeeeeeeeeep.*

Mike said, "The computer seems to be working. Did ya have any problems?"

Danny replied, "No problems. But the music box's a pain."

Mike reassured Danny, "We'll leave it for twenty days, an' if ya don't mind, use it whenever ya can. After twenty days, we'll remove the computer an' replace it with a standard flush handle. You can keep the toilet for your trouble. In fact, if ya like it, we'll replace all your toilets."

Carol called out, "Everyone get ready. Dinner's almost ready."

Danny said to Mary and Tim, "Youins need to wash up." Danny and Mike returned to the living room.

Mike said, "I love pot roast. Mom made it every Friday."

Carol entered the living room. She looked at her father and said, "We're having roast. It's ready."

Mike followed Carol to the kitchen and asked, "Are ya sure there's nothin' I can do?"

"No, I'm almost done. Why don't ya get a beer an' keep Dad company?"

"Hey, Mike, when ya come back, bring me a cold one," Danny shouted.

Mike reached into the refrigerator, retrieved two cans of beer, and went to join Danny. Mike handed a beer to Danny and took a seat on the sofa. The children joined them.

Mary asked, "Papaw, is your house built over an Indian burial ground?"

A quiet chuckle came from Mike, and he thought, *"Under the house of every papaw there's a burial ground of some sort."*

Danny cast a suspicious glance toward Tim and asked, "Mary, what makes ya think this house's built on an Indian burial ground?"

Mary looked toward Tim and said, "Tim told me so. He said there are dead bodies under the house, an' there're ghosts that walk around at night." Mary turned to Danny and, with pleading eyes seeking a negative confirmation from her grandfather, asked, "I told 'im it wasn't true. Right? It's not true, Papaw?"

Mike thought, "*What's Danny goin' to do?*"

Mary's eyes, filled with terror, grew large and fixed on her grandfather. Danny turned the tables on Tim. "Mary, that's not true. There are no bodies under the house. I think he's tryin' to pull a fast one." Tim smirked, knowing he planted the seed of fear in Mary's mind. Danny continued, "He's close, though. Ya see, during the Civil War, there was a prison camp right where my house sets." Danny stepped to the center of the living room and tapped on the floor with his hook. "In fact, the gallows were built on this very spot. Right under the living room."

Mary interrupted Danny, "Gallows, what's that?"

Tim, excited by the unexpected twist in his story and unaware of what his grandfather was up to, replied, "It's where they hang people."

"Yes, that's true. They used to hang spies here. But don't worry. This house ain't haunted. At least, not that I can tell. I mean, I ain't never seen ghosts," replied Danny.

Tim, falling into Danny's trap, became excited. "Tell us 'bout it."

"Sure, but ya won't find it in any history book. My great grandpappy told me about it when I was little. He was a Union officer an' found the camp. In the winter of 1865, things weren't lookin' good for the South, an' General Lee suspected there were spies skulkin' about feeding information to the Union. So he had all the spies he could find arrested and locked up. On a cold February day, they rounded up four men and one woman they thought were spyin' for the Union. They, of course, denied it. But no one believed 'em—"

Tim, falling deeper into Danny's trap, cut him off. "What happened next? What'd they do?" Mike bit his lip to keep himself from laughing. Mary sat frozen in fear.

Danny reclaimed the recliner. "Well, they were tried an' found guilty by a military court an' sentenced to hang. It's said that while they awaited execution, they communicated with one another by tapping messages in Morse code. Kinda like this." Danny tapped the floor rapidly with his hook.

Tap, tap, tap. Pause. *Tap, tap.* Pause. *Tap, tap, tap.*

Danny went in for the kill. "One morning, before sunrise, they were taken from their cells an' walked to the gallows. They bravely climbed the thirteen steps an' were asked if they had any last words. Their eyes glowed red, an' for everyone to hear, they shouted, 'WE'RE INNOCENT! We'll walk these grounds an' torment those who live here forever. Then, lickety-split, before they could say anything else, the executioner sprung the trap door. It fell away with a crash, an' they dropped. All went well for the men. Their necks snapped, an' they dangled, dead. But the woman's rope was a wee bit too long, an' her head popped clean off. It bounced with a loud THUD an' rolled around. Her body plunged to the ground twitching about, an' blood 'a spurtin' like it come outta garden hose. Some of the witnesses swooned."

Mary had enough and ran screaming into the kitchen to be with her mother. Tim's bravado indicated he was unaware of Danny's trap.

With the seed of fear planted, Danny sighed. "Not a pretty sight. An' on this very spot to boot. They told me their bodies are under the mailbox." He turned to Tim. "After the war, it was discovered they were innocent. I don't believe any of it. Even if it were true, I don't believe in ghosts. We all know that's silly. But there was a prison camp here. Sometimes I hear a faint tapping noise, an' some say, the folks who visited us, they saw spirits. Some have said they seen the headless spirit of a young woman in a blood-soaked gown right in this living room. But I don't buy it. I never saw a ghost or spirit. Not one time." Danny looked into Tim's eyes. "I know you're too smart for all that nonsense."

Tim replied, "No way, Papaw." But Danny had the seed of fear planted.

Danny scratched his head with his hook and added, "Ya needn't worry. I dug around by the mailbox one time when your mom was little but couldn't find a thing. I've lived here since I got back from Europe an' have never seen or heard a thing. Maybe one time I thought I saw a ghost. Even if there were ghosts, they didn't bother

PAPAW

me or your mamaw. It's all nonsense. No need to fret over it." Danny's tale metastasized within the young boy's mind. Still, Tim remained resolute in spite of his growing fear.

Mike entered the kitchen and found Mary standing with Carol. Mary asked, "Have ya ever heard that, Mike?"

"Heard what?"

Mary replied, "Hangin' an' ghosts."

Mike kept the yarn alive and said, "Not sure. But it seems to me there was an old prison camp here."

With his bravado evaporating, Tim joined Mary and their mother and asked, "Is Papaw tellin' the truth? Were people hanged here? Are there really ghosts? I'm not scared. I was just wonderin'."

Carol whispered to Mike, "I heard that ole yarn when I was little." Carol turned to Tim. "Papaw's just tryin' to scare ya. Don't pay 'im any mind. Go get 'im. Dinner's ready." Carol turned to Mike. "Would you like to ask for the blessing?"

Everyone gathered around the table; Mike offered the blessing. "Dear heavenly Father, please bless this food we are about to eat. Let us give thanks an' remember those in need. In the name of your son, Jesus, we ask. AMEN." They all took seats and ate dinner.

The macabre story told by Danny crowded out all thoughts in the children's minds. Gallows, prisons, ghosts, and spirits from long ago were entrenched in their heads. Fear escalated, and they could not stop talking about the mysterious hangings. Their inquiry into the matter only made things worse. The more they talked, the more frightened they became. After dinner, Mike and Carol cleaned the kitchen and decided to go to a movie.

Danny loved playing mind games with his grandchildren. This evening, Tim was the target of this mind game. Mary, unfortunately, became an innocent casualty of his scheme. Carol turned toward the children and said, "Youins be good for Papaw. We'll be back around midnight."

Tim asked, "Do ya have to go? Why don't ya stay here an' watch a movie?"

Danny turned to the children, so Mike and Carol could not see, shone a fiendish grin, and said, "You two have fun. We'll be fine here. Won't we?"

Carol said, "Okay, be good."

Tim and Mary found themselves alone with their mischievous grandfather. The entire evening, Tim and Mary never strayed more than fifteen feet from Danny. In spite of his reassurances, the children knew ghosts roamed the house at night, ready to torment them or worse.

Mary turned to Tim and said, "I think it'd be a good idea to sleep in your room."

Tim, not wishing to relinquish his manly honor, agreed and said, "If it'll make ya feel safe, I reckon ya can sleep in my room." A stroke of brilliance flashed in the boy's mind, and he added, "I got a good idea. Let's get Ike up here. He can be YOUR watchdog. He'll warn ya if he sees a ghost an' even protect ya. Dogs can smell ghosts before ya can see 'em."

Mary said, "Good idea. I'll get 'im." Mary ran to the door and called out to the dog. "Come, Ike. Come, ole boy, come on, Ike!" Ike darted up the stairs and through the front door.

Danny said, "Okay, you two need to get to bed."

Tim and Mary made their way upstairs and into Tim's room, with Ike and Danny close behind. Before Mary climbed into bed, she said, "Don't turn out the lights." She turned to Tim and said, "Tell Papaw to leave the bedroom light on too."

Tim feigned indignation at such a suggestion. "Papaw, I think ya need to leave the light on for Mary. She's scared."

To Tim's relief, Danny said, "Okay, if ya insist. I'll leave the lights on." Danny went downstairs and resumed watching TV.

After hearing nothing, Danny went to check on them. He found them whispering, and Ike curled up on the foot of the bed. Danny said, "Good night. If ya need anythin', let me know."

Tim said, "Good night."

Mary reminded Danny, "Good night. Leave the lights on."

Danny threw in one more comment to heighten their fears. "Okay, pay no mind if ya hear anythin' in that closet. Ignore it."

PAPAW

Danny, however, had second thoughts. Maybe he went a little too far, but it was too late. He honored Mary's request, then went downstairs to the kitchen and initiated his plan to deliver the coup de grace.

Danny opened the hot water spigot enough to allow a small stream of water to flow. The hot water caused the pipe that ran under Tim's closet to gently tap. He retrieved a beer and reclined in his chair. Five minutes later, he heard a dull tapping, just as he planned.

Tap, tap, tap.

Mary woke Tim from sleep. "Wake up, wake up! Ya hear that?"

Tim awoke, and he became annoyed. He found Mary sitting up, paralyzed with fear, staring at the closet.

"No, I don't hear anything. Let me sleep," said Tim before he fell back into bed.

Tap, tap, tap.

Mary, focused on the tapping, shook her brother. "There it is." She pointed to the closet. "There's somethin' in there. Don't ya hear it? It's Morse code. What does Morse code sound like?"

Tim, now wide awake, sat up in bed and looked at Ike. The dog, snoring, rolled onto his back with his legs pointing up and his forepaws bent down.

Tap, tap, tap.

His mind sifted through all logical explanations for the tapping. Still, he could not think of anything that would explain it. Tim could only think of the story Danny told of gallows and ghosts.

Tap, tap, tap.

Mary asked, "There! Can't you hear it? I think it's a ghost."

Tim, not wanting his fear out in the open for Mary to see, said, "Quiet, don't be a baby. I'm tryin' to hear."

Tap, tap, tap.

Mary had enough and said, "I'm gettin' Papaw!" She grabbed her new teddy bear and bolted from the room, leaving Tim and Ike to fend for themselves. Tim, determined to tough it out, stayed with the dog.

Tap, tap, tap.

Small bits of Tim's wall of courage started to break away. He poked Ike. "Go get 'im, boy." The dog showed no alarm and rolled over.

Tap, tap, tap.

Fear took over, and like a weakened dam trying to restrain a large body of water, Tim's dam of courage finally broke. Fear gushed forth like a raging torrent, and he sprang from bed and charged after Mary, leaving his manly honor and dog behind. Ike, the lone occupant of the room, lay unconcerned by the commotion. Danny heard panicked feet hit the floor, and as planned, Tim and Mary were standing by his chair.

Danny set his beer down and nonchalantly asked, "What's wrong?"

Tim, wishing to recover his abandoned honor, said, "Mary thinks there's somethin' in the closet. I told her there was nothin' to be afraid of, but she's scared. Ya need to show her. She won't listen to me."

Danny got up and said, "You're right. You two stay here. I have to get somethin'."

Tim, not wishing to remain unguarded while keeping what little honor remained within him, said, "Mary wants to stay with ya, so we'll go along, okay?"

"You're right. Best we stick together. At least till we find what it is." Danny headed to his workshop in the basement, across from his apartment, with Tim and Mary close behind.

Danny rifled through various tools. He picked up one tool, twisted it about, scrutinized it, then returned it to its spot, then another, and another. First, he looked at a saw. "No, this's too awkward. Too much work." Then a hammer. "No, this'll not work either. Too small." He picked up a machete, lifted it high, and made a few swipes. "This's the right tool. It may be a little messy, but it'll get the job done. Fast and efficient. Let's go." With the machete in his hand, they returned to the living room.

Tim asked Danny, "What do ya need that for?"

"I hate to tell ya, but we may be dealin' with a monster. I ain't seen no ghosts, but one time years ago, before your mother was born,

PAPAW

I had to kill a monster. Nasty!" Danny paused and looked at the machete. "Your mamaw was away visitin' her mother. Good thing I was young. That thing was eight feet tall. Had teeth like a lion. Horrible breath, like rotten fish. I'll never forget. Thought I was goin' to die. I kept hittin' that bastard with my hook. Conkin' away, kinda like choppin' wood. All the while it 'a snarlin' an' clawin' at me." Danny looked at Tim. "We'll go up there an' kill 'im."

Tim challenged his grandfather. "Ain't no such 'a thing as monsters."

Danny huffed. "Ha! That's what you think. Ain't ya ever hear of the Loch Ness monster?" Then he squinted his eyes until they were tiny slits and furrowed his brow. "Are YOU willin' to chance it?" Tim said nothing.

Mary said, "We don't need to go with ya. Why do we need to go?"

Tim chimed in, "Yeah, Mary's right. I'll stay with her here an' protect her while you go up there."

Danny replied, "Okay, if ya think so. But if by chance there's somethin' in that room, I'm goin' to need all the help I can get. On the other hand, maybe it's out roamin' around. It may be a good idea to stick together. What'd ya think?"

Tim looked at Mary and said, "Papaw's right. Let's stick together."

Danny said, "Good thinkin'. Now follow me an' be real quiet. Not even a peep. Them monsters got real good hearin'." Danny led the way to Tim's room, moving like a sloth. They crept up the stairs and along the wall. He paused, turned back to Tim and Mary, and put his right index finger to his lips. "Shhh! For goodness sake, stay low an' be quiet!"

Mary, crouched behind Danny and Tim, whispered, "Okay."

"Keep down. Let me check it out. Youins stay put for now." Reminiscent of his days fighting the war, Danny laid down the machete and snaked his way to just outside of Tim's bedroom. He pointed to the door and whispered, "Stay quiet. I'm goin' to peek through the door an' see what's goin' on." Danny got to the door, leaned against the wall, and listened.

Tap, tap, tap.

Danny slowly stretched out his neck and peeked into Tim's room, and he found Ike asleep on the bed, undaunted by the drama. He returned his gaze to Tim, who was on his belly just below the top of the stairs. Mary sat crouched into a tight ball below Tim, her head buried in her chest and arms wrapped around her knees. Danny raised his hand, palm out, signaling not to move. After a moment, he returned to the children.

Danny whispered, "Bad, real bad. Worse than I thought." The color drained from Tim's face.

Mary lifted her head long enough to ask, "What's bad, Papaw?"

"Well, at first I was sure it was a monster. But now I'm not so sure. Maybe it is. Maybe it ain't," Danny whispered.

"What do ya think it is?" Tim asked.

"We could have a ghost on our hands."

"What're ya goin' to do?" Mary asked.

Tim admonished his little sister. "Papaw knows what to do." He turned to Danny. "Don't ya?"

"Yes! Ya, dern tootin' I know what to do!" Danny explained. "It is either some kinda monster or a ghost, but whatever it is, it ain't human, or at least ain't human in the sense that you an' I are human."

Tim asked, "What're goin' to do?"

Danny picked up the machete. "We'll flush it out, whatever it is. If it's a monster, I'll kill it with this."

Tim asked, "Are ya sure you can kill it?

He twisted the machete in the air. "Not much different than killin' a Kraut. Remember, we have the element of surprise on our side."

Mary asked, "How, Papaw?"

Danny replied, "Like I said, we'll flush it out, then I'll conk it on the head with my hook an' stun it. Mary, you an' Tim'll grab its legs an' hold on for dear life. It'll be a kickin' an' tryin' to get away. So you'll have to hold on as tight as ya can. Then I'll hack its head off with this machete. Can't do nothin' till we flush it outta there." Danny paused to collect his thoughts. "Your job is to do the flushin'." Tim and Mary's eyes widened, and they trembled.

PAPAW

Danny pointed the machete at Tim and said, "Unless it's NOT a monster. Maybe a ghost."

Tim asked, "What'll ya do if it's a ghost? Can't ya just kill it like a monster?"

Danny scratched his chin with his hook and answered, "Don't know. That's a whole new kettle 'a fish. It'll be tough. Ya can't kill a ghost."

Tim asked, "Why?"

Danny's eyes opened wide, and he glared at the children. With a fiendish chuckle, he said, "'Don't you two know anything. Ya can't kill a ghost 'cause they're already DEAD! All ya can do is run like hell! So to be safe, when ya get out, Tim'll break left, and Mary, you'll break right. Got it! Remember, even a ghost can only chase one at a time. Speed is your best weapon." Danny paused and said, "Once we start, ain't no turnin' back."

Tim said, "Me and Mary'll wait downstairs, an' you can flush it out."

Danny said, "That won't work. I'm too big an' slow. It'll get me. Once I'm gone, he'll get you two. Now suck it up an' listen! Life ain't cotton candy an' toys! Tim, I think you should go in first, an' Mary, you follow 'im. Get its attention. Whatever it is, it'll go after ya. Tim, you have to make sure Mary doesn't get left behind. I'll wait by the door. Now when it starts to chase ya, run like hell, an' when it comes out, I'll kill it like I told ya. Lest it's a ghost. Just do as I told ya."

Tim asked, "What about Ike?"

With an astonished look, Danny said, "Why that monster don't care about some mangy mutt! It's our blood. Human flesh is what it wants. He'll be after us! If it's a ghost, it'll be after our souls. Dogs don't have souls, least not like we have." The children sat frozen, paralyzed with fear.

"One last thing. If all hell breaks loose an' I get it, you guys go for the car. Tim, I left the keys in the ignition. You can drive to the Smith house for help, got it?"

"I can't drive!"

"Don't worry, you'll figure it out."

Tim pleaded with Danny. "Just let it stay. We can sleep in your room tonight."

Mary added, "Yes, we can sleep in your room tonight. Let's get it tomorrow."

"Not sure 'bout that. Ya see we have the element of surprise."

Mary said, "Let's surprise it tomorrow. I vote that Tim an' I stay in your room."

With his honor left in shambles, Tim added, "I vote we stay in your room too."

Danny thought, *"They've had enough."*

He said, "Okay, I think we're makin' a mistake, but you talked me into it. You can sleep in my room tonight. I'll take care of it in the morning.

Relieved, the children followed their grandfather downstairs and into the living room. Danny went into the kitchen, closed the spigot, and reclaimed his recliner. Tim and Mary took up positions on either side of Danny and watched television. In spite of it being late-night news, they found contentment. Danny, Tim, and Mary fell asleep.

* * * * *

Danny awakened, then glanced at the test pattern on the television. He woke the children. "Time to go to bed."

Mary looked at Danny and said, "Are we safe?"

Tim, indignant, said, "Mary, do ya REALLY think Papaw's goin' to let anything happen to us?"

They followed Danny downstairs and into his apartment. Upon reaching Danny's bed, Mary asked, "Papaw, would ya leave the light on?"

"Yes, Mary, we can leave it on. Now go to sleep." Mary climbed onto Danny's bed, followed by Tim. Soon, Mary fell asleep. But Tim stayed awake in contemplation.

Danny retrieved a book and climbed into bed. Tim asked, "Papaw, can I ask you something?"

PAPAW

Tim's tone telegraphed the child's question. One he had been asked countless times. "Sure, Tim, what's on your mind?"

"Did ya kill anyone during the war?"

"Yes, I have."

"Did ya hate the guys ya killed? Were they bad men?"

Danny remembered the day Carol asked the same question. After a contemplative pause, he replied, "That's kinda complicated. I guess that depends on when ya ask me. I mean, if ya asked me during the war, I'd 'a told ya I hated 'em. I reckon it's easier to kill somethin' or someone ya hate." Danny pulled himself up and rested his back against the headboard. "If ya ask me now, I'd say no. I reckon, had there never been a war, we would've gone to school together or worked together. Hell, we'd likely been friends. They killed us, and we killed them. I suppose they felt the same way we did. Now we get along almost like there never was a war. That's the irony of it all. As we speak, some old guy in Germany is talking to HIS grandchildren an' explainin' the same thing I'm explainin' to you."

"But, Papaw, were they bad men?"

"No, Tim, they weren't bad men."

Tim jumped in, saying, "I don't understand. They killed your friends, Smitty an' Captain Jones."

"Funny thing 'bout war. May be the only time when people who have no desire to hurt, let alone kill anyone, are let loose to kill. People who only weeks before were in school or working jobs an' never considered killin' find themselves killin' each other in every conceivable way. I reckon the ones that I killed had friends. They had mamaws and papaws. No, they weren't bad. Ya see, the world went crazy. A few really bad men somehow got a hold a things. They used power to satisfy their desires. I made peace with it."

"What, Papaw? What did they want?"

Danny replied, "It goes back to what all men want. That's something they don't have. Hitler wanted power, territory, an' revenge, an' create a Germany in his image. He believed the Arian race was superior an' wanted to eradicate all Jewish people from Europe. The more he took, the more he wanted. Same could be said for Mussolini an' Hirohito. I reckon you could say it boiled down to envy, lust, an' greed."

"Will there ever be a war like that again?"

After a brief moment of thought, Danny answered, "Unfortunately, as long as man's on this earth, there'll always be war. That's 'cause we're infected with the same sin. I just hope you'll never have to face that kinda war. Maybe we learned something. I hope." Danny looked at Tim, who had fallen asleep.

Danny contemplated Tim's questions, and those questions indicated Tim and Mary would soon grow up. He studied a picture of himself and Anne, taken shortly before her passing. He, like his parents and grandparents, would end up as nothing but a picture on a wall. Anne's faith in Jesus came to mind, and he thought, *"What will I leave behind? What will Tim and Mary think when they see that picture? What will Carol think? Will they see Jesus in me?"*

Danny studied Tim and Mary, and thought, *"They would have their lives to live. They, like the rest of the world, would move on. Mary and Tim would no longer need a papaw that could kill a monster with a machete. But that was tomorrow. Tomorrow, they'll grow up. Tonight, I'll be happy because for now, I'm Papaw, and for now, it's me they come to. I can still slay monsters and chase away ghosts. It's me they turn to for safety. Years ago, when the world went crazy, I, along with Smitty, Captain Jones, and thousands of others, many of whom would never return, became protectors of the world. We, the imperfect men and women, to whom the world turned, vanquished evil."*

The questions Tim asked came to him. Danny's answers to the child, however, unlocked a different perspective. He thought, *"If I can forgive the ones who killed my friends so long ago, why should I not forgive Jason Black?"* Jason's mother entered his thoughts along with her letter. He contemplated those he killed during the war and the pain their mothers felt. Right or wrong, it did not matter. Their mothers still felt the agony of loss, and there can be no greater pain than the loss of a child. Unwittingly, Tim awakened Danny to what he needed to do to find peace. In order to find Anne, he would have to find his faith. He had to find the faith he abandoned long ago. Anne's faith brought him home from the war, and rekindling his faith would lead him to Anne. Man had nothing to offer; no equations or scientific formulas would fix things or help him understand. Danny understood that without Jesus, there was no hope.

Danny had one more mission—a mission of another sort and as important as anything he ever did. Danny needed to soothe the aching heart of a woman who lost her most precious gift, her child. He would do what he could to return Jason to his mother, and it would be through forgiveness. And through this forgiving act, he would gain and show the faith in Jesus he needed to find God and be with Anne. Now Danny was ready to lift someone's tremendous burden; soon, like the children, Danny fell asleep.

CHAPTER 20

Jason's Letter

DANNY, NORMALLY UP before sunrise, woke to the morning sun. After his best night's sleep in years, he sprang out of bed with a newfound purpose and went upstairs to the kitchen to make coffee. His torment lifted, and for the first time since Anne's passing, he gained control of his mind. For now, he would drink coffee and listen to the chaotic racket of animals starting their day.

As Danny passed the kitchen table, the unopened letter from Jason Black beckoned. Danny picked up the letter and glanced at the master bedroom, the first room he prepared for Anne and where they shared their entire married life. Every inch of it reflected her personality.

After Anne's tragic passing, Danny kept the room locked and allowed no one to enter. The room became a shrine to their love. Danny left it as it had been since that horrible day and took great care to keep the room clean. He left even the most trivial items as Anne left them. With painstaking effort, he dusted around smaller items so as not to disturb them. Sometimes blowing the dust away with gentle puffs. Within those walls, he found solace; only the happy times with Anne entered his mind.

Danny found himself standing before the room, and after retrieving a key kept over the door, he entered. His eyes beheld a lifetime of special treasures Anne collected, and he took great comfort in knowing she touched them last. Pleasant memories of each unique item bound Danny to Anne. Her presence evicted sadness from his mind.

On the bed lay a quilt Anne made in her spare time, sewing intricate circular patterns of flowers and birds, which took nearly three years to complete. A gift for Carol. On the walls were pictures of their parents. He touched the antique rocking chair she found at a yard sale shortly after they moved into the old house and remembered the pride she felt at finding such a good deal. Over the back of the chair hung a throw that belonged to her grandmother. Danny reminisced about Anne wrapping Carol in it and rocking her. He picked it up with reverence and laid it on the bed, then lowered himself into the old rocking chair.

Danny pushed himself into the rocker, recalling the difficult pregnancy Anne endured. Her doctor discovered an ovarian tumor. He assured Anne he could remove the tumor discreetly and safely, but they would lose their child. Anne, due to her strong faith, would not have it. She would deal with whatever came, bad or good. During the pregnancy, Anne never dwelled on her condition. Her courage inspired Danny. After she gave birth to their daughter, Carol, Anne had a hysterectomy. The cancer had not spread, but Carol would be their only child. Now Danny would draw on the courage Anne displayed over a lifetime and confront his never-ending nightmare head-on.

Danny studied the letter, slapping it against the stump of his left arm several times. He put the letter between his teeth and gently tore it open. After shaking the envelope, the letter fell onto his lap, and he opened the folded page:

> Dear Mr. Jerome Shykes,
>
> Since you are reading this, my prayers have been answered. At least so much as to say you may be willing to consider the idea of opening your heart to someone as unworthy as myself. I will never be able to grasp, even in the smallest

measure, what my actions on that rainy night four years ago did to you and your family. I also know it will be of little comfort to you to know that my time spent in this prison has released me from another prison. A prison of torment created by alcohol addiction. I was in that prison until that fateful night. Because of me, you find yourself in a prison not of your choosing.

The loss of your beautiful wife and son-in-law, at my hands, has weighed on me in a never-ending way. As it should. I need to emphasize that this letter is not intended to ease my burden. So many times, those like me in this predicament have said they would give their lives to undo what has happened. I am sure such words ring hollow for you, but I would give my very life to undo this. Unfortunately for you and me, the rules do not permit that.

I have been fortunate over the past few years, thanks to my attorney, to be placed with an individual in a similar situation. He helped me find salvation through Jesus Christ, as he did years ago. Through the grace of God, I have turned my life around. I also had one other person to thank, and that is my mother. She never gave up on me, even during these difficult times. I put her through a living hell. Like you, I put her in a prison which she did not deserve.

It is she who I wish to address. She did her best as I grew up to keep me in the light. It is not her fault that you and I find ourselves in this terrible position. She grieves for you and your family, and sometimes I think the torment is too much for her to bear. She so much wants to talk to you and share with you her sorrow. A sorrow that, for all, is at my hand. Please accept this letter as my plea. A plea not for me but for her.

So I will get to the point. As I stated earlier, none of this can be undone. But maybe you can find some solace by talking to her. You need not even contact me. Richard Hartley dropped by to see you and left his card. Richard would be willing to arrange a meeting between you and her. I ask you to take a moment and meet with my mother. It is my earnest hope and prayer that you will consider this plea. Maybe it will help you and your family find the peace you so richly deserve.

I wish you and your family well, and, again, I am truly sorry for the pain I inflicted.

Sincerely yours through Christ,
Jason Black

The warmth and sincerity of the letter took Danny back to June 1944 and a frightened young private. The private, while facing death, wanted to make things right and honor a promise he made to his fearful mother. But more importantly, Danny remembered a brave captain who found humanity and put his part of the war on hold long enough to comfort the young soldier and help him honor his mother's wish through baptism. Twenty minutes later, the captain would be dead. Danny rose from the rocker, placed Jason's letter on the dresser, and determined he would reach out to Jason's mother.

Danny's eyes locked onto a pearl-handled hairbrush resting on the dresser. Seeing the brush brought forth a calming emotional swell, like taking in a fading sunset at the ocean's edge. Anne had the special treasure for the entirety of their marriage. Like the throw, it belonged to her grandmother, who gave her the brush on the day of their wedding—something old. A silent reminder of the last time he and Anne would be in the room. He never touched the brush and would not do so today. It lay just as Anne left it. Danny reclaimed the rocker, and a sense of peace came over him. He felt Anne's presence and, for the first time in a long while, the presence of God. The brush's hypnotic effect brought Anne to him, and he drifted to the day of the accident and the last conversation he had with Anne.

* * * * *

Danny entered the bedroom. Anne, brushing her hair, did not notice. He watched her through the mirror as she picked through her hair, searching for strands of gray, oblivious to Danny's presence. Her fire and confidence faded into a display of vulnerability. A vulnerability of a woman who, sensitive to her advancing age, gave her heart to him completely and without condition. Danny briefly watched her, then made his presence known by tapping on the door with his hook.

Startled, Anne stopped and looked into the mirror. Danny looked at her from the doorway, smiling. An embarrassed smile came over Anne as if he caught her trying to hide something. Anne playfully asked, "Have ya nothin' better to do than snoop on me?"

"Not really. I love to watch ya."

"Will ya love to look at me when all my hair turns gray?"

Danny walked to her, wrapped his arms around her from behind, and gently kissed her on the cheek while looking into her eyes through the mirror. Anne furrowed her brow. "Did ya know I gained fifteen pounds?"

"Goodness, fifteen pounds! Really! I never noticed." Anne, half hurt and indignant, said, "Don't ya even look at me anymore?"

Danny spun Anne around, pulled her into his arms, and looked into her eyes. "I guess I was just too busy looking into your beautiful blue eyes to notice anything else. Goodness, woman, don't fret over gettin' old. It's our fate. We're lucky. Be happy you're gettin' old. You know you've blossomed into a very beautiful grandmother, an' you're mine. My beautiful angel. I think I'll keep ya, gray hair an' all."

The hurt and indignation left Anne. "Danny Shykes! Ya always know what to say. I love ya so much." Danny kissed her firmly and pulled away. Anne threw her arms around Danny's neck and pulled herself to his face. "One'll get ya two." She returned Danny's kiss with equal passion. "Think I'll keep ya 'round too."

Anne had a thought. She asked Danny, "Do ya love me?"

When Danny heard Anne ask, "Do you love me?", a request for him to perform some unpleasant task followed. He replied skeptically, "Okay, what're ya up to? What'd ya want?"

A mischievous grin washed over Anne's face. "Nothing much. We've talked 'bout this before. You said you'd get baptized. I think ya need to. Mary an' Tim need to see their papaw commit to the Lord."

It would be an exercise in futility for Danny to put it off. He decided to get it over with and answered Anne with a question. "Does it mean that much to ya?"

"Yes, it does."

"I'd rather ya hit me in the head with a sixteen-pound sledgehammer, but if it'll make ya happy, I'll do it Sunday."

"You really do love me, don't ya?"

Danny, with a shake of his head in the negative, said sarcastically, "No! I don't love ya."

Anne laughed. "I gotta go an' watch Tim an' Mary. Do ya think you can manage without me?"

"I'll survive."

"One more thing. I forgot. My car's in the shop. Can you take me?"

"Sure, an' I'll pick ya up when you're ready to come home."

"No need. Tom said he'd bring me home."

Thirty minutes later, Danny dropped Anne off at Carol's house. He would give her one more hug and kiss, as he always did, and say, "I love you, bye." It would be the last time Danny saw Anne alive.

* * * * *

Danny, his eyes fixed on Anne's hairbrush, relived the promise he made to her that he would receive baptism—a promise unfulfilled. The haunting image of a fearful private and a brave captain bound by the sacred sacrament of baptism flashed in Danny's mind. Captain Jones placed everything on hold and put Jesus first for all the men to see. *"No one wanted to do it,"* thought Danny. *"In the shadow of the battle that loomed, he did it anyway."*

"Papaw, Papaw! What're ya doin'? Can I come in?" Mary peered at Danny from the door, pulling him from his daydream.

"Sure, Mary, come in. I'm just sittin' here." Neither Mary nor Tim had been in the room since the accident.

After looking over the room, Mary asked, "Can I sit on your lap?"

"Sure, come over."

She walked to the rocker and climbed onto Danny's lap. Mary, only four when her grandmother passed, had only faint memories. The child experienced overwhelming curiosity instead of the trauma her grandfather felt. Danny placed the throw over Mary and said, "Your mamaw used to wrap your mother in this an' rock her in this chair."

Mary snuggled close to Danny. "Where is she? Will I see her one day?"

Danny rocked his granddaughter. "I miss 'er. She's in heaven. I guess Jesus needed an angel. You'll see her again. I promise."

Carol awoke, went downstairs, and found the door to the master bedroom open. She heard her father talking, looked in, and saw Danny rocking Mary. After a moment, she asked, "Dad, are ya all right?"

Danny answered, "Yes, I'm fine. Just me an' Mary."

Mary said, "Mamaw used to rock you here."

"She sure did. That was a long time ago. She rocked you in that chair too. I'll go an' start breakfast." Carol walked to the kitchen and met Tim.

Tim asked, "What're Mary and Papaw doin'?"

Carol answered, "Nothing. You can go an' watch TV."

Tim's curiosity got the best of him, and he joined Mary and Danny. Like his sister, he studied the room, then focused on a picture of Anne and Danny. In the photograph, Danny wore a dress uniform with medals, including the Silver Star earned for valor, pinned to the left breast of his tunic. Anne, wearing a white cotton dress with navy blue polka dots, stood to the left of Danny. To Danny's right stood a man wearing the white uniform of a British naval officer. In the full-length photograph, Danny had a bandage wrapped around his head, and his left arm hung around Anne's back just above her left hip, exposing the hook of his prosthetic arm.

Tim asked, "When was that picture taken? Who's the man with you an' Mamaw? What happened to your head?"

"It was taken when I got home. He was the doctor who took care of me. I fell an' hit my head. That's why I'm wearin' the bandage."

Carol shouted, "BREAKFAST'S READY." Tim and Mary ran into the kitchen, leaving Danny alone. Carol walked to the bedroom, poked her head in the door, and asked, "Aren't ya hungry?"

Danny replied, "No, I think I'll sit here a spell." Danny fixed his gaze on the photograph of him and Anne and the British naval officer. His mind took him back to September 1945 and his homecoming.

CHAPTER 21

September 1945: Danny Returns from Europe

"Hey, Shykes! What're ya lookin' for?" shouted twenty-year-old Private First Class David Thompson.

David, from Cincinnati, Ohio, called Dave by his friends, struck up a friendship with Danny on the *Queen Mary* during the journey home from Europe. A ship with a capacity of five thousand had nearly fifteen thousand men crammed into every foot of available space. While the massive ship crept to the dock, anxious soldiers crowded the rails, trying to find loved ones. Danny, undeterred by the crowd, fought to see over the troops, working his way to the rail. After weighing anchor, the crew got busy mooring the large ship while anxious family members crowded the dock.

"I'm looking for my gal. The most beautiful woman in the world."

Dave caught up with Danny and laughed hysterically. "Hell, you'll never see her in that crowd. Just relax. We'll be off this ole boat in an hour."

Danny turned to Dave and said, "Oh yes, I'll see 'er just fine. She'll be wearing a white dress with blue polka dots an' a blue ribbon in her hair. The same dress she wore when we said goodbye. I'd be able to spot my Anne a mile away." Dave, convinced his new friend

PAPAW

was crazy for trying to find his girlfriend among the crowd, smiled, lit a cigarette, and stepped away from the throng of soldiers to watch his friend.

* * * * *

 The *Queen Mary* was not due to arrive until 1:00 p.m. Anne, however, arrived at New York Harbor just after 11:00 a.m. Brilliant blue September skies heightened Anne's joy. The sun, at its zenith, filled her war-weary soul with optimism. A gentle autumn breeze added a slight chill to the air. Still determined to greet Danny as she promised and convinced by the warmth of the sun, Anne left her coat in the car. The pier, nearly empty when she arrived, filled quickly. The festive mood was infectious, and her joy increased as the crowd grew. She, among thousands waiting for loved ones, watched as the *Queen Mary*, with the aid of two tugboats, inched to the pier.

 Anne had never seen anything like the *Queen Mary*. It towered over the dock. Undeterred, she looked for Danny in vain among the thousands of servicemen lining the rails of the massive ship. Mothers, fathers, sweethearts, brothers, sisters, and children stood shoulder to shoulder, waiting and, like Anne, looking for loved ones among the men lining the deck.

 Anne, ready to welcome Danny home, counted the days until his return. Beautiful, confident, and true to her word, she wore the same white cotton dress and secured her hair with the same blue ribbon as she had when they said goodbye at the bus stop. A small Brownie hung from her neck and, while she waited, busied herself taking pictures.

* * * * *

 Danny struggled for a spot at the rail, determined to find Anne. Seeking a good vantage point, he found an opening on a lifeboat and clambered onto it. Dave, after witnessing the horrors of war, calmly smoked a cigarette and reveled in Danny's excitement. Danny, meanwhile, ignored his surroundings while searching for Anne from his precarious perch.

Dave called out, "Careful, you crazy hillbilly! You're gonna kill yourself!"

Danny, straining to find Anne, ignored Dave and continued moving within the boat until he reached the cradle that secured it. While grasping for a rope, he lost balance, slipped, and fell, hitting his head against a beam.

Clunk.

Danny landed flat on the deck with a loud thump, his head lying in a growing pool of blood. Dave threw his cigarette down, got up, and pushed his way through the throng of servicemen and found Danny face-down, unconscious. He pressed his fingers against Danny's throat and found a pulse. "Hey, can somebody help me?" A soldier caught Dave's eye, and Dave asked, "Hey, Mac, can ya help me?"

The serviceman said, "No, but I have a buddy who's a medic. I'll get 'im," then he disappeared into the crowd.

Dave whispered into Danny's ear, "Hey, Danny, can ya hear me?" After getting no response, he pulled a handkerchief from his pocket and held it to a gash on Danny's forehead. The growing crowd looked on, closing in on Danny. Muffled chatter broke out among the men, who were anxious to find out what happened.

"What happened?" asked one.

Another answered as he pointed to the boat from which Danny fell. "Don't know. He climbed over that boat, then next thing he conked his head."

"What was he doin' up there?" asked another.

"Lookin' for his gal, I reckon," said another.

A tall soldier stepped forward and, with a deep, gruffy voice, said, "Some kinda hero. I was talkin' to 'im yesterday. I remember the hook. He got his hand shot off takin' a bridge. Traded it for a Silver Star."

"Poor bastard. Made it all this way an' goin' to die not fifty feet from home," said another.

"Terrible, just terrible," lamented another.

PAPAW

Dave shouted, "He's not dead! He ain't gonna die. Would one of you chuckleheads get help?"

The tall, gruffy soldier cut in. "Make room. C'mon, step back, step back! Damn it, let 'im get some air." The crowd relented and backed away.

Another shout rang out, "The medic's here!"

The crowd opened up, and the medic kneeled down and worked on Danny. Dave asked, "Is he goin' to be okay?"

The medic glared at Dave. "Look, Mac, I just got here!"

Shouts filled the air. "Open up! Step aside! Let the doctor in."

A British naval officer in a full white dress uniform stepped through the crowd and took over for the medic. He addressed the crowd in a deep, fatherly voice. "I'm Lieutenant Commander Winfield Blane. Ship's senior medical officer. I've got this now. Everyone, please go back to your business. We'll be docked soon." He checked Danny's pulse, pulled a small penlight from his pocket, lifted each eyelid, and shined a light into his eyes.

Dave, relieved to see Doctor Blane, asked, "Sir, I know this man. May I stay with 'im?"

Doctor Blane answered, "Yes, I'll get a stretcher. Keep 'im still. Don't move 'im. We need X-rays."

Doctor Blane returned with two men, a stretcher, and a backboard. He ordered the men, "Be careful. Strap 'im to the board, don't twist his neck or back, and take him to the sick bay."

The two men carefully strapped Danny to the backboard, placed him on the stretcher, and took him to sick bay as ordered. Dave followed and waited outside while Doctor Blane tended to Danny.

* * * * *

The gangway lowered, signaling Anne's long wait had come to an end. Servicemen anxious to get home rushed from the ship, flooded the pier, and fell into the arms of loved ones. Hugs, kisses, and joyful laughter heightened Anne's excitement. Soldiers in clean, crisp uniforms raised small children into the air, some of whom were barely walking when they left, and they exchanged small gifts. Anne's eyes scanned the rush of men, and she stretched her neck, looking for Danny.

"Danny's in there somewhere," Anne thought.

She could not find Danny in the endless line of men coming off the ship. She watched happy reunions, one after another, anticipating her own. The flow of men became fewer until no one from the ship remained. The pier drained of people, and with the crowd, so went Anne's joy, and still no sign of Danny. There were only a handful left, and like her, they milled about. Soon they left; now only Anne remained on the empty pier. She looked at her watch; it read 3:00. The excitement Anne felt when she arrived had been replaced with a hopeless sense of foreboding. Anne fell into a state of despair.

She thought, *"What happened? Where's Danny? What should I do?"*

The sun fell behind the tall ship, and a chill fell over the empty pier. A discarded paper cup, the remnant of the recent festivities, pushed along by a sudden gust of cool autumn air, tumbled by. Anne heard shouts coming from the crew of the ship; they, too, were about to leave. Her mind could not make sense of the situation she found herself in.

She thought, *"Is he hurt? Did I get the date wrong? Does Danny still love me?"*

Anne, at a loss, found herself alone. Cold and distraught, she made the painful decision to leave and headed toward her truck.

* * * * *

Danny emerged from the X-ray room on a gurney, unconscious, with Doctor Blane close behind. Dave jumped from his seat. "What about it, Doc? Is he goin' to live?"

"Yes, he'll pull through. He's a bloody hardheaded Yank. No fractures. All the bleedin' came from a cut from the fall. I don't see any bleedin' or swellin' in or around the brain. Looks like a nasty concussion. I think we'll keep him overnight. He'll have a headache when he comes to. Are you his friend?"

"You could say that. I met 'im on the boat." Dave glanced at his watch; it indicated 3:00. He thought, *"Goodness, I have to try to find Anne."*

"Doc, I just thought of somethin'. I gotta go. I'll be back in a little bit." Dave headed for the door.

"Okay, I'll need someone to sit with 'im. My nurses are gone."

Dave turned to the doctor. "Don't worry, I got it covered. I'll be right back." He bolted from the room, almost knocking over a member of the crew. "SORRY! IT'S AN EMERGENCY!" shouted Dave, and he leapt up the stairs.

The irritated crewman regained his balance and mumbled, "Just like the bloody Yanks, late comin' to the war and late goin' home."

Dave ran onto the empty deck that, only an hour earlier, was crammed with men. Out of breath, he leaned over the rail, looking left and right, frantically scanning the empty pier in search of Anne. A lone woman, wearing a white dress with blue polka dots, walking away from the ship, her beauty plain to see, caught Dave's eye.

He thought, *"That's gotta be her. She's just as Danny described."*

He ran down the gangway toward the woman and shouted, "ANNE!" Not hearing him, she continued to walk.

Dave cupped his hands to his mouth. "ANNE!" Anne turned to the strange voice.

He caught up to her and, gasping for breath, asked, "You Anne? Ya have to be Shykes's gal." When she heard Dave say Danny's name, the stranger instantly morphed into a dear friend.

Dave's smile lifted Anne from despair and answered with a smile. "I'm Shykes's gal. Do ya know Danny? Do ya know where he is?"

"I sure do. I've been with 'im since we got on board this here boat."

"How'd ya know I'm his girlfriend?"

"Goodness," said Dave. "That's all he talked about. He'd say Anne's the prettiest woman to ever live." After a reflective pause he added, "I have to disagree. I think you're the second most beautiful woman. My wife Julie is the most beautiful, if ya don't mind me sayin'."

Anne adored her newfound friend's comment. "I don't mind. I'm sure she is. Is she here?"

"She couldn't make it. Someone has to stay with my pa. Goin' the get a bus soon as I get done here."

"What's your name?"

"David Thompson! But my friends call me Dave."

"I'm Anne Miller. Where's Danny?" Anne extended her hand.

Dave took her hand and shook it gently. "Did ya say Anne Miller, like the famous dancer?"

"Yes! Same name, but I can't dance."

"When Julie an' I were dating, we saw her in *Room Service*. The Marx brothers were in it too. Funny." Dave looked Anne over. In an effort to calm her, he said, "Ya look more like Ginger Rogers, prettier than either one. Come with me. I'll take ya to Danny." Anne followed Dave up the gangway.

Dave said, "Sure glad I found ya. That crazy fathead was tryin' to find ya while the ship was docking. He got on a lifeboat somehow. With all the excitement, he slipped an' fell. Before I knew it, he was out cold on the deck in a puddle of blood. I tried to warn 'im, but he was hell-bent on findin' you. We all thought he was a goner. Cracked his head pretty hard. Bled bad. Good thing we found a doc. He took Danny to sick bay."

Anne asked, "Is he goin' to be okay?"

"No need to fret. They took X-rays. I talked to the doc just before I found you, an' he said he didn't break anything. He likely gotta concussion." Dave led Anne up to the top of the gangway.

"Now wait here."

Except for an occasional deckhand or sailor, Anne found herself alone on the massive ship. Concern overtook the despair Anne felt moments earlier.

Dave found Doctor Blane and said, "I found his gal. She'll be more than happy to stay with 'im."

"Okay, bring 'er here."

Dave returned to Anne, led her down a flight of narrow stairs, and down a dimly lit hall. They ended up outside the sick bay. He pointed at the door and said, "We're almost there. Danny's just inside."

Dave opened the door and said, "Here he is. We thought he was a goner. He's gonna be fine, thank God. His head must be pretty hard. I heard the clunk when his head hit the beam. Sounded like a howitzer goin' off."

It had been more than three years since their bittersweet farewell at the bus stop. Since then, stacks of letters, many censored, defined their relationship, and unknown to her were greater hardships and dangers than he wrote of. Once inside, she would, at long last, find Danny. Anne paused, closed her eyes, and took a deep breath.

Anne thought, *"Does he still love me?"*

Frightened and happy, she exhaled, opened her eyes, and walked through the door. The small room opened into a vast expanse that marked the beginning of their life together.

Her eyes scanned the bland, cold room. Bandages and other medical supplies filled shelves, and cabinets lined the walls. A blood pressure cuff and stethoscope hung over an IV stand. Anne found Danny with his head bandaged and unconscious, occupying one of two beds. He appeared comatose; the only sign of life was his chest expanding and contracting. Dave looked on, waiting for Anne to react.

Dave broke the silence and said, "It looks worse than it really is."

Anne, lost in the moment yet happy to see Danny, said nothing. His once confident, boyish face acquired the hard edge of maturity. She ran her fingers through his black hair, now laced with streaks of gray. Dignified wrinkles, created by the stress of combat, coursed over the once smooth skin of his face. He wasn't good-looking; he was handsome. He did not react to her touch, and for the first time, she saw the hook. Danny wrote to her about it, but seeing it for the first time brought home the cold reality of war.

Anne recalled the stories her father told. How men, returning from the previous war, changed and wondered if Danny changed. But none of that mattered. She knew whatever he endured, he would be all right. She wanted to spend the rest of her life with him. To have a family.

Dave said, "I'll leave ya alone an' find Doctor Blane."

Anne broke free of her thoughts and said, "Thank you."

"It'll be okay," and left.

Anne touched the hook, then gently lifted and lowered it several times, gauging its weight. The cold steel possessed no humanity and conveyed no warmth, just harsh reality. She returned the heavy prosthetic to Danny's side, and a wave of sadness rolled over her. The struggles of the war Danny kept hidden were plain to see. He never mentioned the danger he faced.

She thought about the hell he had been through. "*What would he be like?*"

Then she thought, *"He's alive and home. He has his right hand. So many others lost much more."* She fixed her gaze on a cross that hung on the wall above his bed. "*Thank you, Jesus, for answering my prayers.*"

From that moment on, from Anne's perspective, he always had the hook. The cold, harsh steel became a thing of beauty. The hook represented love through sacrifice, given by many who answered the call. God blessed her. Anne and Danny were standing on the threshold of an entire lifetime together. Behind them, the despair of separation, and before them, a life filled with joy and struggle. They were together and would share both. For now, however, she just wanted him to wake up. She prayed over him.

As Anne stood over Danny, Doctor Blane entered the room. "Hello, miss, I'm Dr. Winfield Blane, and you are?"

"I'm Anne Miller."

"Are you Danny's sweetheart?"

"Yes, we were dating when the war broke out. We were talkin' marriage, but he wanted to wait till the war was over."

"So you're his fiancé?"

Embarrassed by the doctor's query, Anne said, "Kinda, he hasn't exactly asked me. He was convinced he wouldn't make it home."

Doctor Blane looked at the beautiful young woman and said, "Well, Anne, I haven't known you long, but I can tell just by lookin'

PAPAW

he'll ask. He'll be fine. Nothin' broken, bleedin', or swellin'. I mean, nothin' on the inside's bleedin'. He's got a good gash on his head. Those bleed a lot. I'm sure he has a concussion. Just to be safe, I'll keep him overnight." Certain of an affirmative reply, Blane asked, "Do you think you could stay here with 'im? I'm short a nurse. Everyone's gone."

"Yes. I'll be happy to."

Doctor Blane grabbed a chair, put it beside Danny's bed, and said, "Sounds good. Here's a chair. I'll be back after I check on a few things."

He returned with a British seaman's uniform and explained, "Sorry, it was the smallest one I could find. It's never been worn. Looks like you'll be pressed into the British Navy. At least for the night." Anne smiled and took the uniform. Doctor Blane pointed to a small lavatory and said, "You can change in there. Just shut this door, and you'll have complete privacy. You can sleep in the bed next to his. My cabin's down the hall."

"This'll be great." Anne had a playful thought and asked, "Do ya have the hat?"

Doctor Blane laughed and said, "Yes, I'll be back." He returned with a standard-issue British Navy seaman's cap. The image of Anne in a British seaman's uniform brought a smile to Blane's face. "Here, you'll be ready for inspection." He tossed the cap. "The last time we Brits pressed a Yank into our Navy, it started a nasty little war, and we tried to burn down your White House. So if you don't mind, we can keep this between us. Don't tell the president. I have a few things to do. I'll let you be and check on you a little later."

"Thank you, Doctor. You've been so kind." Anne squinted her eyes, shook her head in the negative, and added, "Don't worry, I won't tell the president." Doctor Blane, relieved by Anne's high spirits, left.

Dave knocked on the door. Anne let him in, and he said, "I ran into Doctor Blane. He seems to think everything's okay. I gotta go. I scrounged up a couple of ham sandwiches for later."

Anne said, "I don't know how to thank you. You've been such a help. I need to know how to get in touch."

"Don't worry, Danny has my address. If you're ever in Cincinnati, I hope you can visit. I know Danny loves you. That's all he talked about during our trip. You two are a handsome couple."

Anne said, "We hope you and your wife can visit us in Tennessee someday." Anne got up and hugged Dave. "Goodbye, an' be careful."

Dave returned the hug, and as he left, said, "Don't worry, we'll get together. Nice meeting you, Anne. Good luck."

Anne changed for the night. After taking off her dress, she slipped on the white trousers and white jumper. Next, she draped the blue collar over her shoulders and tied a loose knot in the front. Danny groaned, and she turned her back to him while rolling up the sleeves and trouser legs. Danny's groans became mixed with indistinguishable words. He would be awake soon. She hastily stuffed her hair under the white cap and cocked it back, exposing a few strands of blond hair that fell over her eyes and the bottoms of her ears.

Danny came to and strained to see the odd-looking sailor. "Goodness, what happened? Where am I? My head's killin' me. Is this a dream? Am I dead?" Danny rubbed his eyes as Anne turned to face him. He said, "This's crazy. You look just like Anne. I must a hit my head really hard."

The sleeves of Anne's jumper unrolled, hiding her hands. She pushed the sleeves back, grabbed her hat, tossed it aside, and gently shook her head; her hair fell over her shoulders. "It's me, Danny. I come to take ya home."

Danny's eyes widened, but he remained silent, taking in the spectacle of Anne dressed as a sailor in a uniform that swallowed her. After a moment, he broke his silence, laughing. "Hell, you'll make a good sailor." He propped himself on his elbow. "Well, don't just stand there. Come here."

Anne walked to Danny, who, with his right hand, pulled her close and kissed her. His head became light, and he fell back, squeezing her hand tightly. She lowered herself, and she said, "Don't stop now." Danny wrapped his arms around Anne. His hook thumped against her back.

Danny said, "Sorry, I need to get used to that."

Anne said, "I'm already used to it. Just kiss me."

PAPAW

Danny kissed Anne repeatedly. "Help me sit up. Quick, get me up!"

"Let's wait till the doctor gets in."

"No," said Danny. "Help me up." He started to pull himself up.

"Goodness, I can see you're still hardheaded."

Danny sat up with his feet dangling over the edge of the bed. "I have a few things to get off my chest."

"Okay, Danny, I'm here."

Danny looked into Anne's eyes and said, "I made the biggest mistake of my life before I left. I should've married you. I remembered your promise that I'd come home. Since that time, that's all I've been thinkin'. Someday you'd be back in my arms. Your promise kept me alive. The whole time I was away, there was never another. Just you. I've missed you. I love you, an' you're here. I don't want to say goodbye till we've lived our lives. Is it too late? Do ya still love me? Anne, will you marry me?"

Before Anne could answer, Danny cut her off. "I know I'm throwin' this at ya quickly. I was plannin' to ask when I got off the boat, but I'm not waiting anymore. Not even a second. So what a ya think?"

Anne waited four years and endured a world war for Danny to propose; she took a moment in silent contemplation. She loved Danny, and he still loved her. Anne studied Danny, who anxiously anticipated her reply, and broke her silence. "Yes, Danny! Yes, I'll marry you. I love you! You'll never have to tell me goodbye." Anne threw her arms around Danny and kissed him.

Doctor Blane tapped on the door. Anne said, "Come in."

The doctor cracked the door, peeked in, and, with a mischievous smile said, "Am I interruptin' anythin'?"

Anne let Danny go and turned to Doctor Blane and said, "Not as long as you're bringing us good news."

Doctor Blane said, "Hello, Sergeant Shykes. When I first saw you, you were a bit of a mess. I'm Dr. Winfield Blane, chief medical officer assigned to the *Queen Mary*. I think you're goin' to be fine, but I want you to indulge me and stay overnight. I noticed the Silver

Star. It'd be a shame for you to make it through that mess, then come home, get a bump on the head, and cash it in."

Anne said, "Doctor Blane, I want you to be the first to know, Danny an' I are engaged!"

Doctor Blane laughed. "Sergeant, what took ya so long?"

Danny smiled at Anne and said, "Doc, I'm not goin' to make that mistake again. I'm never goin' to let this lady go."

Doctor Blane rested his hand on Danny's shoulder and said, "You're a smart man, Sergeant. Now that everything's good, I'll leave you two alone. If you need anything, I'm just down the hall." When Doctor Blane got to the door, he added, "You're a lucky man."

The next morning, Anne was in her dress and, with meticulous care, fixed her hair; she looked as she had the day before. She caught Danny looking and she asked, "What 'a think?"

Danny, taking in Anne's beauty, shook himself free of the trance-like state he was in and answered, "I think you're the most beautiful woman in the world. Why am I so lucky?"

Anne stepped close to Danny as he sat on the edge of the bed. "I'm the lucky one. But you belong to me. You're my man. I ain't goin' to let ya go." She grabbed Danny's hand and said, "Are ya gonna sit just there, or are ya gonna kiss me?" They were interrupted by a gentle knock.

Anne pulled away and said, "Reckon I'll get these kisses later."

Doctor Blane entered and said, "Good morning." The doctor listened to Danny's heart and shined a penlight in each eye. He retrieved a reflex hammer and gently tapped around each knee. The doctor asked Danny a series of questions.

"Where are you?"

"On the *Queen Mary*."

"What's your name?"

"Jerome Daniel Shykes."

"Where are you from?"

"Townsend, Tennessee."

"Looks like you're doin' good. I don't see any need to detain you any longer." Doctor Blane smiled and asked, "Who's this pretty young lady?"

PAPAW

Danny cast his gaze on Anne. "My fiancé, Anne Miller. Soon to be Mrs. Jerome Shykes!"

Doctor Blane said, "You're in possession of your senses. Now you two get outta here."

Anne asked Doctor Blane, "Would you be kind enough to have your picture taken with us?"

Doctor Blane answered, "I would consider it a great honor. When you get ready, I'll be waiting for you topside." Doctor Blane headed for the gangway.

When Danny and Anne reached the gangway, they found Doctor Blane waiting with the ship's captain, Bernard Hawthorn. Doctor Blane put his hand on the captain's shoulder. "I ran into this old fellow. He had nothin' to do, so I asked him to take the picture."

Captain Hawthorn said, "Yes, me an' ole Blane go back a long way. We served in the Great War together, and he decided to stay in the Navy. Now look, we're together an' doin' what we love."

Doctor Blane said, "Yes, haven't seen Bernard for years. Then I was called to serve on the *Queen Mary*. Here he is." The old friends laughed affectionately. Doctor Blane added, "They had to find somethin' for this old man to do. I have to admit this has been a jolly good mission."

Danny said, "Thank you, Captain Hawthorn. It was a good ride till we pulled into port." Danny laughed and continued, "But I guess I got a little excited, slipped, an' fell. Doc took real good care of me and Anne. I'll not forget my time on the *Queen Mary*."

Captain Hawthorn said, "Think nothin' of it, ole chap. Just glad to help."

Doctor Blane asked, "They want a picture of us together. Care to take it?"

Hawthorn took the camera from Anne, looked it over, and said, "My wife has one of these. They take good pictures. Now just stand at the rail."

Doctor Blane joined Danny and Anne at the rail then Captain Hawthorn took the picture and returned the camera. "Good luck and much happiness."

Doctor Blane said, "Yes! Good luck. Hope you two have much happiness." Danny shook hands with Captain Hawthorn and Doctor Blane, and they exchanged hugs. They said goodbye, left, and would never see Captain Hawthorn or Doctor Blane again.

*****

Carol entered the bedroom and found Danny asleep on the rocker. She glanced at the photograph of Anne, Danny, and Doctor Blane on board the *Queen Mary*. Carol recalled her mother sharing the tender moment, then returned to the kitchen and admonished the children. "Don't pester Papaw."

"We won't, Mom," replied Tim. Carol left for work.

CHAPTER 22

Danny's Mission

After waking, Danny glanced at the clock, and it read 9:00. After making his way to the kitchen, he walked by the table and picked up Richard Hartley's business card. He stepped to the rear window, pulled the curtain back, and looked out. Mary and Tim were playing with Ike. After pushing the button on the coffee pot, he called Hartley.

The receptionist answered, "Hello, law offices of Johnson and Hartley. How may I direct your call?"

Danny asked, "Can I speak to Richard Hartley?"

The receptionist said, "May I ask who's calling?"

"Sure. I'm Danny Shykes. It's very important we speak."

Richard Hartley, busy preparing a motion for an upcoming trial, picked up the receiver and asked, "Yes, Janet, I'm kinda busy. What do ya need?"

"There's a Danny Shykes on line one. He says it's urgent."

"Okay, I'll take the call."

"He's on line one."

Richard pushed the button and asked, "Hello, Danny, what can I do for you?"

Danny said, "Hello, Richard. Yes, there is somethin' you can do for me. I've been thinkin' a lot after you an' Pastor Gamble stopped by last Saturday. Maybe we can help each other."

"That's great, Danny. What do ya have in mind?"

Danny said, "I'm ready to talk to Jason, but I would like to talk with his mother first an' as soon as I can. Do ya think you could arrange a time for us to talk this week?"

"Sure, Danny, how does Thursday sound?"

"Yes, I think Thursday'd be fine. I look forward to it. Just let me know."

"I'll let you know in a little bit."

"Great, bye." Danny hung up.

Fifteen minutes later, Richard called and asked, "How does ten Thursday morning sound?"

Danny replied, "Thursday at ten it is. Thanks."

CHAPTER 23

Danny Loses Anne

THURSDAY MORNING FOUND Danny in excellent spirits. The decision to meet with Jason's mother returned to him the one thing he lost since Anne's passing: control. He thought, "*This's what Anne wants. I'm in a position to do it.*" He took the first step in a plan to set matters right with God and invigorate his stagnant faith.

Danny greeted his daughter. "Good morning. What're ya doin' up so early?" He peeked out the window. "It's still dark out. Do ya work today?"

Carol replied, "I'm off till Monday. Put in for a few days of vacation. I decided I'd make breakfast this mornin'. I hope ya don't mind."

"Don't mind at all. I'm feelin' a little lazy."

"This's a big step, Dad. I'm proud of you. Sit down an' relax. The kids are asleep." She flipped the bacon, walked to the refrigerator, and retrieved a carton of eggs. "You want your eggs sunny-side up?"

"Yes, I'll have four."

"You're hungry." Carol cracked the eggs into a bowl. "Martha's a sweet person, an' she's been through a lot. I'm glad you're goin' to see 'er. Mom's lookin' down on ya. I know she's smilin'." Carol paused, then asked, "What changed your mind?

Danny replied, "Just a talk I had with Tim. He got me to thinkin'." He poured a cup of coffee and took a seat at the table. "I reckon I should've done this some time ago."

Carol said, "No, Dad, you did what anyone would've done. It was horrible. You weren't ready. We all needed time. All ya need to do today is talk. I have the kids this morning. Feel free to do whatever ya want. Today's your day."

Danny said, "Yes, this whole thing's been terrible. There's no easy answer. I know Jason's mother has a lot to deal with. But you lost Tom, an' his mother lost a son. It's tough to lose a child. It's true Jason's mother can still see her son, but she's hurtin', an' he's all she has. I know this must sound strange coming from me, but I feel for her. I talked to Jason's attorney Tuesday, an' he said Jason has turned his life around. I hope so. I've been doin' a lot a thinkin'." Danny rested his elbows on the table and sipped from his cup. "When ya think you've had it bad, there's someone who's had it worse. I've had a good life. I know a lot of people that didn't."

Carol handed Danny his breakfast and said, "Not strange at all. You can't fool me. Underneath there's a good man ready to do the right thing. You always have, an' you're on the right track. You're goin' to be fine."

Danny ate breakfast and went outside to take in the sunrise. Anne's palomino, Goldie, grazed, cloaked in wisps of fog. Danny settled in his chair, sipped coffee, and watched the horse. After finishing his coffee, he glanced at his watch; it showed 7:00. He had plenty of time to run a few errands. after which he would visit Martha Black, who also lived in Townsend.

The two-lane blacktop highway wound through a rolling landscape of lush green meadows dotted with farms and patches of wooded areas. Running parallel to the highway, to the south, were the foothills of the Smoky Mountains. Danny approached a hairpin curve at the site of the accident, as he had done countless times before. He could never bring himself to stop. Today, however, Danny felt it would be a good time to visit the site. He slowed as he approached the dangerous curve that wrapped around a shallow ravine. Thirty feet to the bottom ran the stream, where Anne and Tom lost their lives.

Danny pulled his car into a small picnic area. Large oak and fir trees provided ample shade for the laurel trees lining the banks of the stream below. Danny donned a light jacket and made his way to the water that rushed over rocks and flowed through a narrow opening under the highway. The shallow stream looked harmless, but on the stormy night of the accident, water trapped behind the opening below the highway swelled the stream to dangerous levels. Danny glanced at the highway; it became evident how Jason Black's car, traveling at a high rate of speed, would have crossed and hit Tom's car, flipping it into the stream.

Danny found the spot where Tom's car came to rest. Beautiful sights, sounds, and smells filled his senses but would not mitigate the horror that weighed upon him. The time came for Danny to deal with the nightmare of that night. His mind took him back to March 1975.

* * * * *

Danny and Carol entered the crowded emergency room and made their way to the reception desk. A thin woman wearing black cat-eye glasses with short gray hair and in her sixties greeted them. "Can I help you?"

Carol replied, "Yes, we're here to check on my husband. His name's Thomas Chandler."

The woman, aware of the accident, picked up the phone. She used a pencil to punch a few numbers into her phone, and after a pause, she asked, "Can you tell me the status of Thomas Chandler?" She listened, tapping the pencil on the desk, and after another pause, she hung up the phone. The woman, a retired nurse, had experience dealing with many such tragedies and never surrendered to emotion; just doing her job. A weary smile came to her face, and she spoke indifferently in a monotone voice. "He's in surgery. There'll be someone to see you directly." Using the pencil, she pointed to a small conference room and said, "Please wait in that room."

The placard above the door read, "Counseling Room A." As an emergency room nurse, Carol knew the procedure and led her father to the room.

Danny and Carol entered the small rectangular room. A television, not in use, hung in the corner opposite the door. In the corner, to the right of the television, sat an artificial plant that resembled a small palm tree. On either side of it were two chairs. A water cooler filled the corner to the left of the door. At the center of the room were two rows of chairs, five each, back-to-back. On one long wall were windows, and on the opposite long wall were four photographs of scenes of the Smoky Mountains. Underneath the photographs were six chairs, three on each side of a small table that held a stack of worn, outdated magazines, a phone, and a light. Carol guided her father to a chair.

"Here, Dad, sit." Danny, bordering on shock, sank into a chair, emotionless. Carol took a seat next to him. The dimly lit and desolate room became a refuge from the bustle of the hospital; they sat alone in silence.

Not long after they took seats, a nurse in her thirties entered. She was short and petite, had a smooth, dark complexion, brown hair pulled into a ponytail, and deep-set brown eyes. The skirt of her white nurse's uniform fell just below her knees, and a stethoscope draped her neck. She asked, "Are you Mr. Shykes, sir?"

Carol grabbed her father's hand. Danny looked up and into the woman's eyes and replied, "Yes, I'm Mr. Shykes." He stood. "Can you take me to Anne?"

The nurse paused briefly and said, "Yes, Mr. Shykes, follow me."

Carol, her eyes swollen from crying, asked, "Dad, do ya need me to go with you?"

"No, you wait here. I'll be back."

Danny followed the nurse through clean, sterile halls filled with nurses, hospital staff, and people visiting loved ones, each unaware of the other's existence. As he passed by, he heard casual banter about mundane things like the weather or the score of a ball game. It hit Danny like a hammer that drove a spike of harsh reality into his heart and drained his soul of life. The outside world, indifferent to his plight, inched forward, unconcerned, while he found himself gripped in the tentacles of an unimaginable tragedy. When they reached the end of the hall, they stood in front of an elevator. The nurse pressed the down button.

Ping.

The door opened, and they entered the empty elevator. She pushed the button marked "B," and after a gentle jolt, the elevator descended. It came to a stop as fast as it started, and after another ping, the elevator opened. Danny found himself in front of a double door, and he saw a placard: MORGUE.

The sign was the last straw. The wall Danny built during the war, which kept his emotions in check and allowed him to take on the horrors he witnessed and those he encountered throughout his life, crumbled. He inhaled deeply, unable to muster the strength to move. Danny swayed on his feet, and he braced himself against the elevator. The nurse took Danny's hand and guided him to chairs outside the morgue. "Mr. Shykes, take a minute and sit here. There's no hurry, sir."

Danny leaned forward, placing his elbows on his knees. After regaining his composure, he said, "Let's go. I wanna see my wife."

Danny stood next to the nurse in front of the doors. He had never been in a morgue. His understanding of death formed while he fought in Europe. During that period, he experienced death in every hideous way the human mind could dredge up. His visions of death were chaotic, dirty, and filled with mangled, contorted, and rotted bodies. Death permeated all his senses, from the final agonized expressions frozen on the dead faces of friends and strangers to the stench. Even the sounds of death echoed in his mind, from the cries of the mortally wounded to the calm, reassuring words of his friend Smitty.

He watched the nurse punch a few numbers on a keypad. After a soft click, the nurse pushed through the doors, and Danny, unprepared, followed.

The morgue, clean, orderly, and quiet, contrasted greatly with Danny's experiences of death. Most of all, the cold gripped him, enveloping his entire body. The indifference, however, remained the same. Like death on the battlefield, there existed a void where one would normally find emotion. There existed no love or pity; one went about their business. In the morgue, the only emotion present was that which Danny brought with him. Like a contagion, it infected the nurse, who, accustomed to these scenes, saw the love Danny had for his wife, and she surrendered to emotion and quietly wept.

The brightly lit room took the form of a large rectangle. To the right were stainless steel lockers for storing bodies, and to the left were three stainless steel autopsy tables with surgical lights overhead. On the walls hung various tools, mostly designed for cutting. They were hideous to Danny—not for saving lives but for exploring death. Above the tools hung a large twenty-four-hour clock. The second hand tapped *tick, tick, tick,* beating a surreal rhythm Danny could not ignore. As they walked over the cold tile, Anne appeared on a gurney at the far end of the room, covered with a white sheet.

They reached the table, paused, and looked at the sheet. Danny stood frozen, and with reverence, the nurse pulled the sheet back, exposing Anne's head. The accident spared her face, and even death did not destroy Anne's beauty. She looked as if she were asleep. An old pin, in the form of a rose, still held her hair in place. Danny retrieved the heirloom, handed down from her mother, with a trembling hand. He watched Anne put it in before she left. After scrutinizing it, he dropped it in his jacket pocket. The nurse looked at Anne and said, "She's beautiful. Absolutely beautiful."

Tears tracked down Danny's face, and he turned to her and said, "I need to see how she died. Please let me see."

"Are you sure?"

"Yes, I'm sure. Please let me see. I must see."

The nurse carefully pulled the sheet down, folding it over Anne's shoulders, exposing her neck. The disfiguring wound that took Anne's life contrasted with her unblemished face. Danny, accustomed to every grotesque manifestation of death left in the wake of battle, became gripped by grief. The nurse rubbed Danny's shoulder gently and said, "Mr. Shykes, your wife experienced severe trauma to the neck. Based on the debris, it's likely that a branch pierced her neck between C2 and C3. The force broke it, and although I know this'll give you little comfort, it's likely she died quickly. I'm sorry for your loss."

Danny gazed upon Anne, then ran his fingers through her hair and kissed her on the forehead. A tear fell from Danny onto her cheek. He brushed the tear away with his finger. "I love you. Goodbye. You took care of me. You kept me alive. I let you down."

Danny pulled the sheet over Anne's head. "Thank you. I've seen enough. Can you take me back to my daughter?"

* * * * *

"Hey, mister." The voice returned Danny to reality. He looked at his watch. It read 9:45. Standing on the opposite side of the stream stood a boy, about fourteen years old, with a fishing pole clenched in his right hand and a small tackle box in his left hand.

"Where's your fishin' pole?"

Danny gathered his thoughts. "I left it at the house." He asked the boy, "Do ya fish here a lot?"

"Yes, but don't tell anyone. The trout gather in this pool."

"Your secret's safe with me."

"Why don't ya get your pole an' fish some?"

Danny scratched the back of his head. "Can't today but how's next week sound? Save me some."

"Sure will."

Danny made his way to the car and left for his appointment with Martha Black, Jason's mother.

CHAPTER 24

Martha Black

MARTHA BLACK, WAITING for Danny, nervously tidied her living room. She lived alone in a small but immaculately maintained house. She longed to speak with Danny and apologize; any minute, there would be a knock on the door. Thoughts raced through her mind. Remaining idle would allow her simple nervousness to escalate into unbridled terror. What would she say? What would he say? She picked up a feather duster and dusted the little things that defined her life. Things she collected through the years—little treasures and knickknacks—had little meaning to anyone but her. She found herself dusting the mantel of the fireplace and looking at a picture of her family taken during happier times—a portrait of her, her husband, and their three boys.

The portrait resurrected memories of what might have been instead of the cold reality of a lifetime defined by tragic events. Her two oldest sons, twins, died in the Vietnam War. Jason, the youngest, was in prison, serving time for vehicular homicide. All three of her boys were bright, good-looking, and had promising futures. Her husband, who had a successful career as an engineer, finally succumbed to his alcohol addiction shortly after Jason's conviction. Yet somehow, through all the tragedy, she kept her faith. A faith she acquired from her parents that could not be extinguished, even by the tragic events of her life.

PAPAW

Martha gained great courage, knowing grace would prevail and good would flourish through faith in her Savior, Jesus Christ. In a few moments, she would draw from the well of faith that carried her for an entire lifetime. Unsure of where the visit would take her, she believed God would turn this tragedy around. The tired woman dared not question the momentum of the events about to take place. As the appointed time approached, she found a fragile peace.

Danny turned onto Martha's driveway. The tranquil beauty of her modest home impressed him. The simple red brick house sat on a small nicely landscaped lot enclosed by a well-maintained white picket fence. Behind the house, several strategically placed dogwood trees provided shaded sitting areas. Danny stepped out of his car and contemplated the events about to take place. He, like Martha, could not grasp that two troubled lives would, in moments, fuse forever in the lasting beauty of God's true love. A love requiring submission and not understanding. He wanted to end his misery and, at the same time, bring peace to Jason Black's mother. Danny, ready to show the world and God the true extent of his faith, found himself standing at her door.

From inside, a dog barking frantically put Danny at ease. The door swung open, revealing the source of the barking—a small Jack Russell terrier much like his own. With the fur on its neck up, the dog lunged menacingly at Danny, who was safely out of its reach. He looked at the dog, and before Martha could say a word, he laughed. "I see ya have a Jack Russell terrier. I have one too. His name's Ike."

The feisty little dog broke the ice, and Martha said, "His name's Sam. He forgets how little he is. He won't bite."

Danny lowered himself onto his haunches, making a fist to protect his fingers, and greeted the dog. The small animal sniffed hesitantly at Danny's fist, then cautiously worked its way to Danny's feet. After sniffing around his legs, the hair on the back of the dog's neck went down, and it returned to Danny's hand and started licking. Martha said, "Looks like you have a new friend." The dog turned away, and Danny returned his attention to Martha.

Danny replied, "They're great little guard dogs. They were originally bred for fox hunting, but they are excellent ratters."

A stress-filled life etched lines into the frail woman's face. Martha, sixty-two years old, looked well into her seventies. Smartly dressed in blue jeans, an untucked sky-blue plaid shirt, and white Keds on her feet, she possessed remnants of youthful beauty. She wore her white hair up and, regardless of her predicament, presented a positive and cheerful outward demeanor. Her sunken brown eyes, however, betrayed the torment and suffering she endured over the last four years. To Danny, her fragile state of mind could fall apart at any moment. Moved by her vulnerability, Danny would do whatever he could to help her. He felt the kind old woman suffered enough.

Danny's hook, unnatural and intimidating to those seeing it for the first time, captivated Martha. Accustomed to her reaction, he found that, with time, people would forget about the hook. Martha caught herself looking, and with an embarrassed smile, she said, "Look how rude I am. Come in, Mr. Shykes."

Danny replied, "Sure." Danny followed Martha, and wishing to put her at ease, he said, "My grandchildren love this ole hook. I have a trick that simulates a lightning bolt. It gets 'em goin'."

"I'm sorry, Mr. Shykes," replied Martha.

The war that took Danny's hand did not take his charm. Danny flexed his arm and showed how the hook opened and closed. He laughed and said, "Don't be. Everyone gets a little spooked at first. Actually, it's quite functional, an' after a while, ya hardly notice it. Please call me Danny. All my friends call me Danny."

The portrait of Martha's family caught Danny's eye. "You have a nice place. May I look at the picture?"

Martha replied, "Sure, that's my family."

Danny walked to the mantel, retrieved the photograph, and examined it. He recognized Jason but knew nothing of the twins, and after studying it, he said, "This's a nice picture. I see you have twins. What're their names?"

Martha approached Danny and tapped the picture with her finger. "That's John an' Rick. They're identical twins." Martha noticed Danny's expression, and before he could reply, she said, "They died in Vietnam. Their helicopter was shot down. They weren't supposed to be together. There was a mistake, an' they ended up in the same squad. They didn't try to change it because they wanted to be together. I had no idea they were together until they were killed." Martha paused, wiped away tears, and collected her thoughts. "When they were little, they played little tricks. One would say he was the other an' vice versa. No one could tell 'em apart. No one except me, that is. Oh, they tried, but you know a momma knows her babies."

The frail woman had no one, and it hit Danny hard, and a plan formed in his mind. He looked into Martha's eyes and said, "I'm sorry for your loss. I've seen a lot of foul-ups like that in the Army."

Martha said, "I don't understand. I tried to make sense of it, but I can't. No matter how old they get, they're your babies. Ya watch 'em grow up, an' ya do the best ya can, then they get snatched away." Martha turned away from Danny, crying, and said, "Ya see, it hurts to know that my Jason took someone's baby, their child. There's no pain worse than that. Ya may be surprised to know a day doesn't go by that I don't think of Anne an' Tom."

Danny gently rubbed her shoulder and said nothing. Martha continued, "I honestly don't know the answer. I've prayed on it. I prayed for relief for you an' your family, as well as for me." Martha turned around, pointed to the sofa, and said, "Listen to me. Go on. I'm sorry, why don't ya sit? Can I get ya something? I have coffee an' some fresh pastries."

Danny took a seat on the sofa and replied, "Yes, that'd be nice. I take my coffee black." Martha went into the kitchen.

Danny returned his gaze to the portrait, and his mind traveled back to the war. He thought of Smitty and Captain Jones and those who would never enjoy the life he had. Also, the men he killed. They had mothers and loved ones. Danny's compassion for Martha grew, and for the first time since the accident, he did not think of Anne. He could think only of Martha and her pain.

Martha returned with coffee and pastries. She set the tray on the coffee table and sat next to Danny. He took his coffee and said, "I've been doing a lot of prayin' an' soul-searching too. I've seen so much carnage in my life an' found there're no easy answers. I've concluded it boils down to faith. What I mean to say is that if we really believe there's a God an' Jesus IS truly God, then we need to trust.

After all, if there is no God, then when you think of it, there's no hope. The insanity of war caused me to abandon my faith. Where is he, I thought. Still, through it all, I just couldn't shake God. Then I learned the hard way that faith is the bridge to God and peace. We just need to trust God. That's why I'm here. I had to learn to forgive. Forgiveness is the ultimate show of trust an' a true demonstration of faith. After all, what hope is there without God?"

"You're a very kind man. You're right about faith."

"Martha, it's time we talk. I want you to know I understand. Your son has written me. I think he's turnin' things around. What I'm saying is, what happened was an accident. I've forgiven Jason an' put this behind me."

Martha wiped away tears. "Thank you."

Danny said, "Another thing. It's my understanding that Jason's up for parole. I'll do whatever I can to make sure he gets out. Even if I have to visit the governor."

Martha's tears turned into a torrent. "Thank you. You've lost so much." Danny reached and pulled Martha's head to his chest and held the woman, who broke down, venting emotion with heaving sobs and gasps.

Danny said, "You know, I realized maybe I didn't lose anything. I know Anne's with the Lord, waiting for me. I've come to accept that. Your twins are there too. I remember something Anne said to me the first time we met." Danny laughed as he continued, "Goodness, she was goin' on about everything, an' she said she didn't worry. She just believed in Jesus. I reckon that makes sense. After thinkin' on that, I set aside the bad stuff that's happened in my life an' asked, 'Do I believe Jesus is really God?' If I truly believe, then I have to have faith an' trust. The ultimate show of faith is forgiveness."

Martha regained her composure, lifted her head from Danny's chest, and looked him in the eye. "Thank you. I needed so much to hear that."

Danny held her hand and said, "Jason has a lot to offer. We're going to get 'im outta there."

CHAPTER 25

Prison

Jason Black found prison to be a welcome refuge. His confinement had the positive effect of forcing him into deep introspection while at the same time overcoming his alcohol addiction. As his mind became clear, he occupied it by reading. The prison had a good library, and upon his first visit, he noticed Charles Dickens's *A Christmas Carol* in the return stack. He asked the librarian if he could check it out, and subsequently, the librarian gave Jason the book. He found both terror and comfort in the classic novella.

Jason saw himself in Ebenezer Scrooge and felt terror. Like Scrooge, Jason's self-indulgence cost innocent lives. Their families and his mother were casualties of his alcoholism as well. He found other terrifying parallels with the story, like Jacob Marley.

Jacob Marley's spirit roamed the earth in chains, forever lamenting the hardships he wreaked on those with whom he had dealings and wishing for the second chance he longed for but never received. Marley came to Scrooge in a vision to warn him of the fate awaiting him if he did not change. Like Marley's visit to Scrooge, Jason's father would visit him. He saw the godless life of his father, and his own future mirrored that life; this frightened Jason. Unlike Scrooge and Marley's greed for money, alcohol consumed Jason and turned his heart into an empty, soulless vessel.

Like Scrooge, who feared Marley's fate, Jason feared he would suffer the fate of his father. The image of such a squandered existence struck horror into Jason's heart. As with Scrooge, Jason wanted to redeem himself. In the story, Jason found comfort in the fact that Scrooge got a second chance and turned his life around.

"Is it too late for me?" thought Jason after reading the story.

Unlike Marley in the timeless classic, the vision of his father did not plot a course for his repentance. It did, however, allow Jason to visualize, in cold reality, his destiny if he did not change his life. Jason looked at things in a different light. Come what may he would leave prison a good man.

Jason would meet two men who would help him. Both men found themselves at the bottom of a godless pit of their own choosing, where only darkness existed. Both would turn to Jesus and find love and humanity through a new faith. These men would play an instrumental role in Jason's spiritual awakening and redemption.

First, Jason met Briley Smith. Like Jason, he killed two people, but unlike Jason, Briley killed his girlfriend and the man she happened to be with in a jealous rage. He shot them in the back of the head, found a police officer, and calmly turned himself in, never to be free again. The man Briley shot turned out to be his girlfriend's half-brother, who happened to be in the wrong place at the wrong time.

Briley, quickly convicted of a double homicide, faced a certain death sentence. After being found guilty, his mother pleaded on his behalf. The parents of the victims also asked for mercy, and the judge imposed two consecutive life sentences with no hope of parole. Briley accepted his fate, took responsibility, and turned to Jesus. He made his way out of the godless pit and found a reason to live.

Briley, African American, small, and demure with his hair cut to the scalp, did not look capable of the brutal crime for which he stood convicted. In prison, he read the Bible for the first time and surrendered to the Lord. After Briley's salvation and being ordained a minister, he worked with the chaplain, starting a prison ministry. The brutal and unforgiving environment of prison became a mission field. Normally quiet and reserved, Briley's personality came to life, and his large brown eyes filled with passion when he preached the gospel every Sunday.

Briley threw himself into his new mission, working tirelessly with pastors, both within the prison system and outside, like James Gamble, so those released had every opportunity to succeed. He helped countless inmates successfully reenter society, thus allowing him to find a greater purpose, peace, and happiness. More importantly, from his point of view, he harvested souls from the greatest mission field on earth. Even knowing he would never leave prison, he found fulfillment. With each passing day, his faith grew, and he became known among his fellow prisoners as Deacon. His work laid a foundation of respect among the most hardened criminals, and Briley roamed the prison unmolested. Fifteen years into his sentence, Briley met Jason, as the latter, at his lowest point, began to serve his sentence.

Attorney Richard Hartley worked with the warden for Briley to be Jason's cellmate, a fact Jason never knew until his release. Briley would not only become his prison mentor but also a mentor in Jason's spiritual journey. Briley would guide Jason through the prison hierarchy but more importantly, guide Jason to Jesus.

Danny, who abandoned his faith during the war and found himself at the bottom of a godless pit, was the second man Jason would meet.

CHAPTER 26

Briley

In May 1975, Jason entered the cell where he would spend the next fifteen years of his life. A grating buzz sounded, and the door slammed with a loud, cold metallic crash. On the lower bunk, anticipating his new cellmate, sat Briley Smith. Jason stood expressionless, meekly staring at Briley, who remained silent, sizing up the new arrival. Briley had seen Jason's hopeless and fearful look countless times over the years and could tell in a few moments the makeup of a man, and in Jason, he saw hope.

Briley cracked a welcoming smile and said, "I remember the first time I heard that. Man, it's cold. I thought my life's over, an' there's no hope. But my ole mama never gave up on me. Man, she prayed an' prayed. Ever' day she prayed for me. She visited me an' never left my side. I was young an' scared. I've been here for nearly fifteen years. I'm still her baby. She's ninety-one, an' that tired ole woman refuses to die."

Briley stood and approached Jason. "Brother, let me tell ya, THAT's love. THAT's hope. I hear that door slammin' all the time, an' now each time I hear it, I hear hope. I know how ya feel. You're scared. Ain't no shame in that. The sound of that door slammin' is the scariest thing I've ever heard. If you're scared, there's hope."

Briley laughed, shaking his head in the negative. "If not, I wanna new cellmate. I believe you've been guided to me by Jesus. You don't see it, but you will in time."

PAPAW

Briley stepped and grabbed a Bible he had ready from a small desk. He handed it to Jason and said, "Here, I gave this to a man shortly after I got here. He was on death row an' the first person I ever brought to the Lord. Before his execution, he gave it back an' thanked me. You know, Jason, I believe he's in heaven right now. They say preachers are called. I was called through that man, an' that's when I decided to be a minister."

Jason took the Bible, smiled, and said, "Thanks." He opened it and read the passage inscribed by a man about to die:

"To my friend Briley, who never gave up, saw hope, and led me to Christ. Robert Hanley, December 5, 1961."

Briley said, "He wrote that just two hours before they strapped 'im in ole sparky." Briley snickered and said, "He said, 'I'm goin' to ride a lightnin' bolt to heaven.' Last thing he said to me. Ya know he wasn't scared. He was ready.

"There's always hope in Christ Jesus, an' today's the start of your journey of redemption." Briley paused and rested his hand on Jason's shoulder. "The road's long, but one day you'll be walking outta here. For now, forget that 'cause ya gotta concentrate on Jesus."

Time inched forward for Jason, who reaped the benefits of Briley's counsel. Briley, concerned about Jason's eternal soul, mentored him and became a father figure. Jason concluded that if Briley could find purpose and turn his life around in prison, even under the yoke of a terrible crime, then he could turn his life around. The respect Jason had for Briley ran deep, and their friendship would continue long after Jason left prison.

On October 10, 1979, the evening before Jason's release, Briley counseled Jason for the last time. "You paid your debt to society. Now listen." From under his pillow, he pulled a worn leather-bound Bible his mother gave him when he entered prison. He thumbed through the pages. "Listen to this. It is one of many passages that gives me great comfort. It's Luke 23:32–43."

Briley read to Jason, *"Two others also, who were criminals, were being led away to be put to death with Him. When they came to the place called The Skull, there they crucified Him and the criminals, one on the right and the other on the left. But Jesus was saying, 'Father, forgive them;*

for they do not know what they are doing.' And they cast lots, dividing up His garments among themselves. And the people stood by, looking on. And even the rulers were sneering at Him, saying, 'He saved others; let Him save Himself if this is the Christ of God, His Chosen One.' The soldiers also mocked Him, coming up to Him, offering Him sour wine, and saying, 'If You are the King of the Jews, save Yourself!' Now there was also an inscription above Him, 'THIS IS THE KING OF THE JEWS.' One of the criminals who were hanged there was hurling abuse at Him, saying, 'Are You not the Christ? Save Yourself and us!' But the other answered, and rebuking him said, 'Do you not even fear God, since you are under the same sentence of condemnation? And we indeed are suffering justly, for we are receiving what we deserve for our deeds; but this man has done nothing wrong.' And he was saying, 'Jesus, remember me when You come in Your kingdom!' And He said to him, 'Truly I say to you, today you shall be with Me in Paradise.'"

Briley hugged Jason, shook his hand, and said, "We're all like those two criminals who died alongside Jesus. One chose to reject him. The other, through all his suffering, took responsibility for his sins and received the grace of Jesus. His faith was great. You now have the same choice, so go serve the Lord. He died for us. He died for you. This is your second chance. Make it count."

Briley revealed to Jason that faith in Jesus would overcome all his sins. Danny would provide him with the means to show his acceptance of God's love and find forgiveness.

After meeting with Jason's mother, Danny corresponded with Jason and kept his word to her. Danny's compelling testimony resulted in Jason's release. Danny wished for nothing in return but asked Jason for one favor. With Jason's help, Danny would restore the faith he abandoned years ago. Danny requested that Jason perform a special service. Jason jumped at the opportunity to do what Danny asked. For the first time in his life, Jason found the second chance he prayed for and, at the same time, a reason to live.

Danny could finish what Briley began.

CHAPTER 27

A Mountain of Sin

JASON MADE HIS way along the smooth, blacktop highway that snaked through the rolling hills of Wears Valley, Tennessee. Uncertainty set in as he tried to find Owl Creek Baptist Church, Danny's church. Soon, he would stand before hundreds of people who knew Anne. In spite of Danny's sincere reassurances and forgiveness and Briley's mentoring, Jason would have to stand alone. The closer he came to the church, the more his fears heightened, and doubt crept into his mind.

Jason thought, *"Could I really be part of a normal, giving life again? Could I make my life count for something?"*

However, the spirit of the Lord moved on Jason and gave him strength. The simple white-frame church, one hundred feet square, came into view. Large, picturesque oak trees protected the church from the sun, and the steeple towered into the sky. It blended with the landscape, appearing as if God himself placed the structure there, and it beckoned Jason. Suddenly reassured, his cherished moment arrived. He surrendered to the Lord and turned into the parking lot, driving past a sign reading:

Owl Creek Baptist Church
Pastor
Dr. James Gamble
This week's message:
Forgive Always.

A smattering of people aimlessly milled about in front of the church, enjoying the beautiful fall day. Jason thought, *"Just a normal Sunday for them. They're just doing what they do every week: spending time with friends and worshiping God. It's a happy, normal routine, and I'm standing at the edge of a cliff."* He rolled his fingers nervously on the steering wheel, then circled the church idling through the parking lot. Jason continued to have nagging doubts and found himself fighting the urge to leave.

During his time in prison, he prayed for the moment he would confront his sin and lift the specter of shame. Jason's hands were sweaty, his stomach churned, and his heart raced. He felt the weight of every sin, misdeed, and shame of his past, which produced within him a nearly unbearable weight. Jason tried to dry his hands on his pants, and he thought, *"I can still leave."* The greater force of the Holy Spirit intervened, compelling him to stay.

He passed a small group of parishioners, and several greeted Jason with a friendly wave. He thought, *"They saw me! I can't leave now!"* Again, he circled the church and thought of the burden his mother, Danny, and all the victims carried because of his actions. *"What about her? What about everyone? They suffered. This's small."* The thought of his mother and his commitment to Danny squelched his last desire to leave. Before him, a mighty mountain of sin towered. In less than an hour, with Jesus, he would conquer its summit. *"They needed to see Jesus in him. They needed to feel God's presence. Today, they would,"* he thought. This revelation motivated Jason to move forward. His commitment to proceed with Danny's plan liberated him as he eased his car into a parking spot.

He whispered, "One step at a time. Put the car in park, cut the engine, get out, and walk to the church." He offered a one-line prayer. "Please, Jesus, give me strength." He remembered Briley's words. "You paid your debt to society. This is your second chance. Make it count." Now he needed to get out of the car.

Jason glanced at his watch. He had a few minutes and retrieved the Bible Briley gave him and turned to Luke 23. An unexpected tap on the window interrupted him. Pastor James Gamble, wearing a broad smile, stood looking into the window with his jaws clenched so tightly from restraining laughter the muscles in his face were flexing. The last thread of reluctance within Jason snapped.

Jason opened the door, climbed out, and saw the source of the pastor's amusement. A sign read, "Reserved for Pastor James Gamble." After an awkward pause, Jason flashed a sheepish smile and said, "Sorry, I didn't see that."

Pastor Gamble pointed at the church and let out a loud laugh, putting Jason at ease. "Ya know, years ago, when I came to this church, they had a parking spot for me right by the side door. Somehow it made me feel exalted, and being exalted is one thing a pastor should never feel. So I had it moved all the way back here. Kinda my way of letting the congregation know how I felt. It's about as far away as you can get from the church. I needed to walk, and I felt the congregation needed to see me come to the Lord." Pastor Gamble put his arm around Jason's shoulder and said, "Ya know, you're the only person to ever try to take this spot." Jason laughed along with Pastor Gamble.

"I've gotta be honest, Pastor, I'm a little nervous. Actually, I'm a lot nervous."

"I'm aware of your anxiety an' how far you've come. I know Anne's lookin' down an' smilin'. It's time to forgive yourself. Everyone's forgiven you." Pastor Gamble bowed his head and placed his hand on Jason's shoulder. "Let's pray," and he recited the Alcoholics Anonymous prayer:

"God, grant us the serenity to accept the things we cannot change. The courage to change the things we can. And the wisdom to know the difference. And please grant us strength to follow your wisdom. In Jesus's name, we pray."

Pastor Gamble reminded Jason, "This's a big day for our church too. What you and Danny are doin' today'll be talked about for years to come." They turned and headed to the church.

Jason spotted Danny getting out of his car. "There's Danny."

Pastor Gamble said, "Time to get started. It's a big day for Danny too."

Jason and Danny reconciled while the former was in prison. Danny asked Jason to perform a special service. The service would fulfill his promise to Anne, and Owl Creek Baptist Church would become the point of convergence where the two men would complete their spiritual journey. Jason to find God, Danny to return to God, and both to forge a path built on faith.

Like the fateful day in France, when Danny nearly died in the river, his beloved Anne came to him with comforting words. Since her passing, she visited Danny's mind often and told him what she often said in life: *"The greatest show of faith and trust in Jesus is to forgive."*

Danny climbed out of his car, made his way to the two men, and extended his hand to greet them, saying, "Fancy meeting you here, Pastor."

Pastor Gamble flashed a warm smile. "Welcome back, Danny. You've been missed."

After shaking the pastor's hand, Danny turned to Jason, extended his hand, and said, "Welcome to Owl Creek Baptist Church. You're among brothers in Christ."

"I can't thank you enough for this, Danny. What you're goin' to do is well beyond measure. I told Mom about your plans. Made 'er so happy. She'll be here, of course."

Danny replied, "I'm not so sure I shouldn't be thankin' you, Jason. This's a big step for me. I want things right between me and God. You may be helpin' me as much as I'm helpin' you. I know Anne's happy. This's what she wants."

A spiritual deal of forgiveness brokered with the aid of Pastor Gamble and Richard Hartley would soon be consummated. Pastor Gamble turned to Jason and said, "Let's go inside. Richard's bringing your mother." The three men headed to the church.

CHAPTER 28

Amazing Grace

THE THREE MEN entered the church and found Richard Hartley seated with Jason's mother on the front pew, who in turn stood to greet them. Pastor Gamble turned to Jason and said, "Looks like Richard an' your mother beat us here."

Richard extended a hand to Danny and said, "Hey, Danny. I think you know this lady."

Martha looked radiant in a simple outfit consisting of a loose-fitting, pleated, knee-length white skirt and a matching short-sleeve blouse with a light-blue floral print. Sky-blue pumps matched the blue hues of her blouse and added an inch to her frail five-foot frame. She wore her white hair in a bun, held in place by three small hibiscus hair clips: one light blue, one yellow, and one white.

Unlike their first meeting, Martha stood erect, her large brown eyes sparkled, and her cheeks had a rosy hue. With the yoke of her tremendous burden lifted from her shoulders, Martha exuded child-like innocence. She held nothing back, exposing vulnerability and putting the men around her under a joyful spell. Martha's exuberance lifted Danny's spirit on a pillar of happiness. Danny realized the gift of his forgiveness and the restoration of Martha's son may have benefited him most of all.

"I sure do know this lady. How are ya, Martha?" asked Danny.

Martha threw her arms around Danny as Jason looked on and took in his mother's beauty. Overcome with emotion, she cried happy tears. She pulled back and said, "I'm fine. Sorry, I didn't mean to make a fuss."

Danny drew a handkerchief, dabbed her tears, and said, "It's okay. You have your son back. Let's have fun today."

Like the others witnessing the scene, Pastor Gamble, overcome with emotion, said, "Okay, I gotta get ready. I'll see y'all shortly."

Danny paused for a moment as the others moved to their pews. Standing before the altar, transfixed by the cross, he contemplated the upcoming service he orchestrated and the divine forces guiding him. Not since the fateful day in France, when he and Smitty captured a bridge, had Danny seen the manifestation of God. But unlike that day, Danny felt no fear, only the presence of the Lord. Today he would surrender to the will of God as part of a plan to bring about great beauty instead of death and destruction—not taking lives but through God, restoring them. The events of his life were a tapestry woven by God and each moment a thread. When pulled into place, a beautiful image would emerge. In a few moments, the final thread would be in place. Danny proceeded to the pew. He and Jason sat on either side of Martha. Several of his fellow parishioners welcomed them. They sat and waited for the service to begin.

The choir, adorned with blue robes trimmed with a gold collar and a gold cross on the breast, filed into place. The director nodded at the pianist, and the beautiful hymn "Amazing Grace" resonated within the church. Danny glanced at Martha, who, holding Jason's hand, sang along with the choir.

When the choir finished, Pastor Gamble made his way to the pulpit and proclaimed, "That's, without a doubt, the most beautiful hymn ever written. Written by a foul and profane man who, at times, mocked God. I'm speaking of John Newton, a seaman and the captain of a slave ship. Once, Newton found himself on a ship that encountered a storm, and it started to sink. As the ship filled with water and facing death, Newton cried out to God. Miraculously, the ship righted itself. Newton would later say, 'This marked the beginning of my conversion to Christianity. A conversion spanning many years.' Later, he would become an abolitionist. I'm certain the spirit of God moved Newton to write the immortal words to this treasured hymn.

> 'Amazing grace!
> How sweet the sound,
> That saved a wretch like me!
> I once was lost,
> But now I'm found,
> Was blind but now I see.'

"I suspect he dug deep into his miserable, godless existence and realized that without God, he had no hope and needed forgiveness. If his life were to have meaning, he had to change—to repent and seek forgiveness through Jesus Christ. Thus, he could find great purpose and beauty through grace. It's truly what Christianity is about. Anyone, no matter how vile, can be forgiven. God became man and showed us how to forgive through forgiving, thus restoring our relationship with God the Father. Forgiveness is the very foundation of Christianity. In a few moments, we'll see the true meaning of 'Amazing Grace' and Christianity unfold before our eyes. We have a special service, and we're going to do things a little different today. Danny Shykes has asked me to let him deliver today's sermon. We all know Danny well, and I'm sure you'll be moved today. But before we get started, let's take up tithes and offerings. Brother Slayton'll ask for the Lord's blessing."

Deacon Slayton stood up and recited a prayer. "Dear Heavenly Father, please bless these tithes and offerings. Allow them to empower us to further share your word, so all humanity may someday come to accept the precious gift of your Son and eternal life. Lord, we ask you to bless Danny and Jason as they deliver this special service. Also, let us give thanks because we have won both Jason Black and Danny Shykes to Jesus, and may their faith continue to grow. We ask these things in the name of your risen Son, who died for our sins, Jesus Christ."

The collection plates were returned, and Pastor Gamble made his way to the altar. He nodded at Danny and said, "It's now time to turn the service over to Danny."

Danny rose and stepped by Jason, gently tapping his shoulder, and approached the altar. When he reached the lectern, he drew from his pocket a small metal cap he had tucked away for decades in a sock drawer. Danny thought of his friends Smitty and Captain Jones; he looked at Jason and Martha, placed the cap on the lectern, and scanned the congregation.

CHAPTER 29

Danny's Sermon
Ich Vergebe Dir!

DANNY TOOK A deep breath and delivered his sermon. "I would like to thank Pastor Gamble for his kind introduction and allowing Jason and me to perform this service. I'd also like to thank Jason." Danny opened his Bible and continued, "I wish to read scripture. Please open your Bible and turn to Luke 17:4. Jesus says, *'If he sins against you seven times in a day, and seven times comes back to you, and says, 'I repent,' forgive him.'*"

Danny paused, collected his thoughts, and continued.

"May the Lord bless the reading of his word. Today I'm going to talk about forgiveness, the cornerstone of Christianity. Forgiveness and reconciliation are why God donned flesh and became human in the form of Jesus Christ. Forgiveness is what Jesus demands from us and, by example, teaches us. Yet forgiveness is difficult to understand. It's not natural from our human perspective. When someone has wronged us and sinned against God, it's only natural to lash out and turn our backs on that person. For us, it makes sense. However, even after Adam abandoned his faith and turned his back on God, and in spite of us turning our backs on God, God would not turn his back on us. God loved us so much that he chose forgiveness through Jesus Christ, and his crucifixion provided a pathway for forgiveness.

Without forgiveness, there's no hope for mankind. Also, what better way to demonstrate faith than to forgive?

"It's THAT simple. What I want to talk about is faith through forgiveness. I don't know a better demonstration of faith than through forgiveness. It is the most compelling way to show our trust in God. At various times in my life, I had to confront the concept of forgiveness, and unfortunately, because of my weak faith, I failed. Maybe the war hardened my heart. After all, at a young age, when I left childhood and became a man, my profession became killing. From basic training on, I was conditioned to hate the enemy. I suppose that makes sense. I mean, how can you kill someone you love? Take a moment and turn to Matthew 5:44 and 5:45. Here Jesus says, *'But I tell you: love your enemies and pray for those who persecute you, that you may be sons of your Father in heaven; He causes his sun to rise on the evil and the good and sends rain on the righteous and unrighteous.'*

"War, of course, is in direct conflict with what Jesus commands. I cannot explain my own reconciliation except that we are, simply put, lost. All of us are lost, both good and bad. All gathered here today profess belief that Jesus is our Savior, yet some of us, like me, have withheld forgiveness. As of late, I had to ask myself, do I believe? Do I have faith? If I do, I mean if I REALLY believe and have faith that Jesus is God, then I should have no problems with forgiveness. After all, if I really believe Jesus IS God, then what better way to show my faith? I was lucky enough to witness such strong faith in my late wife, Anne.

"During the war, I killed a lot of men. I can honestly say I have not lost much sleep over it. Therefore, I seldom thought of killing as evil. Killing the enemy became their mission as well as ours, so, therefore, we had a *kill-or-be-killed* mentality. During the heat of battle, you don't have time to think about morality. You just react. Simply put, we had a job to do, and we did it. We were fighting a tyrant who had no regard for humanity. Never have I seen such a clear delineation between good and evil. Yet the men we fought sincerely believed they were on the moral high ground. Which is why men will never stop fighting, and, unfortunately, there will be times in the future when we'll call our kids to kill and die. I saw many friends die, and

I saw many men die at my hands. However, there were two times when I killed that I distinctly remember, the first man I killed and the last man I killed."

Danny took a sip of water and proceeded.

"The first time was in North Africa. A place called Faid Pass. Our tanks ran into German anti-tank artillery. Their tanks picked off a lot of our tanks, and we had to make a hasty retreat. Our CO kept a cool head and positioned our platoon to provide cover fire for our men. This would help maintain as much of an orderly retreat as possible. Our rifle squad, positioned on high ground, laid down brutal fire on advancing German infantrymen. They had no idea we were there, and I shot three men. I didn't think of it because things were moving fast. But that night, I could not help but contemplate the irony, and I wondered, *'Had there not been a war, would we have been friends? Would we discuss politics, sports, or have a beer together?'* I thought of their mothers and my mother. Even today, I cannot wrap my arms around the irony. But the war would continue, and I had to set those philosophical questions aside. I would, from that point forward, put my humanity on hold. I couldn't think in terms of compassion. When I killed, I became a callous entity. A machine that, when called upon, would kill. We were kids, and our lives were in front of us. We just wanted to stay alive. Many of us learned at a young age that in order to survive during combat, we would have to discard our rational human compassion, at least with regards to those we were fighting.

"I went from North Africa to Italy and finally ended up on the beaches of Normandy. Omaha Beach, to be exact, the bloodiest battle in which I participated. At the end of the first day, after taking the beach, many of us saw the beginning of the end. As bad as it was, it made some sense, and by this point, I became accustomed to the notion of killing. The Russians were rolling over them from the east, and it was no longer a question of Germany losing. We knew they were going to lose, and we were anxious to put an end to it. The Germans were retreating, but they still fought hard, and the war would not end until we reached Berlin."

"Shortly after Omaha, in northern France, I would kill for the last time, and, unlike the other times, the man I shot would die in my arms. Until then, it had always been at a distance. Here, I would regain compassion. I saw close up they were human, and as a result, I looked at things differently.

"Our company commander, Captain Eric Jones, whom I will discuss shortly, assigned our platoon the task of reconnoitering a road leading to a small town. My squad, about fourteen men, was at the point, the lead. I found myself at the tip of the point, the very first man. The road, like many of the roads in northern France, was lined with thick hedgerows. These hedgerows provided the enemy with a nearly impenetrable place to hide. Needless to say, we were on edge as we slowly worked our way up the road. It was a rather gloomy day—a day I remember like yesterday. I also remember how tense we were. We were fresh off Omaha Beach, and my eyes never left that hedgerow. Everything happened fast. We heard voices, and we stopped dead in our tracks. They were German, so we opened fire. After we stopped firing, one German soldier emerged from the hedgerow and ran straight for me. We made eye contact, and I shot him twice in the chest. He stumbled forward and fell at my feet. He didn't have a weapon, and a white handkerchief fell from his hand along with a crucifix. He was a young soldier—just a kid, a teenager. As he lay on the ground, dying, he spoke to me as best as he could. He frantically said, *'Ich vergebe dir! Ich vergebe dir!'* So I knelt down, and he grabbed my hand. He looked me in the eye and repeated, *'Ich vergebe dir! Ich vergebe dir!'*

"I did not understand his plea. I smiled and nodded, trying to comfort him. I spoke the only German I knew, *'Ja, ja*, it's okay,' and he died. Later, I learned what he was telling me. 'I forgive you.' We learned his squad decided to surrender.

"He was dying, and his last earthly words and his final plea were, 'I forgive you.' At first, it was simple. He was about to surrender, and I killed him before he had the chance. Case closed. Still, I couldn't get those words out of my head. His words kept returning day after day and year after year, until one day I went to Anne. She explained what she thought. Then it made sense.

PAPAW

"Anne told me the young soldier, preparing to die, was actually speaking to God. When he said, '*Ich vergebe dir,*' or I forgive you, he was saying, God, I trust you. God, I have faith. God, I love you. God, I'm ready. It occurred to me why he wanted to forgive me before he died. By forgiving me, he surrendered his will to God and demonstrated trust and faith.

"So it boils down to these questions. Do we believe God created the universe? Do we believe God created man? Do we believe man turned his back on God and became a sinner? Do we believe God came to Earth in the form of a man named Jesus Christ to restore man's relationship with God? Do we accept Jesus as our Savior?

"If we answer yes to all those questions, especially the last one, what is there to worry about? For me, it's simple. I believe that God created the universe and man. Man did turn his back on God. God did indeed come to earth in the form of a sinless man named Jesus Christ. I also accept Jesus as my Lord and Savior. I can't explain to anyone why God did this. I don't understand God's plan, and today I won't attempt to discuss God's plan. There are far smarter men and women than me who can. I just need to trust God and have faith. For me, if forgiveness brings me to Jesus and to Anne, then that's what I'll do, and I'll do so without reservation."

Danny paused and retrieved the small metal canteen cap he stowed unceremoniously in his sock drawer and held it. Its significance and power grew. Danny looked at Jason's mother and Jason. He looked at his daughter and his grandchildren, Pastor Gamble, Richard Hartley, and the congregation. Captain Jones's battlefield baptism came to life in Danny's mind. He returned his gaze to Jason and said, "*Ich vergebe dir*. I forgive you."

Danny's Baptism

Danny lifted the cap into the air for the congregation to see, fixed his gaze on the widow of Captain Jones, and said, "I mentioned Captain Eric Jones earlier. This cap I'm holding once belonged to him. It's the top of a standard GI canteen and may be worth fifty cents. It's ordinary except it has a very special meaning for me and a small group of men, who, years ago, were little more than kids facing mortality. I kept it tucked away for years, not knowing how it would be used. I only knew I made a promise years ago on a battlefield to a dying friend. A promise to remind the folks back home what he, the captain, and all the others died for. In a few moments, that promise will be fulfilled along with its purpose—a purpose, I believe, consecrated by God. But before I get started, I need to tell the story about this cap and Captain Eric Jones. Captain Jones was from Alcoa, and today his widow Betty and their two daughters, Kimberly and Jane, are seated with my daughter and grandchildren. They are here to share in this special baptism about to take place. I'd like to ask them to stand."

Danny acknowledged them with a nod, and the congregation rose to their feet, applauding. After a moment, they sat down, and Danny continued.

"Eric, our CO, carried the nickname Preacher. While Captain Jones, an outstanding leader without any vices, was not an ordained minister, he always found time for Jesus. The men under his command respected and admired him. We would do anything he asked. I was with Captain Jones when he died and remember the day—a beautiful spring morning. You'd have no idea we were in the middle of a war. We were given the task of taking a small bridge before it could be destroyed. Captain Jones led the assault. My job, along with that of my dear friend, Sergeant Reginald Smith, whom we called Smitty, was to clear the bridge of explosive charges. The mission was so important and dangerous that Captain Jones went in with Smitty and me. As we prepared to get under way, a young, frightened private left his position to see Captain Jones. He asked the captain to baptize him before the battle. That private wanted to put his mother at ease and let her know he was baptized. He also wanted to get right with God because he was certain he was about to die. To be honest, most of us thought we were going to die. Of course, most of us were concerned that we would be spotted at any moment. In all honesty, we were not keen on baptizing this soldier. Just getting to our position without being detected was a miracle in itself. Our nerves were on edge, and we tried to talk the captain out of it. Captain Jones, however, didn't show any concern and told us the war would have to wait five minutes. So he performed the baptism," Danny held the cap in the air, "using this very canteen cap. When the brief service was over, a happy private returned to his post, and the war resumed."

Danny returned the cap to the lectern and continued. "We captured the bridge intact. I was lucky and only lost my left hand. I sat out the remainder of the war while Smitty and Captain Jones lost their lives. A mortar round claimed Captain Jones. Smitty pulled the cap from the captain's canteen that, only moments earlier, was used in the private's baptism. Moments later, Smitty, after he removed charges, took a round to the chest. I took a round to my left hand, and we fell into the river, but miraculously, we made it to the riverbank."

Danny paused to collect his thoughts. The sights, sounds, and smells of that June morning, along with the bloodlust that left in its wake unimaginable human carnage, came to the fore and flooded Danny's mind. Smitty's confident smile and sparkling eyes and his final words while he pressed the cap into his hand echoed from the past: *"I have a feelin' you'll need it someday. It'll help ya remember that ya can find God anywhere—even in war."*

The crushing weight of survivor's guilt crashed down on Danny. He steadied himself on the lectern and bowed his head, purging the pent-up emotion he carried for decades as the congregation sat frozen. After pulling a handkerchief from his pocket and dabbing his eyes, he resumed, his voice cracking under the strain of intense emotion.

"Smitty died, but before he died, he gave me the cap pulled from Captain Jones's canteen and told me to make sure our story would be heard. I've tried to make sense of it, but it's beyond me. I tried to honor Smitty and those who died in the war. Not only in that war, but to honor those men and women who gave their lives in all wars before and since. They never got a chance to have a family, to see their children, or even to grow old. This morning, we're not here to dwell on the past but to honor it. But more importantly, we're here to honor God and celebrate the winning of a soul to Christ. That soul is mine. I've not been sure until now of my salvation, but now,

I'm sure. I've asked the Reverend Jason Black to help me celebrate my salvation by baptizing me."

Danny directed his gaze on Jason's mother, and tears tracked down the old woman's face. Her faith had been rewarded. She got her son back, and Danny found his soul.

"Jason, please join me on the altar." Jason looked at his mother, then cast his gaze on Danny and stepped up to the altar.

Danny addressed the congregation. "We're goin' to perform a baptism today. I wish to, as best I can, recreate what Captain Jones did that day. In his honor and to honor the brave men and women who gave their lives in wars past, present, and future to secure and maintain freedom, they lie buried throughout our land and the land of distant battlefields. Their blood fertilized the soil of our freedom and the freedom of those in Europe, Asia, and other lands. They sacrificed their lives, their futures, and their earthly happiness so good could be advanced and evil vanquished. We're here because God lifted us on their shoulders."

Danny placed his hand on Jason's shoulder, "Are you ready, Jason?"

"Yes."

After Jason's affirmative reply, Danny addressed the congregation. "In Luke 15:7, Jesus says, *'I tell you that in the same way, there is more rejoicing in heaven over one sinner who repents than over ninety-nine righteous persons who do not need to repent.'*" Danny smiled and, using his hook, handed the canteen cap to Jason and, in a whisper, so no one else could hear, he said, "Here, you're goin' to need this. This ole cap has one more mission."

Jason took the cap with reverence. The stories Danny shared during their visits came alive. The worthless metal had more value than gold. The power of God surged through it and into Jason as he imagined the scene in northern France unfolding. A small group of frightened soldiers huddled around their captain, baptizing a young private before engaging in a desperate and deadly battle. This baptism would become for him, like the men in 1944, the focal point of what good lies within man and how God, through Jesus, can secure miracles.

PAPAW

Jason found peace and continued. He turned to the congregation. "Let us pray. Dear heavenly Father, let us give thanks that Danny is surrendering his life to Christ and telling the world through his baptism. Let us give thanks to his daughter and her family. Thanks to my mother, who never gave up on me. Thanks to Pastor Gamble, Richard Hartley, and the entire Owl Creek congregation for opening a door that would lead to a second chance and the gift of forgiveness. Most of all, let us give thanks to God for his Son, Jesus Christ, for the gift of forgiveness. In the name of Jesus, we give our thanks. Amen."

Jason retrieved a bottle of water from the lectern and said, "Danny has shared with me Anne's unshakeable faith and complete devotion to Jesus and his teachings. He also said Anne would be the first to forgive me. Such is her faith. She told Danny, 'Forgiveness is the strongest show of faith and trust in God.' She hoped one day Danny would take this step." Jason turned to Danny. "Danny, please join me."

They stepped from the altar and stood before the first row of pews, about five feet from Jason's mother, Martha.

Jason directed his attention to Danny and began. "Do you believe Jesus Christ is the Son of God, and do you acknowledge he died on the cross and was resurrected so man's sins would be forgiven?"

"Yes, I do."

"Do you acknowledge his blood cleanses your soul of sin, and do you ask forgiveness and repent of your sins?"

"I do."

Jason removed the lid from the bottle, poured water into the canteen cap, and addressed the congregation. "Today our brother in Christ, Danny Shykes, testified before God and man that he is a follower of Jesus Christ. For God so loved the world, that he gave his only begotten Son, that whosoever believeth in him should not perish, but have everlasting life. Danny, do you put your faith in Jesus Christ as your Savior?"

"I do."

"Danny, upon your profession of faith, I baptize you in the name of the Father, Son, and Holy Spirit." Jason poured the water from the cap onto Danny's forehead.

Jason turned to the congregation. "I truly believe that, along with Anne, all the angels are rejoicing in heaven."

The entire congregation rose to their feet and applauded, and shouts of "AMEN" rang out. Jason returned the canteen cap to Danny and said, "Thank you."

Danny addressed the congregation. "Today, I fulfilled the final step of my surrender to Jesus Christ. I also fulfilled a promise to Anne. I know one day I'll see her again. Now, I must continue to honor Christ with my life. In a moment, we'll be joined by Pastor Gamble. If there is anyone who wishes to surrender and commit their life to Christ, please join us."

Pastor Gamble and Mrs. Gamble joined Jason and Danny. Also joining them were Captain Jones's widow, Betty, and daughters Kimberly, Jane, and Jason's mother. Danny found Betty, handed the canteen cap to her, and said, "Please accept this. I want you to have it."

Betty, her eyes red and swollen from crying, said, "Thank you, Danny. Eric is in heaven smiling."

Danny hugged Jason's mother and said, "I hope the rest of your years are happy."

Martha hugged Danny. "Thank you. God bless you."

As the congregation filed by, Danny turned to Jason and said, "Thanks. Take care of your mom. She loves you. You're on the right track, and you have many years ahead to serve the Lord. You'll be fine."

"I promise I'll not squander my life."

CHAPTER 30

February 1991

"Saddam Hussein accepted terms for a cease-fire scarcely one hundred hours after coalition ground forces commenced the invasion to liberate Kuwait." Danny watched the news report while sipping beer. "Coalition forces suffered minimal casualties during the brief operation. This evening, President Bush will address the nation."

Danny set his beer down, picked up the remote, and shut the television off. He turned to his son-in-law, Mike, and said, "Minimal losses! Tell that to a mom who lost her child. Fighting a war sure has changed since I was in the Army."

Mike replied, "Hell, it's changed a lot since Nam."

"All those fancy gadgets an' computers are great, but some crazy bastard still has to go in blastin'," said Danny.

Carol, preparing for the arrival of Tim and Mary to celebrate Danny's seventy-second birthday, busied herself in the kitchen. She paused and called out to her husband, "Mike, is Ryan with you?"

Mike said, "No. He's outside."

Carol admonished her husband. "Ya need to keep an eye on your son."

Mike got up from his chair. Danny said, "Stay put. I'm goin' out anyway. It's nice. I'm goin' for a walk. Help your wife." Danny removed his hook, set it on the recliner, and strolled to the front door.

Danny opened the door, and his eight-year-old grandson, Ryan Paulson, flew by. "Papaw, can I watch TV?"

"Better ask your pa."

Ryan asked, "Dad, can I watch TV?"

"Sure," replied Mike.

In spite of it being February, clear skies and balmy temperatures greeted Danny as he stepped onto the porch. After making his way to the gently sloping pasture, he propped his arms on the fence, looking for Anne's palomino. The horse was nowhere to be found. He turned west toward his house, admiring the sun approaching the horizon, and thought, *"Where's that horse?"*

He turned back to the pasture and called out, "Come here, ole girl." Still no horse and Danny thought, *"This's odd."*

Danny claimed the seat at the base of the tree, where he spent many hours over the years. Small green buds, an indication of an early spring, adorned its branches. Seeking the horse, he continued to scan the pasture from his seat until he fell asleep.

CHAPTER 31

End of Times

Danny awoke to a brilliant, crystal-clear blue sky. An aroma of fresh rain filled his nostrils, yet no sign of rain. He felt better than he had in years and rose from his seat, turning his gaze on his house. Frightening storm clouds billowed with varying shades of gray. From within, lightning lit up the clouds, exposing feather-like wisps but no thunder, and menacing blackness filled voids from inside the clouds. The storm churned over Wears Valley and grew in size. It rolled over everything in its path as it moved toward his house. Danny returned his gaze to the pasture and marveled at a sky perfectly delineated between east and west: a gathering storm to the west and, to the east, a brilliant, bright-blue sky.

He returned to the fence. The pains of old age disappeared. He thought, *"This is strange. A storm with no wind and lightning with no thunder. What's goin' on?"*

Two men on horseback, one on a splash overo and the other on a dapple gray, appeared on the hilltop. *"Who could they be?"* thought Danny. Their identity eluded him.

They walked slowly toward his spot. Danny kept his gaze locked on them as a gentle tremor rose from the ground. When they drew close, Danny recognized the uniforms of his old infantry unit. The two men reined up at the fence. He thought, *"This can't be."*

One said, "Danny, ole boy. You're lookin' good."

Astonished, Danny replied, "This can't be. It just can't be."

The other said, "What can't be, Danny?"

Danny said, "You two look like old friends. You can't be. They died years ago. Smitty? Captain Jones? Is it you? What's goin' on?"

Smitty cast his gaze on Danny and with a mischievous grin, said, "Same ole skeptical Danny. Yes, ole boy, it's me."

Captain Jones said, "We come for ya, Danny. Ya might say this's our last mission."

"I saw ya both die. Smitty, you died in my arms."

Smitty said, "Yes, I died in your arms, but here we're alive an' well. We just got here. We come to get ya."

Danny repeated, "I don't understand."

Smitty moved his eyes to Danny's left hand and said, "Look at your hands."

Danny, amazed, looked at his left hand, closed it into a fist, then opened it several times. "Goodness, is this some kind of dream? Am I dead?"

Captain Jones said, "No, Danny, you're not dead. You're very much alive. Look behind you."

Danny looked at his body, reclined in his chair under the tree, and it appeared as if he were asleep. "What's goin' on?"

Captain Jones replied, "This's no dream. You're alive. But your body's dead."

"What's happenin'? Where's everyone?"

Smitty pointed to the hilltop from where he and Captain Jones came. "Look!"

Danny turned to where Smitty pointed. A beautiful woman stood alone, mounted on a palomino. Her blond hair was pulled into a ponytail, and a cowboy hat was cocked back on her head. An extra horse stood at her side; its black coat glistened in the sun. *"Anne, Goldie, Black Jack!"* Danny thought.

Anne spurred Goldie. The horse broke into a gallop, with Black Jack close behind. Smitty nodded at Captain Jones, and he said, "We're done. I think ya know this lady. She'll take ya the rest of the way."

PAPAW

Captain Jones said, "We gotta go. Don't be afraid. See ya on the other side." Captain Jones and Smitty acknowledged Anne with a nod, turned, spurred their horses, and raced to the hilltop. The two men and their horses started to glow. The glow intensified as their horses galloped up the hill. Upon reaching its crest, they disappeared with a brilliant flash. Danny gazed in wonder.

Goldie greeted Danny with a nicker. Anne pointed to the black horse. "Do ya remember Black Jack? He'll take ya to the other side."

Danny replied, "Anne, Goldie? Of course, I remember Black Jack."

"I come for you. We all just got here."

Danny, overwhelmed, said, "I'm confused. I still don't understand. Let me kiss you. I just want to hold you an' kiss you. PLEASE!"

"Don't be silly. Ya don't have to ask." Anne jumped off Goldie and threw herself into his arms.

The earth under Danny's feet trembled with greater intensity as he cupped Anne's head in his hands. Her hat fell to the ground. "Let me look at you. You're so young. I just wanna hold you." Anne's eyes were wide and unflinching. He said, "Your eyes are as blue as when we met."

Anne looked into Danny's eyes. "What are ya waitin' for? Are ya goin' to kiss me?" Danny felt Anne's hair in his fingers and kissed her.

"It's you!"

"Of course it's me. One'll get ya two." She reached up and kissed Danny. "Remember our first kiss? I love you. We'll be together forever, an' nothin' will take us apart. It's judgment. Don't be afraid. Jesus's ready for us."

"Where's Jesus?" asked Danny.

Anne pointed to the hilltop and said, "Over that hill. He's just over that hill, on the other side. Your friends are there now. That's where life is. Our life."

"This's too much. Smitty an' Captain Jones were in uniforms. Is it real?"

Anne explained, "Kinda yes, an' kinda no. I can't explain it. Time, like we know it, doesn't exist in heaven. It's kinda like the past, present, an' future exist at the same time. You're in a place of transition. Only temporary. Soon even this place'll be gone. You see us as you remember us. We won't look like this when we get to heaven. When you go over the hill, you'll see us as we are in heaven. Danny, you're always tryin' to make sense of things. Love doesn't make sense, an' over the top of that hill's love."

Danny asked, "What'll we look like?"

"We'll look perfect. Perfect."

Danny pointed to the tree and his body and asked, "What about the darkness? Where's everyone?"

Anne answered, "The war against Satan an' sin's over. All that's left are the saved an' the damned." Anne pointed to the wall of boiling clouds that rose perpendicular to the ground, reaching as high as the eye could see. "The damned are THERE, an' they cannot see the light we see, only darkness. They hear only their own screams an' only know agony. It's as if they're on a sinking ship with no way off. There's no hope for 'em. The lost are trapped inside that cloud and will never escape."

"What about our family Tim, Mary, an' Carol? What about Mom an' Dad? Where are they? Are they okay?"

"They found Jesus. Like you, they see the light. They lived full lives an', like you, are on the way. Each of us comes to God in our own way."

Anne pointed to the darkness. "The earth's bein' destroyed. The world we knew will soon be gone. There's no goin' back. Jesus has returned. There's no evil, no wars, no sin or hate. On the other side of that hill is perfection. Just perfection an' love. There's nothing to worry about because there's nothing left of the old world. The way to life is over the top of that hill. There you'll find the Lord Jesus an' me."

Anne slung herself onto Goldie, turned to Danny, and said, "Follow me. I'll be on the other side." Anne headed for the hilltop.

Danny shouted, "Wait, just a little longer. Let me hold you a little longer."

Anne wheeled her horse about and said, "We'll have eternity for that. Now, we gotta go. Look behind you!"

The trembling of the earth intensified. Danny stumbled against Black Jack. Terrifying darkness advanced and engulfed the tree. The boiling black cloud towered into the sky like a giant wall. Muffled screams of the damned, from within the cloud, broke the silence. Danny could hear no discernable language, only desperation and terror. He cried out to Anne, "Wait!"

Anne gazed down at Danny from atop Goldie. "Get on the good foot! Follow me! You lived a good life for the Lord." Anne waved her hand at the hilltop. "Your reward's over that hill. The darkness is for those who rejected Jesus. Trust me!" Anne spurred Goldie to a full gallop and raced to the hilltop, leaving Danny to follow.

Time ran out. Danny grabbed the horse's mane with his left hand, the horn of the saddle with his right, and placed his left foot into the stirrup. He threw his right leg over the saddle, placing it into the other stirrup, and clenched Black Jack's mane. The beautiful horse felt Danny's grip and, without prodding, broke into full gallop. The sudden burst of speed threw Danny back, and he wrapped his arms around Black Jack's neck, hanging on, trusting the horse. He spurred Black Jack faster to catch Anne and followed her to Jesus.

"Git Black Jack, git!"

Anne neared the top of the hill. Like Smitty and Captain Jones, she started to glow. The intensity of her glow increased, and upon reaching the crest of the hill, Anne disappeared in a blinding flash.

Not a soul existed; Danny found himself alone with Black Jack, and fear gripped him like a vise. The wall of clouds, extending north to south, chased Danny up the hill as the earth crumbled behind him from the advancing maelstrom. Frightening screams from within the cloud grew louder. Before him, in stark contrast, lay the beauty and warmth of an eternal existence with Jesus and Anne. Desperate for speed, Danny dug his heels into the horse's flank, and Black Jack's hooves dug into the earth. The determined horse, it's mane soaked in sweat, gulped air, and clawed its way to the top of the hill.

Danny neared the crest and felt lighter in the saddle. A strange but friendly force had control and lifted him into the sky. The sound of the powerful animal dimmed until he could no longer hear anything, and he found himself rising higher into the air. Along with joy and peace, he felt no pain, and his senses sharpened. Danny passed above an untouched meadow as vast as an ocean, stretching as far as eternity in every direction, filled with wildflowers of every kind. They rippled in a gentle breeze, and for the first time, his eyes perceived a multitude of colors he'd never seen, detecting subtle variations. Danny felt no fear or dread as he passed over the meadow at an increasing velocity until the meadow was a blur beneath him and knew he would soon be standing before Jesus. He looked at his hands, and they were glowing. The old world disappeared, Danny found peace, and he succumbed to a pleasant fate.

In a brilliant flash, like Anne and his friends, Danny was gone.

CHAPTER 32

Mom's Stetson

Mary wandered into the kitchen. Her stepfather, Mike, and her mother were busy preparing dinner. Mary said, "Hello, Mom." Carol stepped away from the stove and hugged her daughter. "Where's Papaw? I saw his hook on the chair."

Carol said with a laugh, "Guess!"

"His tree," replied Mary.

Carol pointed to a bag in her daughter's hand. "What do ya have in the bag?"

"Oh, just a little something for Ryan." Mary turned to Mike. "I remember the giant teddy bear you got me. My dormmate's always stealing it." Mary stepped to Mike and kissed him gently on the cheek. "You're a good father." Mike blushed at the unexpected praise from his stepdaughter.

Ryan burst into the kitchen and shouted, "Mary!" The excited child pointed to the bag. "Toy!" Mike, Carol, and Mary laughed. Mary set the bag on the table and pulled out a toy dinosaur figure.

Ryan snatched the toy from Mary and cried out, "A T-rex! My favorite." With the dinosaur in hand, he bolted for the door.

Mike shouted, "Stop!" The child stopped in his tracks and turned to his father. "What do ya say?"

"Thank you," Ryan replied sheepishly, then retreated to the living room.

Mary turned to her mother and stepfather. "Where's Tim? Figured he'd be here by now."

Carol picked up a spatula and stirred a pan of okra. "He called around noon an' said he'd be a little late." After a brief pause, she added, "Bein' a little late's not so bad. After he finished basic, all that mess started in Kuwait. I was sure he was goin'. I'm glad he missed the fighting."

Mary said, "I was sure he was goin' too. He was disappointed when they didn't send 'im."

Carol sighed. "He ain't a mom." She paused for a moment. "Mike, would you watch this? I'm goin' to get Dad."

"Sure."

Carol walked to Danny's shade tree. She found her father reclining in his chair with his legs stretched out and head propped on the tree. His arms were crossed on his lap. Carol glanced at her watch and thought, *"It'll be a little while before Tim arrives. I'll let him sleep."* Carol turned toward the house. Instinctively, her eyes scanned the pasture, and she zeroed in on a dark patch just beyond the fence. She thought, *"What's that? A dead animal?"*

She went to investigate. Upon reaching the gate, she studied the mysterious dark mound. She spoke in a whisper. "Looks like a hat." Carol stepped through the gate and approached the hat. A bronze leather Stetson trimmed with a scalloped concho knot hat band. She whispered, "Can't be." She picked up the hat and looked at the hat band. "Strange. Mom's Stetson."

Carol turned to her father. He had not moved. "Dad," she said.

Danny gave no response, and dread washed over her. She raced to Danny, kneeled next to him, dropped the hat at his side, and felt for a pulse but could not find it. She looked at her father's closed eyes. He looked happy in death, and she kissed him on the forehead.

"Mom found you. Didn't she?"

EPILOGUE

Rows of perfectly aligned white marble crosses glistened under the morning sun that hung close to the eastern horizon. Buried beneath the finely manicured grass lay veterans of various wars and conflicts, ranging from the Spanish American War through the Vietnam War. Under some headstones lay old soldiers who lived out their lives, and under others lay soldiers killed in action.

A gentle breeze blew a blast of chilled air, causing Carol to fasten the collar of her coat. The pleasant, unseasonable warmth that greeted Danny when he passed three days earlier gave way to winter. She sat stoically next to Mike, taking note of squirrels that played around a stately oak tree, ignoring the chilly March air, and she heard the hum of cars in the distance. She turned to Mike and said, "Isn't it funny how life seems to move on?" Mike patted her hand and smiled.

A two-soldier detail attired in crisp Army dress uniforms approached the flag-draped casket containing Danny's remains. Both sergeants stood facing each other, one at the head and the other at the foot. They bent over, grasped the flag by the corners, and rose to a standing position. In unison, they took three side steps away from the mourners, exposing the casket suspended over a freshly dug grave. They brought the corners together as if folding a sheet, then folded the flag in half along its length. After rotating the blue canton down, they repeated the fold, with the blue canton at the head. After a brief pause, the sergeant at the head flicked his wrist, and the sergeant at the foot commenced the ceremonial folding. He brought the corner of the folded side to the open side with his left hand, forming a triangle. After advancing toward the soldier at the head, he repeated the procedure, folding the triangle thirteen times. Each fold represented one of the original thirteen colonies. After the thirteenth fold, they stood facing each other, two feet apart. The sergeant at the head tucked the edges, completing the procedure, and surrendered the flag, folded into a tight triangle with the canton and stars out, to the sergeant at the foot. The sergeant took the flag, presented it to Carol, and said, "This flag is presented on behalf of a grateful nation and the United States Army as a token of appreciation for your father's honorable and faithful service."

A single tear from Carol's left eye tracked down her cheek as she received the flag. The sergeant stood erect facing Carol and, in a single motion, with mechanical precision, lifted his right hand, palm down, so the tip of his right forefinger touched the right-side visor of his hat in a salute. After saluting, he turned around and left. Mike said nothing and clasped her hand over the folded flag.

The mourners gave condolences and left. Carol, Mike, along with Mary, Tim, and Ryan, were alone with the casket. Carol pulled the flag to her breast. "That was a beautiful service. I'm beginning to understand how Dad felt. I mean about all the kids who never got the life he had. They gave up so much—things like family, love, an' even the troubles of life—things we take for granted. Dad cherished life, Mom, an' his family. But most of all, he cherished the Lord. Funny, in the end, he taught us the true meaning of Christianity: forgiveness."

Mike said, "Your father's an impressive man. I'm glad I got to know 'im. He faced an' overcame incredible horror. I don't think he ever took any of that for granted. I guess that's why I admire 'im. Like you said, he loved his Anne an' family. He loved the Lord an' demonstrated faith by forgiving. I can't think of a better way to show one's love for the Lord."

Tim and Mary approached the casket. They ran their hands over the polished metal and tearfully said goodbye. Carol rose and ran her hands over the casket; Mike and Ryan followed. Mike said nothing and caressed Carol's shoulder as ribbons adorning wreaths rattled in the chilly breeze.

Who we who, who, who.

Mike asked, "Did ya hear that?"

Carol replied, "Hear what, honey?"

Mike said, "Sнннн! Listen." Carol strained to hear the sound.

Who we who, who, who.

"That! A mourning dove. It's a mourning dove."

Carol turned and put her head on Mike's shoulder. "One time, when Dad an' I were fishin', we heard one. I was twelve. He got so emotional. I never saw my father cry before. I asked 'im what was wrong." Carol paused and stroked the flag. "He never told me."

AFTERWORD

THANK YOU FOR reading my story. If, however, you have not read it, please *stop* and read the story first. Here I explain certain aspects of the ending and why.

A few disclaimers

I have received no theological training. I have, however, drawn from experts, and I read the Bible regularly. Also, I am not an expert in matters of science, but I have spent a lifetime reading about the universe from experts. It is fair to say, based on this story, that I have accepted Jesus as my Savior. Only you can know or care if you are saved. I am saved.

I do not believe the end of time events depicted in my novel. We cannot know the specifics of heaven until we cross over. The Bible, however, tells us what to expect when Jesus returns. Like I tell my kids, there are 1.5 billion people professing to be Christians, and each one will have a slightly different take on the end times as well as other matters relating to Christianity. I suspect one of them is right.

Lastly, I write mostly for my wife, children, grandchildren, family, and a few friends. However, it is mostly for my grandchildren. Because I never had a papaw, I used the relationship between myself and my grandchildren to create the relationship between Danny "Papaw" and his grandchildren. Therefore, there are things in this story my grandchildren can relate to. It is my hope that when they are my age, this story will bring to mind memories of long ago. Also, it is my way of speaking to them from beyond should they ever doubt their beliefs. Maybe this story will help them sort things out.

I felt, however, some may legitimately consider the ending a mistake, a continuity error. So what follows is a brief explanation of Chapter 31 and beyond.

Thought experiment

The purpose of the ending is to demonstrate that the parameters (physics) of the known universe, as we know them, do not apply to an eternal heaven or hell. If you believe God created the universe, then you must believe God created the parameters that make it work. Conversely, it is my opinion that the parameters for an eternal heaven, also created by God, must be different and therefore completely alien to our ability to reason. I suspect mass, space, and time are different when we cross over. Believers can find great comfort in knowing that when we cross over, we will behold a beautiful place created by God. How God structures heaven (physics), if you can call it physics, will not concern us; just saying.

In my novel, Danny reunites with Anne, and they ride off to Jesus and heaven as God destroys the earth. Next, Danny's daughter, Carol, finds Danny dead, and his graveside service follows; the earth exists, and humanity is going about its business as if nothing happened. I can see why someone would think that makes no sense. So let me put forth this rhetorical question: What if, from God's throne in heaven, the end times have already happened?

I wrote it that way deliberately to demonstrate how bizarre heaven is compared to our current existence. At least, in my humble opinion. I doubt, however, that is the case. Honestly, I thought it was fun. Maybe it will get people thinking. I do not wish to go into greater detail other than what I have already stated. It would take too long. If you run into me, I'll be happy to give up my thoughts in greater detail. What follows, however, is my perspective on man's place in the grand scheme of things.

PAPAW

In a fishbowl

In some ways, we are like goldfish in a bowl. The fish cannot comprehend what is beyond the glass. We are in a glass bowl of sorts; we call it earth. We do, however, have a tremendous advantage over the fish. We can ask, "How did the glass bowl get here?" We can determine what is inside the bowl and contemplate what is beyond the bowl.

As we speak, far greater minds than mine are looking into this bowl and outside, trying to understand. We have giant super colliders that smash subatomic particles together, liberating their component parts for study. We shoot probes into space and send robots to sift through the sands of Mars. But like it or not, no matter how advanced we become, we will only be able to explore a tiny, tiny, tiny sliver of a sliver of the universe. For better understanding, allow me to put it another way. If we shrink the entire known universe to the size of the earth, man will at best only be able to touch a single grain of sand. And within the single grain of sand, the earth and all humanity are no more than a single atom. Because of its unimaginable size, an overwhelming portion of the universe will remain sterile to man's touch. No one can dispute this; regardless of the number of advanced degrees one can muster, or no matter how many Nobel Prizes adorn their mantles, what I just illustrated is an inescapable truth. Alas, some may not like that, but like Sergeant Friday said, "All we want are the facts, Ma'am."

It seems that in the wake of this search for knowledge, many more questions arise. The search began the moment Adam and Eve bit into the fruit. Once separated from God, we sought to eliminate God through knowledge we attained by our own means, and sadly, many great thinkers of our day continue to kick God to the curb. We are woefully unaware of the limitations God has bound us with.

In my view, there are things that, from a scientific perspective, will remain unanswered and forever speculative. Ultimately, man will reach the boundary of attainable knowledge. As long as we are on earth, we will look out through the glass at the vast expanse of the universe and find ourselves tapping the glass in speculation; that's it.

We will be freed from the shackles of doubt only in death when we stand before God. I believe that because we are here as the result of a creation and not by any accident. This, ultimately, will prevent us from seeing what is under the last rock. We are a created entity, and our Creator restrained us with limitations and for good reason.

Anne summed it up nicely when she first met Danny. She said, "But it's simple for me 'cause I believe in Jesus. That way I don't have to worry 'bout all that stuff, an' when I die, I inherit paradise."

An atheist acquaintance years ago, when I professed my belief in Jesus, challenged me. He asked me what if I am wrong. What if it were proven there is no God?

I replied, "I can't accept that."

He replied, "Humor me this one time."

I said, "Okay, for the sake of discussion I will."

He said, "So, what of it?"

I replied, "If for some reason it was proven that God did not exist, I would still refuse to believe it. Because if there is no God, then we are nothing more than a complex chemical reaction. We would be nothing more than a burning log or a piece of rusting iron, empty of *hope* and *purpose*. Therefore, I would find it far more palatable to believe in a nonexistent God that gives me hope and purpose than any reality that would preclude both."

Not to worry. Jesus is alive and well, preparing to return. If you don't know Jesus, now is the time before it's too late. Just saying.

PS

The sinking of U-1206 is a real event and occurred pretty much as I told it. With one exception—Captain Karl Schlitt may not have been the guilty party. No one knows who flushed the toilet that doomed the submarine, and it is likely whoever flushed the toilet will remain a mystery forever.

I DECIDED TO take a break, then my cat, Daphne, joined me; so I took a selfie. By looking at her, one might think she suffers from small dog syndrome. There may be some merit to that. I'm convinced that she thinks she's a lion and my yard is the Serengeti. She skulks within the black-eyed Susans and calla lilies, ready to pounce on an unsuspecting squirrel or bird. The cat's confidence is a great motivator.

Printed in the USA
CPSIA information can be obtained
at www.ICGtesting.com
LVHW090727120924
790746LV00002B/225